THE GHOST OF
EDMUND WINTER

THE GHOST OF EDMUND WINTER

MAGGIE KRAUS

Published in paperback in 2016 by Sixth Element Publishing
on behalf of Maggie Kraus

Reprinted 2018

Sixth Element Publishing
Arthur Robinson House
13-14 The Green
Billingham TS23 1EU
Tel: 01642 360253
www.6epublishing.net

© Maggie Kraus 2016

ISBN 978-1-908299-91-8

British Library Cataloguing in Publication Data. A catalogue record for this book is available from the British Library.

This is a work of fiction. Names, characters, businesses, places, events and incidents are either the products of the author's imagination or used in a fictitious manner. Any resemblance to actual persons, living or dead, or actual events and places is purely coincidental.

All rights reserved. No part of this publication may be reproduced, stored in a retrieval system or transmitted, in any form or by any means, electronic, mechanical, photocopying, recording and/or otherwise without the prior written permission of the publishers. This book may not be lent, resold, hired out or disposed of by way of trade in any form, binding or cover other than that in which it is published without the prior written consent of the publishers.

Maggie Kraus asserts the moral right to be identified as the author of this work.

Printed in Great Britain.

For my dear daughter, Emma

ABOUT THE AUTHOR

In her career, Maggie taught Drama, English and PSHE
in secondary schools, across the Teesside region,
in specialist units for anxious and phobic pupils
and in behaviour support.

She has also lived and taught in Somerset and
in Central Peel High School, Ontario, Canada.

Maggie moved back to Middlesbrough where she lived
until she retired. She now lives happily in East Cleveland,
with the sea view she always wanted.

ACKNOWLEDGEMENTS

Thanks to the following people for their
co-operation and encouragement:

Mr A Wharton, of Skelton Castle

Mr Nick Abraham, proprietor, The Duke William Inn, Skelton

Rushpool Hall Hotel

The Late Richard Baker, and the Skinningrove Bonfire builders

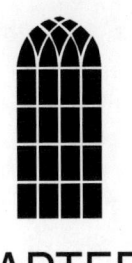

CHAPTER 1

I travelled this road each day to and from work in my younger days and had never once thought to turn left into the tiny lane until today. The sign, however, which seemed to appear at rare and random intervals, caught my attention this time: 'Historic Church Open'.

Sunday, late afternoon of a late spring day and there was no hint of a breeze – also a rare occurrence hereabouts. The lane, bordered on one side by deciduous woodland, was well hidden from the main road. I had some free time to explore on that fateful day, so, swinging the car round abruptly and wincing at the frustrated beeps of the traffic behind me, I turned in.

'*Dum-da-dum: dum dad um,*' an insistent beat, then the man's voice on the car radio, singing about love being in the air. I switched off the car engine and the song stopped. How apt, though.

I listened to what remained. Not silence, but a thrum of birdsong and the cooling-down sounds of the car engine. Branches, heavy with new leaf, overhung two tiny single-storey cottages to the left, further along the lane. Ahead of me lay a grey-painted gate that led to All Saints, the ancient sandstone church.

In making this visit I was not attending to my own wishes, but fulfilling an earlier promise made to a dying friend that, should my god-daughter, Amelia, ever marry, I would organise her wedding when the time came.

The girl was a bit flighty and spoiled and had become quite demanding. It was she who had cajoled me into finding what she called 'a marvellous and unusual' setting for her wedding. The family had lived in this area until Amelia's mother died, but she'd decided to return and be married locally because, as she'd told me tearfully, "I think Mummy would have liked that."

I was beginning to regret having promised to find a venue for the wedding. I'd been at it for months now, dashing to the North East whenever I had precious free time, sending photos and brochures to Amelia as soon as a good prospect hove into view.

Every church thus far had been rejected – too ornate, too Catholic (!), the paintings were horrible, one smelled too much of incense, too 'stony' and finally, 'too-modern-with–all-that-light-wood-everywhere-it-looks-like-a-hotel-lobby'.

Had I not been running out of options, I wouldn't have been on the lookout for 'somewhere unique', but desperation and a feeling of 'meant to be' somehow drew me on. This was a long shot, whichever way you looked at it. The neglected churchyard would put her off – the grass waist-high. Also, there was nowhere to park the inevitably flashy fleet of wedding cars. The space was too narrow with no room for even the smallest turning circle.

I had no idea what it was like inside but anyway, it was probably too small for the number of guests she'd want. So far she'd organised *nine* friends to be bridesmaids or 'bridesmaid reserves' as she put it.

"Well, it would be too awful if someone were ill on the day – and besides, they're all about the same size so we wouldn't need to buy any more dresses."

Only Amelia could get away with that one.

Thinking that the negatives far outweighed any charm the church may have had, I'd almost made up my mind to retreat when I felt an odd, overwhelming urge to explore the churchyard.

Generally, I am not prone to whims or fancies, but it was almost as if something was pulling at me. However, since I had nothing else to do, nobody to miss me, and it was such a perfect afternoon, I decided to have a wander around the grounds.

I hardly needed to lock the car, but I did anyway – force of habit – and made my way down the path, grit crunching beneath my unsuitable sandals. The air was glorious and I took great lungfuls of it, revelling in the lack of traffic fumes. Then it struck me... we were so close to the main road, so why could I not hear or smell the cars trundling past? I reasoned that the mature trees would absorb both, and continued my walk.

Directly in front of me, I could see the front aspect of Skelton Castle, nestled in its very private grounds. Even though I'd spent a great deal of my childhood in the village, the castle, surrounded as it was by a high wall, its gatehouse standing guard, like a soldier in a sentry box, must have been discounted by us as a playground. We children were happier exploring the glorious coastline and woodland instead.

The grandeur of the place took my breath away once more. 'Pity about the wedding,' I thought. The photographs would have had a spectacular backdrop if only the church were suitable. Despite the 'Open' sign, the church door was locked. I took a couple of quick shots on my phone and sent them to Amelia. Even as I did it – even as I was pressing the 'send' button – I knew it was fatal. Amelia would want this place and force her father to make it happen. He'd throw a boatload of money at the Churches Conservation Trust, and some poor fool (me?) would be charged with the negotiations.

The setting, with the castle in the background, *was* beautiful though.

The graveyard in contrast was ancient, with tombstones crowded in together, like blackened teeth in an old mouth. Hardly any of the inscriptions were still visible, weathered as they were by centuries of North Eastern winters clawing away the names and dates of the 'rude forefathers of the hamlet'. It was fascinating.

Beneath an old sycamore tree, I came across a monument that was still legible. I could just make out the name 'Ed---- Winter', but as to date or other details, I would have needed to clear the greenery and for that I'd've needed some sort of scythe or something to scrub the stone.

Amelia's mother, Caroline, had been a Winter before she married. 'Just a coincidence,' I told myself. It was quite an ordinary name. And if there was an extended family, maybe some of them landed up here?

'I'll tell Amelia once all the wedding madness has subsided and maybe we'll do a bit of research into her family tree – parish records and the like?' I decided.

It sounded like an ideal way to bring her down to earth again after being the centre of attention for so long.

There had been nobody special thus far, in her full and rather spoiled life. Well, no one who would come close to her father, James, who'd indulged his only daughter excessively, and it was to her credit that Amelia had turned out well, despite a headstrong streak.

When Robert Belfort had come along in her final year of university, it seemed to be a 'marriage of true minds' and her choice of husband pleased all her family, especially me. I admit I had been quite a harsh critic of some of her former boyfriends, and we had disagreed about the last one, a Jamie somebody, because I'd objected to his offhand manner with Amelia which *she* took as a challenge but I believed to be born of disdain and contempt. With Robert though, I could make amends.

"At last you've found the right one," I'd said. "He'll keep you in check and hold you back from your worst excesses."

She'd exclaimed in a high-pitched squeal at this, but I'd continued, "He seems like a warm-hearted, kind sort of man. He won't let you down."

I'd felt a secret pang of envy as I spoke, never having had that kind of relationship in my own life and realising I was never likely to find one.

My praise wasn't effusive enough for her of course and she'd continued the theme for some time after. The words 'wonderful', 'fantastic' and 'gorgeous' were used several times as I recall, before I'd switched off and simply smiled into the distance for a few minutes until she ran out of superlatives.

My churchyard reverie was interrupted by a persistent blackbird, whose nestlings I had disturbed by encroaching on her territory. Now, she dive-bombed me so closely that I felt the draught of her wings across my hair. Maybe it was time to return to the present and the safety and order of my car?

'Before that, I must just have a look at the notices on the church door,' I thought, 'in case there's a keeper of the keys or some such person to whom I could apply if I wanted to look inside the building.' I didn't know why I'd want to – I just did.

I was right. A scruffy piece of paper was sellotaped to the window naming a Mrs Barrington as the person responsible for security. Without knowing why this information had become so important, I scribbled her phone number in my diary and left, feeling a calm I hadn't felt for years.

'This sightseeing is good for me,' I thought, slipping my car keys into the ignition, but I couldn't leave just yet. I sat for some time, as in a daydream, and mused a while.

The problem of the wedding was still in the foreground of my mind. I had meetings to attend for work in the coming weeks but on my return I'd still have to find a damned church and book it for madam, otherwise an autumn wedding would be out of the question. So much preparation, so many people and things to organise. I couldn't let it beat me. Where else to look? I felt sure I'd exhausted the supply of local churches, so might have to look further afield.

There was also the nagging matter of the connection to the Winter headstone. Should I ask Amelia and James about him now, or leave it? I shrugged it off. He was probably nothing to do with the family anyway. Perhaps I could make some enquiries of my own – or Sylvie, my secretary, could find a genealogist or someone?

I sat in the car for some time, not yet ready to leave, then I got out and for some reason, went back to the grave. I stared at the writing. Definitely Edward... or was it 'Edmund' Winter? I scraped some moss away and found a date, 1805 but I couldn't be sure. And was that the date of his birth or death? Surely the church was much older, anyway?

It was almost dusk, and a coldness had begun to creep into the air, so, shivering slightly, I reluctantly returned to the car and the present.

Once again I found it difficult to leave the place – I was under its spell – but as soon as I'd turned left at the end of the lane, I became my usual self, and with a massive sigh of relief, realised I was now in control and the world made sense once more.

CHAPTER 2

Later that evening, having showered in my room at the Duke William pub and eaten a hearty meal – farmers' portions of everything – and having caught up on a backlog of accounts, I decided to have a walk and give my digestive system a fighting chance. 'I really must get back to the city tomorrow, though, and get on with my life,' I thought.

It would be good to be in control again; making deals with high-powered people all over the world who wanted to buy Pleasure First Cosmetics.

I tried to convince myself that I was worthy of my success. I'd worked bloody hard for this and people respected my skills. It was all going really well. I'd built this business from nothing and life was getting better all the time.

Why did it sound a bit hollow and ridiculous in this place? I wasn't sure, but there must've been long-buried childhood memories that made it seem familiar. I must've walked for miles around the lanes and streets of the village as a kid, thinking about the future and dismissing the past as unimportant.

On a sudden impulse I made a call to Steve at work, just to make sure the Japanese clients were still interested, but it must have been the wrong time because he sounded irritated.

"It's a beautiful night and the air is sweet and fresh. How's London?"

"Sorry. Who *is* this?"

"Oh, stoppit. Just ringing to see how today went. And before you ask, the church is *not* suitable so the search goes on. Will you be able to sort things out at your end without me for a few more days?"

"Perfectly well, thank you. I take it you know what time it is *and* that I have to be at work at 6.30 in the morning?" The mumbling voice sounded piqued.

I glanced at the clock above the Duke William's heavy oak doors on my return. Impossible. It said 1.30am.

"Oh God, I'm so sorry, Steve. I honestly didn't realise the time."

"Hmm, typical. G'night, Jo."

I heard the click of the phone and suddenly felt lonelier than I'd ever felt before. I could usually immerse myself in work before the feeling came, but in this place, out of kilter with who I was, there was a heaviness in my stomach which couldn't just be blamed on the food.

The old thoughts came to the fore again. That feeling of being set apart; of somehow floating between people, synapses not connecting, had been so much a part of me that I could generally pretend it was normal, but some days I remembered the past and envied other people. They were the ones who just got on with things, people who had highs and lows and allowed themselves to feel stuff.

I suppose the disconnect had saved me from all the cupboarded skeletons, but, might I have been better off letting them out sometimes?

By that time, my circuit of the village was over and with a degree of reluctance, I took my last breaths of the pure night air and fished in my pocket for the huge, old-fashioned front door key, but no sooner had my fingers grasped it, than I felt compelled to walk in the direction of the church once more.

Madness.

Luckily, I was saved from my folly by the revellers pouring and bubbling loudly out of the pub on a wave of euphoria. The local football team had been celebrating a victory and ushered me in on a wave of good-natured banter.

"Missed a good night there, love," I was told over the chant of 'five one' in full flow behind him.

And by another voice, with a Geordie lilt, "Howay back in and we'll have another stoppy-back?"

This second voice was overruled by a third. "Let the lass get up to her bed, John."

John, in turn, tried to focus on his wristwatch through drunken eyelids and peered into my face for too long, wobbling the while.

"By, she's a bonny 'un, Greg. *Sure* you don't fancy a quick one, love?"

I wasn't sure what a 'quick one' meant but 'Greg' was reassuring.

"He only means a drink, lass. That's about all he could manage at the moment."

Greg had a commanding presence, being in less of a stupor than the others. He smiled apologetically, shrugged his shoulders and directed the rest of the team out of the pub.

I managed what I hoped was an understanding smile in return. They were still celebrating and meant no disrespect. I wished I'd been able to respond but here I was again, on the periphery of the action, outside looking in.

Pressing against the wall, I allowed them the wobble-room they needed to get out and slid through the doorway, dignity intact, to the bar, where my room keys were waiting for me.

Silence echoed around the pub with the final customers gone. The air was thick with the smell of beer, stale perfume and humanity. I hurried away and, once ensconced in my room with a book, fell into a sound sleep.

CHAPTER 3

It wasn't a rude awakening, but unexpected brightness filled the room through the thin, brown curtains. I was only moments into my first cup of tea when Steve called to apologise for having been short with me in the early hours of the morning. Seemingly, our Japanese market was growing so much that he thought it might be a good idea if I put in an appearance sooner rather than later; otherwise they might see my absence as an insult. Having worked with these particular delegates before, I knew he was right. Even so, I was reluctant to drop everything at his behest.

"You're more than capable, Steve. Come on. Is there something else?" I cajoled, realising I was being a bit manipulative – something I can't be accused of ordinarily.

There was an uncharacteristic pause as Steve recognised my strategy. His voice changed, the irritation now audible. "Well, Sylvie hasn't hit it off with Mr Matsuki. He's a bit pushy and it's not going well."

My eyebrows hit my hairline. These petty concerns seemed so far away from where I was, both geographically and mentally, that I was ready to dismiss them without a second thought. I tried to sound non-committal and left him to deal with it.

Ten minutes after breakfast, I was on the road back to All Saints Church. Why, I didn't know. All I knew was that I needed to look again at Edmund Winter's gravestone. I had discounted the church on my earlier visit, yet now something was pushing me again to check inside.

The same sensation of being in a kind of time warp hit me as I turned once more into the secluded lane leading to All Saints. It was as beautiful and calm as ever, reminding me of the 'special place' we were urged to go to in yoga. *This* should be my place.

The traffic roared past, up the hill to the centre of the village, yet once again, I could not hear a thing. How odd. There must be so much shelter from the trees that nothing could get through.

A perfect, gentle breeze stroked my cheek as I made for the gravestone and slowly traced the letters of his name with a finger before entering the church. A hymn came to me from far back in my childhood.

"For all the saints who from their labours rest…" I hummed it quietly and thought of the people whose labour had created *this* church. 'They were truly the saints,' I thought, 'building a thing of beauty such as this.'

Skelton Castle in all its glory, situated on a gentle slope above its manicured lawns, had none of the charm of All Saints, to my mind. In a small fenced-off area at the end of the churchyard stood three white stone crosses. So, even in death then, the landowners were separate from the hoi-polloi.

I took myself over to the church door and, finding it open, I walked in.

Sunlight streamed through the clear arched windows from all directions, allowing the leafy greenery of the trees to be fully appreciated. It was the only light-filled church I had seen on my travels and I was enchanted. There was no hint of stained glass windows here, unlike the new All Saints in the High Street, which I'd remembered from childhood.

The stone-flagged floor was uneven and I had to take care where I trod to avoid tripping. I was glad I'd changed to covered-in flat shoes, in a burst of good sense prior to setting off.

Georgian box-pews filled both sides, some of them boasting the black-stencilled family names of the people who had rented them centuries ago. I picked up a brochure which told visitors about the unique features – the unusual geometric and floral designs on the 13th Century font and the west gallery which provided seating for more parishioners, seemingly quite common in Georgian times. A triple decker pulpit overhung by a canopy – or tester – helped to amplify the preacher's voice. 'No doubt preaching fire and brimstone,' I thought, 'and hell and damnation.'

As the church and grounds were empty, I didn't see any reason *not* to climb the pulpit and try it out for myself. There were bibles open on each level, and at the top, I could not resist putting on my deepest, most solemn voice and declaiming the words of the text: '*A reading from the letter to the Hebrews, 12.18.29.*'

Fabulous. The acoustics were first class. I had to continue, of course.

> *'You have not come to something that can be touched,*
> *a blazing fire,*
> *and darkness and gloom, and a tempest,*
> *and the sound of a trumpet,*
> *and a voice whose words made the hearers beg*
> *that not another word would be spoken to them.*
> *(For they could not endure the order that was given.)'*

The final word, 'given' echoed and resonated around the whole building. As it faded, I suddenly felt both self-conscious and foolish. What if someone had heard me? It seemed to me that someone *was* listening. I sensed a presence, but the silence was absolute. I looked all around, hoping my embarrassing display had been private.

I climbed down from the topmost pulpit, stirring the air around me and causing some strange, dormant smell of wax or tallow to shift about and follow me as I moved. At the next two pulpits, I looked again at the texts. There was a psalm in the centre and, at the lowest one, something about honouring the Sabbath, not going your own ways, serving your own interests or pursuing your own affairs. Apparently if you did this, you could 'ride on the heights of the earth'. "Sounds good to me," I said, then I suddenly realised something wasn't right.

How odd. I was sure the first of those texts had been open at a different page on my way up. Surely I remembered a garish, coloured illustration on the left hand page, when I mounted the pulpit? Almost sneaking back to floor level, like a guilty child coming out of the headmaster's office, I dismissed the idea. There was nobody around now and there had been nobody around earlier. Who would interfere with any of the readings? It didn't make sense.

I explained it to myself logically. 'I probably wafted past on my way to the top, causing the page to turn over.'

Now, though, the air was stilled and I could take a moment to explore the rest of this place. Obviously, the grand wedding Amelia wanted would be impossible here. The old flagstones would never be clean enough to keep the inevitable designer dress from being dirtied as Amelia, centre of attention, shimmered down the aisle. Anyway, it would seem from the leaflet that the church was decommissioned so having any kind of religious ceremony was probably impossible. She might not appreciate the faint waft of incense in the air either.

I paused for a moment at this point, to clarify my thinking. Was I pleased that she would not get her own way for once? Was it jealousy that made that little worm of delight dance in my brain at her disappointment – that I'd thwarted her for once? If so, I now felt a pang of remorse. I loved Amelia. I was being a cow for no reason. Where had these mean-spirited thoughts come from?

Shaking them off, I turned back to the brochure, noting the rest of the points of interest – a harmonium, two medieval stone sarcophagi – one infant, one adult, of unknown date, opposite the only fireplace in the church. How interesting. The fireplace was situated in a private family pew. I walked over to it and read the name WINTER stencilled in thick black ink on the outer door.

'So, Edmund Winter, who arranged *that* bit of one-upmanship?' I wondered with a half-smile.

Had I said that out loud? I felt rather silly and was behaving completely out of character. Time to leave and go to the pub for a light lunch. I must've been there ages and hadn't been aware of the passage of time in this timeless place.

At the church door, I noticed some Gift Aid envelopes. I leaned on one of the modern little tables nearby and rootled around in my bag to find a pen. Bending slightly to fill in the details, I began to feel a very strange, yet pleasant sensation. It was as though someone was running a finger from the nape of my neck, very slowly down my back to my waist. I could feel the pressure and the heat through my clothing. The feeling was oddly familiar. Steve had always used this as a prelude to our lovemaking. I smiled in spite of myself and turned, half-expecting to see him. There was nobody there. And yet there was. I could feel a strange presence in the very atmosphere of this place.

An involuntary shiver ran through my whole body. What was happening?

Hastily licking the envelope, I dumped it on the table and took flight from All Saints as quickly as possible, vowing never to set foot in the place again.

CHAPTER 4

Time can bring perspective to things, I find. Time and distance. I had spent the last few days, camera in hand, photographing various facilities – not just churches but golf clubs, the more upmarket pubs; a couple of ex-stately homes and a theme park; and had duly sent them to Amelia to add to her growing collection of reject venues. I had also been very diligent at work, smoothing over troubles between Steve, the Japanese group and our secretary, to no avail. The messages coming back were increasingly frantic, *'We need you here! Now, Jo!'* being the latest in the series, followed by the ominous, *'That is, unless you want Matsuki to cancel the order altogether?'*

Strange to relate, but because I was geographically distant, I also felt emotionally distant. Everything seemed like much ado about very little, if I was honest.

Priorities had shifted, despite Steve's disapproval and I now wanted to get this bloody wedding out of the way, once and for all. I went to sit in the deserted saloon bar of the pub and composed an email to Amelia's doting father, James, to beg him to make his darling see sense. *'It's a small village, James. If she wants more choice, I'll look further afield but this is it, as far as Skelton goes. That is unless you want me to go downmarket??? I really must…'*

"We never scared you off then?"

It was the man from the football team, the one who'd still had his wits about him, after what had looked like an epic drinking session.

I wanted to say, 'Go away and don't give me any corny lines or I'll tip this drink over you.'

I didn't. I gave what I hoped was a frigid smile and looked back at the screen.

"Mind if I join you?"

"There's plenty of empty tables." This was annoying.

He sat anyway. "I'm just wondering what you're doing here?"

"So am I."

I looked at his brown arms leaning on the table. Sleeves rolled up past the elbows and stretched across toned muscles. Too hairy, I decided, but a strong man, used to physical labour I shouldn't wonder. I gave in and shut the laptop in case he began to read my private stuff.

"I'm looking for a wedding venue for my god-daughter. It's a long story, but briefly; I am fulfilling a promise I made to her mother before she died and it's a bloody pain in the arse, okay?"

It was tetchy and rude but I looked defiantly back at him.

"Oh." He looked back coolly, indicating the drink.

"Fancy another one?"

"No. Thank you."

'My God, he has a tattoo,' I thought. A bird of some kind, nestling in the chest hair just below the open-necked shirt.

He saw me looking and his eyes smiled but the rest of his countenance was serious.

Greg, I remembered. His name was Greg.

"Where've you looked so far?"

Exasperated, I told him. "Everywhere, okay? I've looked everywhere to no avail. She's a spoiled darling and there's always something wrong with 'everywhere'."

It was stalemate. He was about to give up when a high-pitched, highly recognisable trill resonated from the pub doorway. "Guess who!"

Amelia, designer suitcase and dog in tow, sashayed into the pub, looking incongruous. A couple of old men, here for their afternoon pint, appraised her appreciatively. Amelia, in turn, did the same to Greg.

"Oo, you dark horse, Joanne!" she simpered, dumping her leather bag on a sticky, beer-stained table. Exclamation marks were the punctuation of choice for Amelia.

I jumped up and ushered her out of the bar and up to my room. What did she mean, flouncing up here? The whole point was that I was meant to be sorting this wedding. *Me*. For Caroline (and thanks for dropping this one on me, Caroline, wherever you are).

Amelia's arms flung themselves around me and I was enveloped in a cloud of 'Agent Provocateur' making me catch my breath and cough.

"Well, what *I* wanted, dear Jo-Jo, was to see in person the church of my choice. You know, it's quite hard to judge from a photo and I wanted to get the 3-D experience for myself. After all, it is my wedding, you know. And I know that *you'll* make it absolutely perfect. I just know."

I was aware of what would come next.

'She wants All Saints,' I thought, 'and I can't bear it.'

I struck at once.

"Ah, well, as long as it isn't All Saints," I responded. "It's decommissioned, you know, so it would be impossible. And it's far too small. The cars would struggle down that lane and your dress would be filthy even before you reached the reception. No, I'd suggest Rushpool Hall. Beautiful grounds and everything… and good food."

I was clutching at straws and we both knew it. Her determined little face had set itself in that familiar expression and I'd already lost my case.

"Well, darling Jo-Jo…"

"Stop calling me Jo-Jo." Even my voice was signalling 'failure'. "I'm a grown woman. It's ridiculous."

"I was going to say I loved Rushpool, but only for the reception. Do you see? It's beautiful and the rooms are excellent. I've booked in for the night to try it out. But I'm sorry, Jo-J… er, Joanne. I'm here to look at All Saints and nothing else will do. *Somebody* will be able to sort out re-commissioning it – or whatever it's called."

('Me', I thought. 'That would be me.')

"Daddy will speak to some churchy high-ups or something and make it alright, I'm sure. Now then who's that hunk down in the bar? Does Steve know you've found another man?" She did that tinkly laugh then, the one that captivates the men. I just grimaced.

"You're about to be a blushing bride, Ammy. Don't go flirting with anyone else, after all the trouble I've gone to in the last few months. I'm sick of looking at bloody churches on your behalf."

She crumpled.

It was cruel and I didn't mean it. I just felt cornered and unable to make sense of things. Since my visit to All Saints, I'd been sleeping badly and having very vivid dreams about one Edmund Winter of this parish. They all ran on the same theme. I was driving down a busy motorway at high speed and suddenly someone in the back seat covered my eyes, rendering me helpless. I panicked and clawed at the fingers trying to take control again, when all of a sudden, his face was before me and I saw that he was very beautiful and meant me no harm. That was always the point when I veered into the sandstone wall by the church – and woke up with a jolt.

Perhaps I should have told Amelia about the weird happenings in All Saints, but I honestly thought she'd 'freak out' – to use one of her expressions. She would want to go and see for herself, just for the thrill of it, and I wasn't prepared to go back. I was too afraid.

So, I simply put my arms out to her and said, "Sorry, Ammy. I didn't mean any of that. I'm just worried about a situation at work – to do with Steve and the Japanese deal. And tiredness. What with sleeping in a strange bed – it's never quite the same as home, is it?"

Recovering instantly, Amelia grabbed my elbow and dragged me to the door. "Come on, we're wasting valuable flirting time. Let's get back to your man downstairs."

The bar, however, was empty when we swanned back in – Amelia putting fresh lipstick on and me searching in my purse to get the next round in. I thought a brandy might send me off into a sounder sleep. Amelia, on finding that the man had left, and the landlord had a limited selection of spirits, decided to go back to Rushpool and test-drive the honeymoon suite, complete with room service, in advance of the Wedding of the Year.

CHAPTER 5

I had to admit it, Amelia had been quite good company since she arrived. We'd had a long walk on the deserted beach in Skinningrove. It was early morning and the air still held an icy chill. The beach was deserted save for a solitary figure at the farthest end. He seemed to be collecting shells or something. His figure was slight but graceful. When he saw us however, he suddenly dipped out of sight, seeming to disappear completely between the rocks. We ignored him.

An old-fashioned paddle in the North Sea had left us breathless and helpless with laughter at the exhilaration of it all. It took me back to my childhood and that morning with Caroline scavenging for driftwood, which had turned into an evening bonfire on the beach – the general practice in my younger days. I had told Amelia how Caroline and I would meet school friends here and have secret drinking sessions straight after school.

"Well, not so much 'drinking sessions' as a couple of cans of lager between six of us. We still thought we were drunk though."

Amelia loved hearing about her mother and we'd laughed a great deal about our exploits.

Maybe it wasn't all altruism on my part. I had an ulterior motive – I'd wanted to keep her from All Saints Church and promote the advantages of the other churches in the area, especially the one along the High Street that was still being used and would've been fine. Sadly though, she wasn't biting. She'd dropped the bombshell on me half way through the afternoon.

"I'm going out with Greg tomorrow. I might ask him to take me to the church of choice if you're not prepared to, Jo."

"What? A date? With Greg? You *do* know he's got a tattoo?" It was out of my mouth before I could stop myself.

She was dismissive of this. Stopping in mid-dry (we were trying to get the sand from between our toes at the time), she turned on me.

"He's glorious! Really, Joanne, you are the most awful snob. He's great company; he's got a really good body and he's intelligent. No. No. More than that actually – he's a *real* man. That's why you shy away from him. I've seen you eyeing him up, so you must be interested, but no, you prefer milk-sops like Stevie. Wonder why? What are you so scared of, Jo-Jo?"

She tossed her blonde hair and put her head on one side like some under-trained counsellor awaiting the inevitable tears at Relate.

I stuffed my still-sandy feet into my walking boots, omitting the socks, just so I could get away from the conversation and Amelia. It worried me that she was showing too much interest in Greg. I'd seen her chatting to him when I'd looked out of the pub window earlier that morning. She'd found out that he was the gamekeeper at Skelton Castle and he'd already promised her a tour of the grounds. I wondered how much he knew about her impending wedding – and whether he cared.

She told me that he'd also hinted at 'dark deeds' around the church and castle in bygone days, but had gone all mysterious when asked for more information.

I was a bit jealous, to be honest. I was desperate for details about Edmund (we were now on first name terms – in my head at least) and I was particularly interested in cleaning up the headstone to learn more about him. Amelia always managed to get people to tell her stuff that I couldn't bring myself to ask.

Hearing a noise followed by a cry of pain, I turned in mid-flounce (having been a bit of a drama queen) only to see Amelia flat out on the beach, a bottle of champagne in one hand and a punnet of strawberries in the other. On the ground beside her lay two sand-covered champagne flutes. So that's what was in the enormous beach bag. She was a stylish woman, I'll give her that...

"I just thought we'd have a bit of a picnic?" she offered.

It was a tentative apology and the best I was going to get, and it brought me back to myself very quickly. The rest of the afternoon was a bit hazy. I don't normally drink much, especially in the daytime.

The one thing I do remember, though, was the phone call from London. My secretary was calling to give notice. She had just walked out, claiming sexual harassment. Apparently Mr Matsuki had overstepped the mark once too often. Steve rang minutes later asking me to return. I had no choice and, still a little hung over, I hurried back to my room to pack, passing George who was cleaning graffiti from the pub wall.

"Bloody nuisances," he said, shaking his head and rubbing at a sprayed-on capital M, to no avail.

CHAPTER 6

Having over-indulged earlier that day, I caught a train. I needed my car too much to forfeit it if breathalysed. The Darlington train would take me directly to King's Cross station so I hoped it would be a stress-free journey without any gossipy companion occupying the next seat.

I had just settled myself across both seats, however, when a quiet, polite voice tentatively suggested that this was his seat. He showed me his ticket as proof when I stared uncomprehendingly back.

"Sorry, but I'm in 17A."

I managed a thin smile and reluctantly moved my oversized handbag and my laptop to accommodate him. With many genteel apologies, he heaved a large leather bag onto the luggage rack and, taking out a small leather-bound book from his top pocket, began to read.

'Good,' I thought. That's a tactic I employ myself if I wish to be left undisturbed. I'd only just settled myself again and was answering a tricky text from Steven when he began.

"Going far?"

"Sorry?"

"Are you going far?"

"Me? All the way – I mean, to King's Cross."

"Ah, I myself will be alighting at Rugby. A reunion, actually… my old college."

"How lovely."

I looked at him properly for the first time. In his late sixties, I'd say. White hair, quite shabby clothes, but of good quality. A nice face, but someone who could prove irritating if he wittered on all the time. This was the first time in a week that I'd had to go back to the business suit and cripplingly high heels so I was in no mood to indulge him for the whole of the journey.

"I'm going back to London because there's a crisis in the office and I need to sort it out quickly. I have a report to write before I land, so…"

He got the message, nodded and smiled regretfully, and I felt mean.

After a few minutes I said, "Are you from Oxford then?"

It took a couple of minutes for him to form a succinct answer. "I don't know where I'm from, actually. Been moved around so many times in my life. My father was in the Army, you see. Then I got the call…"

My brain was working overtime at this killer piece of information. Was he some nutter on 'a mission'? 'Will he try converting me?' I wondered.

Noticing the widening of my eyes and general shrinking back of my demeanour, he reassured me. "I'm a priest, my dear. Retired now of course – Dr Cedric Martin. I was rector in the parish of Skelton. You won't have heard of it, but it's a place I'm very fond of, having spent ten happy years there."

"I notice you're not wearing a dog collar?"

"Ah, the dog collar," he twinkled. "It seems to attract abuse and deference in equal measure. All Saints is a big, rather nondescript building, that is, the church on the High Street, but the people are rather wonderful. Straightforward and good hearted, you know? I still preach there from time to time."

He smiled benevolently, like a cartoon version of his profession and I couldn't help smiling back. Inevitably, my heart had given a lurch when he talked of Skelton and I longed to question him at length about the disused church I felt such an affinity with; but the refreshment trolley came through the carriage and halted the conversation. I offered him coffee and we resumed our discussion. This is what he told me about Edmund Winter:

"Well, the first time I entered All Saints old church I was struck by the atmosphere of calm. It oozed out of the very walls, so to speak. And the clear glass windows did not allow of any distraction from the business of worship – which – after all – was the reason the people had congregated there in the first place. No, it wasn't until some time had passed that I began to notice, and be distracted by, strange sounds. I dismissed it at first – these old buildings you know, seem to have a life of their own, and of course we only used the building when the new church was being renovated. That was generally in the summer months because of the lack of heating, you understand."

He continued his reverie… "It has always amazed me that the Winter family could sit cosily in their pew, raised above the 'commoners' – and by that I mean the thoroughly decent working people who attended every Sunday – and pretend to be humbled in the presence of God. Of course, those times are well past now. The church makes no distinction nowadays, but each time we used the place, we lit the fire in their pew and left the doors open so the heat would spread – as a gesture, I suppose – of defiance."

I had so many questions by this time that I was almost squirming with excitement in my cramped seat. Where to begin? "Do you know much about the Winter family then?"

"Oh," he was rather slow in responding, "so sorry, world of my own, so to speak… the Winter family? I'd say I was more au fait with the Fauconbergs, the original owners of the castle. The Winters came by Skelton not by fair means but foul, actually. Something to do with debts and gambling. All gone of course, nowadays. The present owner is anxious to do something useful with the land I believe. He's had it managed very successfully for him for a number of years now. Good for him, I say."

He continued for some time with the history of the church. "The 13th Century building was all but destroyed by fire and had to be rebuilt – the north transept being the only part of the original building to survive. It was decommissioned, not deconsecrated and had been rebuilt, only to be damaged again by fire – this time the bell tower sustained most of the damage. Over the chancel arch, where a crucifix would traditionally hang, a royal coat of arms is now mounted."

Itching to drag him back to the most important part, I asked, "What do you know about the Winter I saw in the churchyard... Edmund, I believe his name is. Was." I corrected.

The old priest stirred uncomfortably. "Hmm, not many people had a good word to say about him if you are to believe the records. Can't quite recall the exact details but something about a young woman who worked on the farms. She got mixed up with one of the Winters and came to a sticky end, so they say."

He stopped again. I looked at him and found that he had dozed off. I couldn't very well wake him up but the train was approaching Derby, so I took heart, thinking he'd only sleep for half an hour or so then we could continue our talk.

Turning to my laptop, I continued working but with my brain working overtime on the crumbs of knowledge I'd gained from Rev Martin I didn't get very far with the business of – business.

So, Edmund was a bad lad. Well, the sons of the rich often were. He'd sown his wild oats, I suppose – like many a poor man's son. And, because he was well known and looked up to, local gossipmongers had their say. I couldn't help thinking that if he looked anything like the man in my recurring dream, the young woman who finally landed him was pretty lucky.

I took stock of things as I waited for the Rev to wake.

Since my fateful and scary visit to the church, I had not slept too well, always waking with one of those awful jolts to the body, just before I crashed the car. There was no going back to sleep then, so I would immerse myself in work – my solace.

Most times, it was really hard to fall back to sleep until there was at least a glimmer of light in the sky. It had become my routine to slip on a coat and walk until I caught a glimpse of the sea. It seemed to lull me, whether calm or stormy. I suppose it gave me a perspective on the tiny problems of humanity, seeing the vast expanse of blue-grey water opened out in front of me.

Each time I'd returned to my room, I'd felt tired enough to give sleep another go. Perhaps I should have sought some medical help but it seemed to be such a silly thing to see a doctor for. I have always been able to handle situations – unlike Amelia who simply passed them blithely on to whichever man was nearest.

I wondered whether I should confide in someone about the happenings at the church but I realised that Steve and Amelia would think it preposterous. I could imagine the conversation now:

'Did you really see a ghost Jo-Jo? With a white sheet and scary noises and everything?'

'I think you've been doing too much lately, Joanne. Get yourself back down here. Bit of office politics'll scare any illusions away. Ha ha. Can I tell Michael and Bill? Please?'

I closed my sore, tired eyes for just a moment and must've dropped off myself, because I woke up to the sound of the driver announcing: *'Ladies and Gentlemen, we are now approaching Birmingham New Street. Your next station stop is: Birmingham New Street.'*

Rev Martin stirred. "Oh dear, I'm afraid I must've fallen asleep. Do forgive me my dear. Where are we?"

"We're just approaching Birmingham. Plenty of time yet. Time for another cuppa?" I asked, smiling at his confused face.

"No, no. Oh dear. This is my stop. I must get my bag." His agitation was palpable and it transferred to me.

"I thought you were going to Rugby?" I said loudly.

"Yes, yes, the reunions are always held at the Station Hotel in Rugby. I have to change here."

I pulled his bag down from the luggage rack and helped him out of his seat, thinking, 'What an idiot I am, of course he'd have to change trains.'

"Please, could I come and see you when you get back?"

"That's very kind of you, Joanna. I'd like that."

"One more thing. What kind of noises did you hear in the old church? It's important."

He looked very grave and still as he answered.

"The sounds of despair."

With that, he was jostled to the end of the carriage as the train heaved to a stop, and was gone in the slow, anxious bustle that marks out old age.

CHAPTER 7

The legal system in this country is as much of an ass nowadays as Dickens claimed it to be in Victorian England. It seems, on the surface that we have moved away from Jarndyce and Jarndyce – the scourge of Chancery – but in truth, the twists and turns of company law are still just as complex and lacking in logic as they ever were. It's always been my ambition to steer well clear of anything that lands the company in the dock. Sadly, it seemed inevitable that the woman who used to be my rock, clichéd though that expression may be, would be sending us off in that direction and taking our Japanese clients along for the ride.

I hadn't given much thought to the seriousness of our position, foolishly assuming that Steve would have smoothed it over and that I'd arrive to find both sides kissing and making up. It turned out to be an unfortunate metaphor since kissing had been the cause of the trouble in the first place.

Apparently Sylvie had gathered up her belongings and left, quite rightly expecting some communication from Steve, me, Mr Matsuki or all of us, but we had been remiss and we'd left her to become bitter and indignant at our neglect. The situation was about to become litigious and writs were being talked about by both parties.

As soon as I'd arrived at King's Cross, I went directly to Sylvie's flat to try to make some sense of the incidents which had led to her resignation. I sensed her initial resentment but instinct told me to be warm and sympathetic, (not something I do very well most of the time).

"Oh Sylvie," I said, putting some fellow-feeling into my voice, "what a nightmare. I just had to come directly I got off the train." And then, "Actually, I'm dying for a cup of tea. Any chance I could come in?"

She was so shocked by my presence – and the suitcase I was trailing behind me – that she stood to one side and let me in.

My faux-empathy soon changed to real concern as I listened to her story. The initial 'accidental' rubbing against Sylvie as she waved him past her became more prolonged, with eye contact just that bit too long – long enough to make his intentions obvious. She'd tried to ignore it – after all they'd all been primed to cater to the group's every need – but as it escalated to groping and eventually propositioning her and offering money, she finally snapped.

"If Steve had spoken to him in the first place, none of this would've happened. Mr Matsuki would have sent him back to Japan. All the others were really polite – almost deferential."

"What – it wasn't Mr Matsuki?"

She looked resigned. "No, of course not. Is that what Steve told you?"

My face must've fallen about a foot at this. Of course he hadn't named names. I had simply assumed. And I knew why. This business with ghosts and weddings had been clouding my judgement. I had not listened carefully enough to what was happening in the real world. Searching the recesses of my brain, I tried a couple of the other delegates but was mortified to realise I didn't remember any names.

"Right." I smiled sympathetically and tried to look calm, though my head was in turmoil. "Women have had to put up with this crap for centuries. It's not going to happen in my company. I'll tell Steve to cancel the contract when I see him this afternoon. We'll help you if you want to register a complaint with the police."

I meant it. Sylvie had been a friend and that was worth more than money – although it surprised me that I was thinking like this – that my softer side was showing.

She was aghast. "Joanne, I can *never* come back if I've caused negotiations to collapse like this. Steve won't forgive me and I'd feel uncomfortable with everyone in the office. No." She paused for thought. "They've already sacked *him* anyway, the rat."

We sat in silence for ages. Then, needing to break the deadlock, I made a suggestion.

"Sylvie, cuppa now. Please?"

Sylvie, tear trails on her cheeks, remembered herself. I stopped her as she walked to the kitchen. "What do *you* want to happen next?"

She was staring at herself in the mirror as she answered me. "I want it all to *un*happen. That is, things to go back to how they used to be."

That sounded reasonable.

"Why don't you work from home for a few days until we've sorted contracts out with this lot, then come back? Meanwhile, I'll extract a written apology from Mr Whoeverheis – and a boatload of money for – what do they call it – 'the distress he's caused you'. When they've all gone, you come back triumphant. And with a new designer handbag – spoils of the incident?"

She looked reassured and gave a wan smile. That would be the handbag, I thought, smiling back. I was pretty ashamed of myself for using these tactics on her. How would a handbag compensate her for being groped by the horrible man?

"Actually, forget the handbag. We'll sue the buggers. You can go to the press if you like?"

"No." Once again, she was determined that the business shouldn't suffer. Her loyalty seemed admirable. I was yet to find out why, but that was still in the future.

After the tea, Sylvie was much calmer. It seemed that the idea of pointing fingers had unnerved her and the relief of not causing *us* any trouble, coupled with the knowledge that she need never see the groper again had settled things admirably.

As I left, she took my hand in both of hers and said, "I hope you've solved that northern problem, Jo. Don't be going back any time soon… and I hope I'm invited to the Wedding of the Year. And thanks."

I went back to the office feeling troubled. Having solved Sylvie's problem, I was now free to solve my own, but that wouldn't be quite so straightforward.

CHAPTER 8

Journal Entry: *'The dreams have stopped! I slept like a log last night. I put it down to being back in my own flat, in my own bed and with all the familiar trappings of who I really am around me. Understandable really. Being with strangers in different surroundings, however lovely the landscape, might have given me a skewed perspective. What had happened, after all? A strange sensation and 'feelings' about the atmosphere in an old church. That was all. It was nothing.'*

My other worry, about Amelia and this Greg bloke turned out to be unfounded too. He'd got the keys, shown her the church, tried to put her off it and seemingly succeeded.

After Rev Martin had dashed off so suddenly on the way back to London, I'd had a text from Amelia, *'Soo happy Jo! Joining Rob in Scotland. Gonna hang out for few dys tog. So lookg fwd to seeing him! Hv decided on All Snts church on High St fr wdg. Lv etc.'*

There had followed a detailed set of instructions (commands?).

Rushpool Hall was to be booked for the reception, please, and all she needed me to do was to speak to the Warden – oh, and sort out the other hundred little unnecessary things that brides-to-be normally do for themselves – that is, if they're not Amelia. No mention of Greg at all. All very satisfactory – and neat. Too neat, as it happened.

I was just getting out of bed the next morning when I heard it. 'Come back…'

It was a bolt from the blue. I looked around at the familiar bedroom, then out of the window. The sky was blue and the morning filled with promise… then this. My heart was pounding almost out of my chest and I didn't dare move.

'Come back…'

I heard it again, but this time, so clearly it was as if someone beside me was whispering in my ear. I felt his lips brushing my skin, but there was nobody there. I smelled that candlewax and incense once more and felt the breath in my ear. And I knew who it was…

Thrown into confusion, a pang of fear spread through me. I was sure I had 'logicked' it out of my consciousness but now there was no denying what was happening. Surely ghosts only happened in old houses – in the dark and the cold? And yet, here he was, in *my* space and my head. I felt his heat.

Without allowing any thinking time, I called Steve. He was still at the office and was keen to meet me for lunch. It sounded ridiculous but, still disquieted, I showered and dressed in a great hurry, covering myself with a towel as though I were changing on a public beach. His presence was palpable and I didn't want him to see my body.

Ten minutes later I was on the train into town, and then having coffee in the station cafe. By 11.30, we were sitting in Café Leclerc with a bowl of olive oil and balsamic vinegar dressing and some good bread between us, awaiting our salads.

It suddenly struck me that Greg, the man from the pub, would find this scenario highly amusing and pretentious. 'You wanna get some proper food down you, lass.'

Entirely imaginary and yet it managed to make me feel a bit foolish. He was right – even in his absence – eating French peasant food and pretending to be sophisticated. It probably *was* something to scoff at, but what I usually enjoyed about it was the sharing. He would too – if he ever took the chance to try it.

"Miles away, again." Although he was smiling, I could hear a note of irritation in Steve's voice. "But where are you?"

"Oh, sorry. I was in Sylvie's house. Wondering if she was really okay with my solution," I lied.

The rest of the meal was predictable and although I wanted to tell Steve what had happened earlier, something stopped me. I scoured my mind to think of someone I could confide in, but to no avail.

Most of my London friends were superficial. You can't go breaking the code and become *earnest* all of a sudden. That's the way to lose friends and become the subject of gossip. 'Just keep things light-hearted,' I told myself.

Steve was looking at his watch.

"Work to do?" I grabbed his wrist and asked, suddenly desperate, "What comes to mind when you think of ghosts?"

He thought it was a joke. "Woooo... cold, white, spooky things." He laughed, making silly movements with his fingers.

Reluctantly, I dragged myself away from the comfort of Café Leclerc and followed him, privately dreading going back to the flat that evening. Would the presence still be there?

CHAPTER 9

Back at the flat, I took some comfort from what Steve had said. Of course, ghost stories are filled with strange apparitions and hauntings but they have one thing in common. *They are cold*. Fresh from the grave and cold as snowflakes. Just like everyone who dies. Nobody comes back. Ever.

My ghost, my Edmund, was warm. The finger down my spine generated heat – and not just my heat. It seemed to come from outside of me. How could that be? The voice was warm in my ear. The lips brushed my skin. So he couldn't wish me harm, could he?

With that crumb of comfort, I tried to settle down to sleep, having determined to go back north and collect my car next morning. Now things were sorted at the office, there was no reason to hang around here.

Steve was rather put out by the suddenness of my planned departure even though he saw the logic of it. We had an odd relationship, I suppose. We just seemed to rub along together and didn't label each other. 'Boyfriend' was a ludicrous term anyway, at our age, and though we shared physical intimacy, this was still a shallow relationship – probably the best and most convenient we could manage, given the hours we worked.

My confidence was rewarded with a sound sleep and a dreamless night and I awoke refreshed and made my way to King's Cross for the late morning train. The journey was uneventful and I dozed for most of it and read for the rest. The business was in good shape and a crisis had been averted, so I was feeling pleased with myself.

At the Duke William, all was the same as ever. The landlord proffered the same hearty food and I had a couple of glasses of wine with it. At last I was learning to relax and enjoy being there.

I'd half hoped that Greg or the others would be in the bar, but it was quiet and sedate with only the odd pensioner in the corner nursing a drink.

At 3am I sat bolt upright in bed. The still air was alive with foreboding. I felt myself getting out of my bed in the pitch dark and feeling my way around the solid, old-fashioned furniture of my room. Powerless to resist, I slipped on a dressing gown and tiptoed downstairs. Although fully aware of what I was doing, I felt unable to stop. On opening the great wooden door of the pub, I was aware of the barking of the owner's ancient dog, Shady, but I carried on – like someone on a mission.

It was a perfect night. The moonlight was strong enough to see the road for the first part of my walk, but as I neared the bank and walked down the slope to the end of the village, it became darker and the streetlights stopped.

Church Lane was blacked-out by the trees and I had to feel my way. There was an owl nearby, and his hooting alerted the crows, whose cawing shocked me into full consciousness. What the hell was I doing?

In a sudden panic, I turned to leave and was horrified when a hand grabbed my shoulder.

"Got you, ye bugger!"

My knees almost collapsed under me.

"You were warned. This time it's the police."

Shivering, I managed a weak, "What?" and felt myself being pulled back along the lane to the main road. In the sickly glow of the nearest streetlight, Greg and I stared at each other.

"You're that woman from the Duke."

"You're that nosey man at the pub." This said in unison.

"Well, you're obviously not the lad we're after. I can't see you poaching in that outfit."

Feeling appallingly vulnerable, with trembling fingers I held the edges of my thin dressing gown together where they had fallen open.

"I was just going for a walk. I couldn't sleep."

Even as I was saying it, I knew it sounded preposterous.

"Great night for it."

His face was serious. He thought I was an idiot. This was like an encounter in a bad rom com; only we had no interest in falling into a passionate embrace. I just wanted a cup of tea, actually. I also wondered what magnet had drawn me from my sleep in the middle of the night, towards a graveyard – though I already knew.

Nothing much was said on the way back. We went into the pub and he put on the lights, made tea, and waited. How could I discuss something I didn't understand? I jumped in first. Anything to get this over with.

"Okay, it was stupid, but I've been a bit out of sorts lately – what with all the travelling to and fro and work problems." The last bit tailed off and echoed in the silence.

"What's really happening?"

"You're a very stubborn man – and quite nosey; you know that?"

"Just concerned. I find you in the middle of the night – in a very fetching outfit…"

I had the grace to blush at this.

"Now, either you're a stalker with a massive crush on me or…"

"What? Or what?" I sounded too needy.

"Do you know much about the history of the old church?"

"How would I? I don't live round here any more."

"You mean you used to live here?"

"Only as a kid. We moved away before I went to big school." I smiled at the childlike terminology I'd used.

I found myself relating large chunks of my life history and he listened politely, but I sensed he wanted to get back to the poacher problem, so I yawned loudly a couple of times and he took the hint.

"Thanks for bringing me back."

He stood up, shrugged and half smiled, but at the door he surprised me by asking, "Have you ever seen the inside of the castle? Some interesting portraits in there."

Then after an awkward silence, he was gone.

I puzzled over his words for some time, and promised myself a visit to Skelton Castle in the near future to see these 'interesting portraits'.

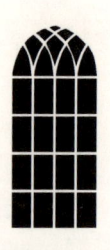

CHAPTER 10

I'll say this for the Duke William, they do a bloody good breakfast. Great chunks of bread (the stuff they call 'artisan' in London but it's just an uncut loaf here) and the freshest eggs, delivered daily by a local allotment owner – and probably at local prices. I was tucking in when George, the owner, brought a note to the table.

'Joanne, don't ever go wandering down to the old church again. It was just luck that I was in wait for poachers last night or you might have met them before I did. Not very clever of you, was it?

Go and see Mrs Barrington if you're that fascinated by the graveyard and the castle. She'll be able to tell you a lot more about the estate – and the church – in daylight.

All the Best,

Your personal voice of reason.'

I blushed a bit but was grateful to have some sense of direction and decided to take his advice. I heaved myself out of the dining room, taking it slowly to allow the digestion process to begin once more.

It puzzled me that I was so calm about these ghostly happenings but with the certainty of the sceptic, I still believed in logic. Anything that defied logic, I chose to ignore.

Mrs Barrington opened the door to the cottage and appraised me with an unwarranted intensity.

"You've seen him, haven't you?"

I was taken aback. "Who, Greg?"

"No," she sneered. "*You* know who I mean."

"No, that is, I haven't seen anyone. Yet."

"You will." Turning on her heel, she went to collect the church keys.

"Seen *her?*" she questioned. This time the tone was different.

"Honestly, I haven't seen anyone," I protested.

A long suspicious look later, and I was in the churchyard, passing *the* grave and then once more inside the church alone.

My memory had not registered it aright. There was a whole section I had not explored yet. The steps leading to the gallery had been repaired recently and could be accessed more easily since my initial visit. Good.

There was so much more to find out about everyone involved in this mystery and so little time to do it. Determined to stay positive and refusing to accept any more nonsense, I thought, 'I'll explore the relics at the far end of the church first,' to get the lie of the land, so to speak. However, before I could walk across to the enormous bible, I felt myself being gently but firmly steered, by the heat of a persistent pressure on my neck, towards the Winters' pew, where I found embers glowing red in the grate. My first thought was, 'This must be Mrs Barrington's doing,' but I wasn't sure whether to be grateful or not. Maybe lighting a fire was something that was required of the caretaker – to keep the damp at bay.

I stood for some time absorbing the warmth when my phone trilled out, making me jump.

At the same time, a horrible cawing noise rasped out as a crow, which must have been trapped in the building, flew directly at my eyes. Dropping my phone, I ducked, making a stupid little squealy noise as I ran to the door. Of all the birds, the crow is the most repellent to me and I could feel my flesh creep as I turned my face to avoid it.

The bird was probably spooked and hungry if it had been locked in overnight. The best thing to do was open the door wide and try to guide it out, but it was flying madly, directionless and in a great panic. I took off my coat and wafted it to the door but at the last moment, it took off towards the glow of the embers and I heard the bulk of its body hit the back of the grate as it fell.

Dashing back to the fire, which had flared up momentarily as it burned the poor creature's feathers, I used my raincoat to pull it out of the fire. As best I could, I covered the most damaged parts of its still-burning body to damp out the scorched wings, but I had scarcely a hope. It lay still in my hands. Thinking that the kindest thing to do was to wring its neck, I took it outside into the moisture-laden air but I just didn't have the stomach for it. As luck – good or bad – would have it, the disapproving caretaker was waiting directly outside the door, almost as if she'd anticipated something like this.

Once more that mean voice rasped out. "What on earth's happened now?"

Already feeling unnerved, my words fell over each other in a jumbled mess.

"Oh, Mrs Barrington, poor thing was trapped – inside the church. It flew at the fire."

Without another word, she wrenched the crow out of my hand and seconds later I heard the sickening crack of its neck. It had been so easy – the work of a moment. No fellow-feeling was offered and no discussion deemed necessary. She stared at me, offering up the body and I felt absurdly responsible for its death – although there could have been no blame attached to me. I swallowed hard and blinked back tears, trying to recover my equilibrium.

She turned abruptly back to the cottages, dropping the bird's body into a nearby bin as she spoke. "Was there anything else?"

I fought back the urge to throw up and tried to smile at her.

"Oh, yes. Thanks for making up the fire in the pew. That was very thoughtful, on such a miserable day." I held out the keys to her, but I noticed her change when I mentioned the fire. Her demeanour was immediately more friendly.

"Why don't you come in for a hot drink? It must have been a shock when the bird attacked you."

I was astounded at her cordiality, after the earlier barriers. Why was she being so positive? The cynic in me was suspicious. What did she want? And how did she know the bird had attacked me when I hadn't mentioned it?

Glueing the smile back on, I replied, "Thanks. I could do with a coffee right now."

She led the way into the tiny cottage, which I'd fancied exploring the moment I'd set eyes on it.

It was rather dingy inside – hardly surprising, surrounded as it was by woodland. There was a deal of clutter, plenty of old-fashioned ornaments and dust-gatherers but the most striking thing was its smell. There was an all-pervading scent of fox which initially overwhelmed me and I feared I might embarrass myself and have to cry off the refreshments, but as she opened the door to the tidy kitchen, the atmosphere lightened and the scent of fresh lemons filled the air.

"Sorry about the mess, I'm making lemonade," she explained, not sounding the least bit sorry, but I was so grateful that she was being more human, that I made a fool of myself, exclaiming at the wonder of someone actually *making* lemonade, taking in exaggerated lungfuls of the sugary lemon sweetness as we went. Mrs Barrington however, wasn't to be won over.

"By the way," my hostess said, po-faced, "no need to thank me for the fire. Nobody's been allowed to light a fire in the church for at least a hundred years now. Not since eighteen seventy, anyway. Nearly destroyed the whole building, you see, the last one, so you must be mistaken."

I was being examined minutely for my reaction to this piece of news. Luckily I managed to keep my disbelief under control. She was playing games and I refused to go along with them.

"Oh, really?" I ran my fingers across the model of a fox with her cubs which sat on the table and kept my gaze there as I replied. "Well, I must've imagined it – what with the distress of the bird and everything. Someone must've been burning some litter or something?" I hoped I sounded tentative so she wouldn't contradict me again.

The woman was not to be drawn. She smiled slightly,

a quizzical look on her face. She moved the model and placed it on the windowsill.

"Might I ask *you* something, Miss Logan? Why do you keep bobbing in and out of this church all the time? What exactly do you want? You've already decided it isn't suitable for your goddaughter's wedding. It doesn't take long to make these decisions. Why do you keep coming back?"

I'd forgotten I was in a village where everyone gossips about newcomers.

Leading me back to the sitting room, she produced a plate of biscuits and offered them to me, but with little grace. Maybe it was time to come clean.

"I'm fascinated. Strange things seem to be happening in there, and they seem in some way connected with the Winters. What's their history? Oh, and when we spoke earlier, who did you think I might have seen?"

She couldn't wait to get rid of me after that. She stood over me as I drank my coffee, all the while fiddling with a couple of ornaments, rearranging them on the overlarge mantelpiece and rubbing imaginary dust from their creases.

"If you want to know about the Winters, you should go across to the castle. It has a very interesting history and the present owners of the estate will be able to tell you much more than I can."

With that, she plonked the final ornament, a model of a hawk, back in its place, went into her office and made a phone call to someone at the castle. I was invited over whenever it was convenient, apparently, 'for a tour of the long gallery' where she reckoned there might be some objects of interest to me.

As I left, she dropped the bombshell she was saving, and enjoyed my unguarded reaction. "There's a portrait of one of the Winters there that *you* might want to see."

I didn't need to ask which one.

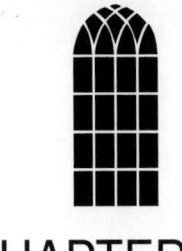

CHAPTER 11

Back in my room at the Duke William, I took out my laptop and wrote a journal entry. '*So, this is the situation. Although I'm a reasonably sensible woman, I have got it into my head that every time I go into a 13th Century church, the ghost of an 18th Century man is haunting – no, not haunting so much as troubling me.*'

There now. Seeing it down in print like that, I realised how ludicrous it sounded. What I needed was a dose of logic from someone sensible, and I hated to say it, even to myself, but that person would have to be Greg.

'Hopefully, all this nonsense will be laid to rest when I visit the castle anyway, so there'll be no need to seek him out. If it isn't, I'll ask the landlord where to find him – bit of a long shot to go wandering in poaching country again.'

I closed the journal, then re-opened it. '*Hm, that idea of deliberately doing something daft again, is sending a frisson of excitement through me. I think I'm a bit afraid of Greg. He's so sure of himself and confidence is always a turn-on, isn't it?*' Putting the book away, I refrained from even thinking I might fancy the man. I told myself that 'his tattoo puts me off,' but even I was not convinced.

CHAPTER 12

"Hiya Steve. Amelia's back at Rushpool Hall. This time she's dragged Lucy, the chief bridesmaid, along with her. Have to go and get changed for my meeting before they find me. Speak soon. Bye." I closed my mobile before he could respond.

I was dressing for the Skelton Castle meeting when George, the landlord, phoned up.

"Visitors."

"Sorry?"

"There's two lasses here for you. I can send 'em up or you can come down."

I don't think George had got the hang of customer service yet, but he was all the better for that. I hate too much subservience.

"I'll be five minutes, George. Thanks."

One last check in the mirror and I was on my way, but irritated that I couldn't have the luxury of pleasing myself about the time and place of my next meeting with Amelia. I was also anxious not to take the airheads with me. Their questions would be embarrassing and naïve. This was something I was determined to do alone.

"Jo-Jo!" The familiar high-pitched, girly screech rang around the bar once more.

Trying to look composed, I strained out a smile at the two silly girls. "Well, what brings you back here? There hasn't been another change of plan has there?"

"See, I told you she was really clever." Amelia smiled at her friend. "She's probably guessed already."

Lucy, gullible as ever, took it as a truth.

I ordered them drinks and in a no-nonsense voice said, "Look, I've made plans of my own, so your news will have to wait, sorry."

"What plans Jo-Jo... er Joanne?"

"It's a business meeting with some people at the castle... nothing to interest you."

Amelia's eyes shone at the prospect. "A castle?"

I might have got away then, but the pub door opened and Greg put his head round it and swept the room with a quick glance. His face lit up when he saw Amelia and she jumped up, teetered across and flung her arms around him. Watching her, as she kissed him full on the mouth, and certainly not in a 'just friends' way, caused me to feel a pang of – what? Anger? Jealousy?

'What the hell was that?' I wondered, taken aback. I didn't get a chance to find out because George caught my eye and tapped his watch, significantly.

"You don't wanna keep 'em waiting," he warned.

And I fled.

This meeting had been the most important thing in my mind during the last few days, but now, suddenly, my interest had waned. My brain was whirling. What was this new intimate relationship between Amelia and Greg? How and why had it changed? And when? Why didn't *I* know anything about it? And who could I ask? Had something gone wrong between Robert Belfort and Amelia?

These, and another hundred questions, would have to be put on hold.

It took an effort of will to quash them, but by the time I'd arrived at the castle entrance, my latent curiosity about the old church had surfaced again.

I was about to hear the history of this place, and of its occupants. I'd hear about the past and how it had encroached on the future. I would learn how these things pertained to me and whether anyone else had experienced similar... could I call them hauntings?

There was the sound of a heavy door handle being turned.

A small, balding man heaved open the door and invited me in. I recognised him as Reverend Martin, the priest from the train.

"You look surprised, my dear," he said in a rather weakened voice, "but everyone in my parish has dealings with the local clergy, you know."

In the high-ceilinged surroundings of the castle, he looked much smaller and more insignificant than he had in the crowded railway carriage. I sensed that here was a man who would rather not be involved in the business at hand. A press-ganged old man stood before me.

"Will I be meeting the owners of the estate too, Reverend Martin?"

"Oh, yes of course. I am merely the… erm… what am I? The show-er-in." He smiled at his own joke. "You'll be meeting at least one of the Gilling brothers, who own the castle, today."

It was clear he was tired and wanted this whole thing over as soon as I'd allow it.

"This is the Long Gallery, Joanna. And these are family portraits of all the owners of the castle since the year dot."

"It's 'Joanne'. Could you be a bit more specific about their dates, Reverend?" I asked, rather irritated. Was he deliberately playing the stereotype? If so, why? They knew I was coming to see the pictures and yet he was acting as if it was all a big surprise.

"Miss Logan." The voice was clear and authoritative, belonging to a man used to having his own way. It rang out and echoed along the corridor, shocking both me and the old priest.

We turned in unison and came face to face with the elder of the two brothers.

"Delighted," he roared as he walked towards me, hand held out. "John Gilling. Now then, I understand you're interested in our humble churchyard and all the tribulations of its past."

He appraised me with a lecher's eye, holding my handshake for too long as I followed in his wake. "Mind you, all this stuff is a bit dusty for a modern young woman like yourself. Must admit I was expecting someone a bit less – shall we say, glamorous." His eyes swept across my body as he spoke. I couldn't help thinking he was probably a nasty piece of work underneath all that 'hail fellow well met' façade.

I wished heartily that I'd worn a few more layers because I felt myself being bored-into by Mr G, and was about to make an excuse to leave when a new voice rang out, echoing from the door.

"John, so sorry I'm late. You go on now and I'll take over from here." This was Saul Gilling, the younger, more personable brother.

"I'm Saul," he said, "the one who's meant to be filling in some of the gaps in your church history, Miss Logan. I was delayed by some of the farm business – these things sometimes drag on because of silly details. Still, I'm here now. John?"

The bad cop turned on his heel and left without a word. The good cop, Saul, took my elbow and gently led me to the far end of the gallery. He talked with wit and knowledge about all the portraits from the 13th Century onwards and I was thoroughly entertained and fascinated.

'This is turning out to be so much better than I expected,' I thought gleefully.

When it came to the time of Edmund Winter, the only one I really wanted to know about, his tone changed somewhat. I suddenly felt quite nervous. I had been half in love with the ghost of Edmund Winter or at least, my dream version of him, for some time now.

I felt my heart thumping loudly in my chest, to the extent that I looked at my two companions, the priest and the landowner, to see whether they could hear it too. Preposterous.

Trouble was, now he was before me, I was almost scared to look at him, even though I was desperate to know everything.

"This young reprobate is Edmund, only child of Mary and Edwin Winter. I'm afraid he was a bad lot, Miss Logan. Spoiled, as many of the heirs to these great estates were."

I could hear Saul Gilling's voice but it had an echo to it, as if it were reverberating through a long tunnel.

"Oh, he's a handsome devil alright. My wife keeps the portrait here because all the ladies who visit like to look at him, but it's said he brought a great deal of shame and sadness to the family in his time."

He was about to move on to the next picture but I wasn't able to leave Edmund Winter yet. Here before me was a man in the fullness of youth – I'd say late twenties. There was an amused expression in the face, a knowingness in the eyes and curl of the lips which made him look wise beyond his years. Was this the Edmund Winter of my recurring dream? Maybe. Although at that moment, my mental picture of him was extinguished by the portrait before me.

The Reverend Martin broke into my train of thought by asking if this was the Winter I was interested in.

"Erm, yes. I was wondering what he'd done, for everyone to disapprove of him so wholeheartedly. He looks quite kind and open to me."

Saul Gilling laughed out loud at this, but, since I'd first clapped eyes on Edmund, I had been mesmerised and couldn't even glance at the two men showing me round. I suddenly felt odd – quite faint and too hot – and I stumbled slightly, still staring at the portrait.

Reverend Martin's arms caught me as I slipped out of consciousness.

When I came to, I was half-lying on a rather elegant chaise longue in some sort of small sitting room. An oldish woman was hovering over me and making fussy, clucking noises of concern and the old priest sat in the background enjoying – cliché of clichés – a small sherry.

"I'm so sorry," I mumbled, as I became more aware of the situation. "I'm not usually one of those women who blacks out at nothing. I don't know how this happened."

"Did you eat any breakfast, my dear?" This, predictably, from the Reverend.

I was sufficiently revived to smile at that. "Have you ever *eaten* breakfast at the Duke William, Reverend Martin? They pride themselves on giving, well, shall we say, American portions of everything. I've never eaten so much in my life."

A polite chuckle went round the room in response to my weak attempt at a joke, and I was given a rather large brandy. Gratefully I warmed it between my palms and nursed it because I wasn't ready to forget the remaining questions I had about Edmund and his history.

"You may have to return, Joanne, to hear the rest of the stories about Winter – and indeed the Demoniacs." Saul was happy to continue his account of the Winter family history. "You will of course have heard of Lawrence Sterne, the novelist? He, alongside all the other idle, rich young men in London Society, would meet at the Castle, and in the caves to drink, gamble and generally indulge in debauchery. You've heard of the Hellfire Club? Well, this was the northern equivalent, apparently." He paused long enough to refill our glasses. "Nobody knows exactly what went on at their meetings, which is probably just as well, from the scraps of information in circulation, but…"

That was as much as I heard of the story because I must've fallen asleep. Probably the effect of the warmth from an unnecessary coal fire mixed with the heat of the brandy as it eased its way around my body, but drowsiness and a mixture of emotions lulled me into a deep coma-like state. When I awoke, with a raging thirst, a hasty glance at the grandfather clock in the corner told me I'd been out cold for two hours.

"I'm so terribly sorry," I mumbled, but the room was empty and the fire had died to ashes.

"Hello?"

The word echoed through the high ceilings and came back to me. Stumbling from the chaise to the heavy door, I took hold of the doorknob and was startled to feel another hand on mine – but there *was* no hand – no person – in the room. The warmth and the pressure of the hand stopped me from removing mine for a few seconds; then it was gone.

I felt rather stupid as it was, so I wasn't about to tell any of the staff about the odd sensation I'd felt. After a minute or two, indeed, I began to doubt it myself. Wrenching open the door, I found a pleasant woman in an adjoining kitchen, who gave me a glass of cold water, then showed me out.

The welcome freshness of the air in Skelton Castle grounds was enough to blow away any remaining fancies from my mind. After a few gulps, I was ready for the wander back to the Duke William and the very different problem of Amelia, Greg and Robert.

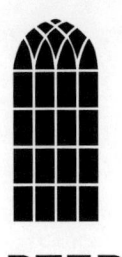

CHAPTER 13

To take my mind off the wedding, I'd sent Sylvie a lovely bouquet of internet flowers, (even though I knew they wouldn't have any smell). Not that it mattered. I was sure she'd be thrilled anyway. Not many people in the corporate world are spontaneous nowadays, except about money-making opportunities. Kindness is always a lovely surprise and I knew Sylvie would be appreciative. I felt a bit better after that.

I sent a slightly more difficult message of apology to Steve. He'd been grappling with our present orders without my help for some time now. My absence wasn't just about my plans for the wedding, although I could kid myself that it was. No, I was becoming more and more dissatisfied with our relationship. Like a marriage of convenience, it wasn't providing either of us with what we really wanted. At first we just needed '*a person*', someone we came first with, but now it seemed like we were just rubbing along together for the sake of it. If we'd wished for a 'marriage of true minds' we had been disappointed and had settled for an okay friendship instead.

I worded a handwritten letter but it took me a long time to get the right tone. I simply outlined my feelings – or more accurately, my lack of feelings – and assumed he would feel the same.

However, I couldn't kid myself. This had all come about since I saw the display of affection between Amelia and Greg. It stirred something I had yet to define in myself. It was a sort of homesickness for a better relationship. I didn't understand it fully because it wasn't something I'd ever truly had.

I put off sending that particular letter for the time being. It required a cooler head and a bit of emotional distance before posting.

I decided to turn my mind once again to the matter of Amelia's behaviour. It suddenly seemed a good idea to challenge her about it, once and for all, and I met her and Lucy in the opulent surroundings of the bar at Rushpool Hall, Amelia's crash pad, as she put it. Beautiful stained glass and wooden wainscotting gave an impression that all was well with the world, as these lovely old places do. Nothing was too much trouble for the well-trained staff and the coffee was excellent.

The only trouble was me. I'd come here to confront Amelia without really thinking it through, which was quite out of character. I'd launched into a diatribe about Amelia's bad behaviour and her unfaithfulness to Robert, without waiting for her to tell me herself, but I was so angry about what I was mentally calling 'Amelia's Gregsnog', that logic flew out of the window.

"Well really, Joanne, there's no need to be so *very* unreasonable about everything. It's not as if I've done anything wrong, is it?"

The querulous tone was beginning to irritate me. I suppose if I'm being fair, everything about Amelia was irritating me. The very *fact* of Amelia was, in itself, irritating, given my present mood.

"Nothing wrong? So, there's nothing wrong with grabbing a stranger in a bar and wrapping yourself around him?"

The people at the other tables stared but I was past caring.

I'd spent the morning trying not to be so annoyed with the pair of them. Instead I'd been deciding to do the right thing for every one of my work colleagues, to avoid dwelling on the incident at the Duke.

To add insult to injury, Amelia had once again changed her mind and chosen the old church as her venue of choice.

After I'd said my piece, Amelia flounced off. It was a habit I'd recognised in her of old, but I didn't blame her this time. She'd been humiliated in public. Lucy shrank into the huge leather sofa, looking hugely embarrassed at my outburst. When her friend was safely out of the building, she turned to me with a look of disgust. I noticed her hands slowly shredding a red paper napkin as she spoke.

"Robert called Amelia yesterday to say he'd been having misgivings about the wedding. You know her well enough to know how she'd react to that. We drove directly up here to see you in the hope that you could smooth things over between them. We talked about you on the journey – she really looks up to you, you know, and she thinks you fancy that bloke in the pub but, as usual, you're terrified to acknowledge it – well that's what she said anyway. None of my business, of course, but her dad's told her about Jenny, and your horrible ex-boyfriend – dunno his name. He says since you lost Jenny, you won't get close to anyone."

She looked at the wreckage of my face and was embarrassed. "I think she wanted to give you a push in the right direction. Thought the snog would do it. Seems like it worked?"

There was a horrible silence as the whole place held its breath. After a few embarrassing moments, Lucy broke it. "Sorry, but I just thought you should be told."

We both stared at the mess of napkin confetti she'd made on the table and the floor of the lounge, unable to look at each other and unable to say anything.

It was the first time I'd heard anyone mention my lost baby's name in fifteen years. I felt angry and betrayed, but then I began to roll the letters around in my head. 'Jenny'. My poor child. She was only hours old when she died but I'd mapped out her personality into a fully rounded adult in the ensuing years, yet I'd never shared my thoughts with anyone, and now *this* was thrust upon me, and it all rushed back unexpectedly, without giving me the chance to put on my emotional armour.

I suddenly became indignant. Who were *they* to bandy about my personal stuff? What made this girl – this silly girl

– think she had the right to discuss my history, to imagine my reactions and feelings? Why ever did James tell his airhead of a daughter in the first place? How dared they all discuss me and my past?

I slowly became aware again of the other people in the bar. They turned away and pretended they were no longer interested. The floor show was over as soon as Amelia had left and they were all chatting animatedly and falsely over their assorted aperitifs and their own concerns once more. Lucy and I, upset in our own ways, were silent and still.

Not knowing what to do, I did something mundane... I walked to the bar and ordered two coffees. It might've been brandies but I was driving and the old cautious gene came into play. As I walked back to our table again, I suddenly remembered.

I put them down and as I did so, I challenged Lucy with a sudden, "Hang on, how does *that* have anything to do with Ammy eating the face off Greg in the Duke William? I mean, I know she's a tease, but – *he* seemed to be enjoying it too. How d'you explain that?"

Lucy brightened up. "He's a man, isn't he? And, er... and I was filming it – on my phone?" She'd done that little upward lilt at the end of the sentence. It drives me crackers.

"Why were you 'filming it on your phone'?" I asked, as one with infinite patience speaks to a small child.

"She wanted me to send it to Robert. Make him jealous..." The sentence tailed off as she realised how ridiculous it sounded. "One of those 'it seemed a good idea at the time' moments?"

We both gulped down the rest of our coffee, anxious not to stay in each other's company longer than necessary.

"And Greg?" I asked, gathering up my things. "How did *he* react to his starring role?" I knew it was ludicrous to describe it like that but I couldn't resist.

"Well, he laughed."

"He 'laughed'? Is that all?"

I don't know what I expected, but that wasn't it.

"He said something like, 'Well, you're gorgeous and all that, but I think I'd prefer someone me own age, thanks very much.' Then he added, 'But *she's* just gone out,' and he laughed."

"Oh, right," I said, my cheeks burning at the unexpected revelation. Picking up my things, I thanked Lucy and hurried away, desperate to forget the whole conversation.

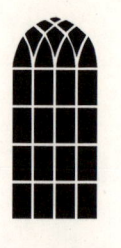

CHAPTER 14

"Never had you down as the swoony type." He turned his head slightly as he spoke.

Arriving back at the Duke William, my mind still in turmoil, I was quite taken aback by this comment from Greg, who was standing at the bar with George as I walked in.

At first I had no idea what he was talking about but then I realised that the gossipy landlord had heard through the bush telegraph about my Skelton Castle adventure.

"Oh, yeah, I carry a bottle of sal volatile and some smelling salts in case my corsets get too tight and I need to be brought back to life again. Happens all the time," I laughed, thinking I had to match the mood.

With a slight hand movement, Greg offered me a drink and this time I accepted.

"So, what happened?"

"I think it was just the stuffiness, really, in the castle. It was quite airless. And of course, I'd had a bit of a rush to get there, 'cos of the unexpected visitors – I mean Amelia and Lucy. Just general panic really."

He seemed convinced and nodded sympathetically. "You seemed a bit worried when you came in. Is everything alright?"

"Well, Amelia can be hard work sometimes."

"Mm. She does seem to enjoy controlling people. Bit spoiled as a kid, I imagine?"

I wasn't comfortable discussing Amelia at present so I simply shrugged and he accepted. We were both staring straight ahead of us at the paraphernalia on the bar counter. I was thinking about his response to Ammy and Lucy – was he saying he fancied me, I wondered, feeling like a daft kid.

"Have you been back to the church or to old ma Barrington's den any more?" he asked, breaking the awkward silence.

"I expect you already know. Everyone here seems to know everything about me. Ammy's friend, the one I've only met *once*, knows my past history in minute detail. In fact, my life story's being broadcast on local radio tomorrow."

"Woah. Where did that come from?" He turned towards me, looking concerned.

I really needed to get things off my chest but didn't want to tell George – the grapevine who everyone heard it through – so I indicated a corner table by the window and we went to talk in private.

Once we'd settled, I launched into the story about Amelia's betrayal – for that's what I saw it as – and the stuff she was prepared to gossip about to all her friends. I was under no illusion that Lucy was the only one of her circle who was privy to my private life. Impossible that it had not been made public.

Greg listened patiently. He had a sort of stillness about him that encouraged confession. For the first time since her death, I was able to talk about my baby girl.

"What was her name?" he asked.

"Jenny. I insisted that she be given a name and a birth certificate, although her father was against it. He said it would just prolong the agony. What a joke. He left soon after. Got a job in Scotland on the rigs. I never heard from him again. You see, that's what men can do. They can leave a mess behind and never look at it again. They can walk away."

He made no attempt to defend 'men' or protest against that horribly unfair assessment of them.

"Did you get a photo of her?"

"No. I was quite ill after the birth but they let me hold her for a few minutes, only, the painkilling drugs kicked in soon after and I must've fallen asleep, because when I came round, she was gone."

Once again, there was no furrowed brow of mock concern. There was also no attempt to squeeze my hand. Just that stillness. I was so grateful.

"Do you know why Amelia thought it should be public knowledge?"

I returned to the familiar merry-go-round. I knew Amelia was doing her amateur psychiatry on me, thinking I was too buttoned-up and thinking she knew the cause.

"I know she didn't spill it all out because she is a bad person; she's just a young, thoughtless one." I got up from the table and asked, "Would you like another drink?"

"No, thanks. Would you like to walk round the castle grounds? I have something of a confession to make and it's always better when you walk beside someone rather than staring at them."

Intrigued, I agreed.

Once we'd passed through the gates, he began.

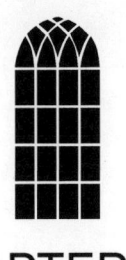

CHAPTER 15

"We've met before," he said as we strolled in the beautiful grounds. "A long time ago, but I remember it vividly."

I gave him a puzzled look.

"You were one of the blue and red girls."

Puzzled, I made light of it. "You make me sound like a bruise."

He looked to the side as if he were seeing a scene, long gone, and explained. "It was a scorching hot day just before the summer holidays; my first year at secondary school. A few of us had gone on a bike ride along the Cleveland Way, but it had turned out to be a lot further, longer and hotter than we'd bargained for. Then my bike got a puncture. Well, I say 'my bike'. It was borrowed from my Uncle Stewart and a bit too big for me if truth be told. Anyway, it was decided that I'd have to walk back with it or at least inland, until I found somewhere to buy a puncture kit. The other lads offered to take my rucksack and stuff so I'd have less to carry, but that left me with no food or water." He shrugged. "So, there I was, trundling the stupid flat-tyred bike along the cliff path to Saltburn, hot, bothered and desperately hungry and thirsty, when I saw you both. You were in a field, I remember, surrounded by Queen Anne's Lace, up to your shoulders and you were wearing identical dresses of some sort of flimsy stuff, twirling round and round until you were so dizzy you fell to the floor laughing. I watched you for ages but you were both so busy with the game, competing to see which of you dropped first, you were oblivious to anything else."

He continued. "Then I rang my bell – a bit tinny but it did the trick and you both turned to face me. There were bits of blossom stuck to your cheeks and you were both flushed with excitement, but you did come across to see what was wrong. Your friend was in red and you were in blue. She did all the questioning: what had happened, where was I going, how far had I come, how far did I have to go and all the rest of it. I remember, you just stood looking at the bike and the inner tube slung over my shoulder. You hardly looked at me. You had this blue dress on and you were bunching it up with one hand, like you were embarrassed, but you looked very pretty and sad. When the red one said, in a daft grown-up voice, 'We have to go now. I hope you get to Saltburn safely,' you looked concerned.

"*She* turned away and set off back to the houses further up from the cliff but you made as if to go, then paused as if you'd thought better of it and turned back, holding out a small bottle of cherryade. You thrust it into my hand, then you ran off. I watched until you were just a blur of blue on the horizon, and I heard your mate, the red one, telling you off for giving me the drink. 'Well, don't expect me to give you half of mine. You'll have to make do with the water out of the cemetery tap and you'll probably get worms or something from that and it'll be your own fault.' Then you gave her a push and twirled and twirled, laughing again, and doing a backward wave in my direction. How could I ever forget you? You've always been the 'blue girl' in my memory ever since."

I was stunned and we walked in silence for some time, contemplating Greg's story in our own ways. I *did* remember the incident and an overwhelming sadness suddenly enveloped me. For what? Something indefinable. The girl I used to be, perhaps? Lost innocence? That's what all writers bang on about, isn't it? Lost youth.

'What would the Joanne I am today have done, given the same circumstances?' I asked myself.

"So, did you realise straight away, that it was me?" I asked Greg. "You know, when I found you all the worse for wear in the pub, that first night?"

He smiled. "No, not immediately."

I was still curious. "So, when?"

"Does it matter?"

The man was so annoying. Why didn't he just give me a straight answer?

"Not really, no."

But it did.

CHAPTER 16

I hadn't realised that Greg actually lived in the gatehouse to Skelton Castle. Well, I hadn't ever thought about where he might live, but I'd made a vague assumption that he'd live in the village in a little cottage on the High Street, perhaps. As we neared his house, he invited me in for a drink and I became unaccountably shy. It was ridiculous after the secrets we'd shared, but I wasn't sure how much more I wanted to know about him. It was all getting a bit too intimate, somehow.

We were about to go into the house when an oldish woman opened it from the inside.

"Oh, you're back," she smiled.

'Oh God, does he still live with his mother?' I thought. 'How awful.'

"Freda, this is Joanne. She's here looking for a place to stage a wedding."

"Oh? Not yours I hope?"

He put a protective arm around her, smiling as he responded with, "Jo, Freda's my 'little treasure'. Well, she's nothing of the sort really. She's always nagging me but she keeps the house clean and tidy, so I let her nag."

The woman obviously adored him and smiled up into his face. "I've left you a corned beef pie in the fridge," she told him, "and there's some soup for tomorrow's dinner."

Greg kissed the top of her head. This mutual admiration was completely alien to me. In my world, friendship generally ran on sarcasm and irony, not genuine affection. I found it embarrassing, but at the same time, I envied them their closeness. As if she'd read my thoughts, Freda pushed him roughly aside and, giving him an old-fashioned look, walked away.

He beckoned me in, but I was now reluctant to continue our tête-à-tête.

"Actually, I think I'd better get back. I'm expecting a call from work soon and I've neglected things lately so I'd better make my peace."

"Oh, right." And with a slightly raised eyebrow, "See you around then?"

As soon as he'd accepted the excuse, I wanted desperately to stay. It was obvious that he saw through the lie and was amused by it. Probably thought I was either scared he'd snog me or... or what? Stupid, stupid woman. What had changed in the couple of minutes at the threshold of his house?

As I turned away, I heard a voice in my ear.

The voice.

'Come and see me. I'm very close.'

I caught my breath and felt a tingle travelling up my spine.

"Oh, by the way..." Greg was calling me back and fishing in his breast pocket, "the Gillings asked me to give you this."

I was rooted to the spot so he had to bring it over to me.

It was a thick cream envelope, with a handwritten name on the front in a very flowing script: '*Ms. Joanne Logan.*'

I walked slowly away, in the direction of the church, intrigued as to what it could be. Probably an apology for leaving me to sleep, after what I was calling my 'funny turn'. Either that, or Saul Gilling was inviting me back.

The envelope contained a small, postcard-sized copy of the portrait of Edmund Winter that had fascinated me in Skelton Castle. There was no message.

I hurried to All Saints, staring all the while at the image before me, and not understanding why I was going there.

CHAPTER 17

Inside the church, it was cool and still. It was hardly a match for my mood, which had been stirred up, first by Amelia then Greg and now Edmund Winter. It was almost as if they were competing to see which of them could dominate my thoughts, but it was having the opposite effect. I was simply confused.

My ten-year-old self was in my head, laughing about our game; deliberately making ourselves dizzy and enjoying losing control. I felt a tenderness towards her, and the child Greg, hair damp with sweat, dragging his useless bike in the summer heat.

I pushed them away, one by one, then I took out the picture of my friendly neighbourhood ghost and went to stand in the centre aisle.

I had gone back to my car before coming here to collect a couple of things I thought I might need. It was time to confront whatever it was in this place that had been haunting me. I wrapped my fingers around the crucifix in my pocket, just for comfort, and spoke.

"Right then. Here I am. What do you want?"

The final syllable died away but nothing happened. This was stupid.

"What do you want with me, Edmund Winter?"

Just as I was about to walk away, feeling half-disappointed yet triumphant that I was no longer in thrall to him, I felt as if an iron band were tightening around my head.

Whoever or whatever was doing this was *not* a benign presence. I felt a foreboding as never before.

At the back of the church, I could see a figure standing very still, and wearing some kind of hooded cloak. The face was obscured by a sort of scarf or cloth so there were no visible features, just a darkness where the face should be. Clutching the crucifix, like some medieval witchfinder, my stomach churning, I moved slowly towards the shadowy being. I could see now that it was indicating the smaller of the two sarcophagi, which had obviously been made for a child, on the left, behind the pulpit. If this had been in a horror film, I'd have been shouting at the heroine, 'Make a run for it and don't be so stupid!' but my need to know drove me on.

What was it that the 'ghost' for want of a better word, wanted me to see? I bent over the child's coffin and for a fleeting second, it appeared to me that there was a small bundle – the form of a swaddled baby – lying in the stone sarcophagus. All I could feel at that moment was pity. I put out a hand to touch the infant but it was no longer there and I recoiled in horror. I must've broken the spell somehow.

I stood for a long time, unable to move, at first, rigid with fear and panic then beginning to feel calmer, and reassured by the silence of the shadowy figure, I thought about the situation I was in.

This was a mother whose baby had died, and my instinct was to turn to her in empathy, but as I looked into what had seemed to be an empty space where the face should be, I saw horrific injuries and I had to turn away, revolted as I was. My mind was screaming inside my skull, 'Run! Run now!' but I could not move. I looked around, desperate for an escape from the nightmare, and as I did so, the band of iron tightened around my head once again, making me gag with the pain.

I couldn't see clearly but I felt around in a panic for the shape of the little coffin and placed the crucifix into it. I may have muttered some sort of prayer, I can't remember. I was acting on instinct by now.

Something I did or said must have worked, because the figure vanished, bringing with it a relief from the pain, but not from my sense of horror and sadness. I slumped into the nearest pew and lost track of time, thinking about the events of the day. The pain had cleared by now, and with it a certain lightness and clarity came into my head.

Every nerve had been strained – but then, in seconds, everything was calm again. It was impossible to make sense of anything, so sudden was my recovery and so quick was my return to peace.

Feeling weak and disorientated, and wishing to be rid of Edmund Winter, I carefully placed his picture on the first pulpit by the open bible and made for the door. Outside, a slight drizzle was falling and the air was fresh and green. I breathed deeply and wondered what to do next. I could go back to ask Greg about the church ghosts but I was afraid he wouldn't take it seriously.

Maybe, if I could find Reverend Martin he'd be able to tell me a bit more. After all, he'd hinted that things had been 'odd' when he'd ministered there.

Accordingly, I made my way to the new All Saints Church on the High Street and found it open. A wedding had just taken place and there were clumps of people, looking uncomfortable in their Sunday best, the women in unaccustomed headgear and heels. They seemed to lack purpose, hanging around the grounds, probably waiting to go to the reception, once the bride and groom had left. Maybe it was a bad time but 'carpe diem', I told myself.

I wandered in trying to be unobtrusive, and found the old priest in the vestry, putting away all the wedding paraphernalia. He paused when he saw me.

"Joanna. How very nice of you to call. As you see, you find me trying to make sense of this mess – as usual." The thin shoulders shrugged off his dilemma and he beckoned me to sit down, moving a pile of hymnals as he did so. "How are you? No more fainting fits, I trust?"

I was grateful for this mundane conversation after the high drama of recent events.

"No, no. Back to normal, thanks. Oh, and it's 'Joanne'."

He nodded an acknowledgement as he shuffled various papers into some semblance of order.

"Tea?"

"Oh, let me." I looked round the tiny room then wandered over to the sink where I found the tea things. Busying myself with the ritual of tea making helped me stay calm. It's what we do, in emergencies or times of stress. We make tea. We call it 'a lovely cup of tea'.

When Jenny died, so many people offered me 'a nice cuppa' or 'a lovely cup of tea'; hoping it would ease some of the pain, I suppose, yet knowing, as they put their fumbling hands to the useless task, that it wouldn't.

Passing him the tea with my hands still trembling slightly, I broached the subject of the ghostly woman in All Saints.

"So, there must be more to it than Edmund Winter's ghost just appearing from time to time," I concluded. "Who was the woman I saw in the church? Has anyone else reported seeing her? What's her story?"

Reverend Martin, not one to be hurried, took a sip of tea, and nodded his approval.

"Nobody knows the whole story," he said. "It came to me in fragments from several people who knew just a little part of the history. Eventually I managed to piece together as much of the story as possible, to make sense of it. Mrs Barrington probably knows more than I do, but then…" he trailed off with a knowing sideways glance.

"Okay," I said. "Tell me all you know and I'll get the rest out of her, somehow. Amelia still thinks she's getting married there and I can't move anything forward until we've sorted this out. That is, if there's even going to be a wedding at all."

I failed to mention my emotional involvement with the long-dead 'handsome devil' that was Edmund Winter. I felt inside my handbag for the picture but remembered I'd left it in the church. If I wanted to retrieve it, I'd have to go back there.

CHAPTER 18

I sipped the hot, strong tea and Reverend Martin began his story.

"I first met the Gilling brothers, when they were youngsters and I was newly arrived here at All Saints. The last incumbent had left suddenly, saying he had emotional problems and couldn't stay a moment longer. That's not as uncommon as you'd think in the priesthood, by the way, so I wasn't unduly worried. Anyway, he'd left a letter for me, a sort of welcome but also a warning and I wanted to get to the bottom of things so… well… I asked the estate owners what the problems had been, *before* reading what he had to say."

He took another sip of tea and continued. "At first, they were dismissive, blaming Father Blackett's 'instability', but once I'd read his letter, and made up my own mind as to its veracity, I decided the warnings of ghostly activity within the church were so specific, I had to believe them or at least test them out. Accordingly, I confronted the owners directly, and Mr Gilling Sr elected to tell me the story handed down by his own parents. Apparently, Edmund Winter – who'd had a reputation for being a bit of a rake and a womaniser – had fallen for a young woman, a local farmer's girl, called Alice Thomas, and he seemed finally ready to settle down. His family hoped, rather than believed, this to be true, and although the girl was not as educated nor her family as wealthy as the Winters would have liked, she was respectable, healthy and pretty, so they gave their approval to the match and welcomed the family into their inner circle."

At that point, the old priest stood to check that the wedding guests had gone safely on their way. He looked through the grimy vestry window and nodded to himself, before continuing. "During the courtship, all those involved held their breath. They feared that, judging from past form, Edmund might tire of Alice's company and go back to his old ways before long. However, the opposite was true. The more he saw of Alice, and more to the point – the more she denied him congress – 'Not until we're married,' she'd said and I believe she stuck to that vow initially – the keener he was, until he became obsessive and spent almost all his free time with her. She must have been strong-willed because by all accounts, he could be very persuasive... Before he met Alice, he used to belong to a strange set. As you may have heard, they called themselves the 'Demoniacs' and ran their meetings along the lines of the Hellfire Club, being the northern version of that selfish, self-indulgent, pleasure-seeking sect. It was made up of the sons of the landed gentry with a sprinkling of bohemians – painters, writers and the like."

"Yes," I told him. "I had heard something about that, but do go on."

He broke off, shaking his head at the sin of it all and became philosophical. "Why did these rich, idle young men get so much pleasure in making others' lives a misery? I mean, they could see the poverty around them. They could see the farm labourers' hard lives and their children's lack of education and advancement. Or maybe they couldn't – or chose not to? Sorry, I digress. There are books written about their activities should you wish to find out more, but I believe the novelist Laurence Sterne was one of the group. Worth looking up, I should say."

I wanted Reverend Martin to stick to his story and must've been fidgeting or squirming in my seat, because he stopped to offer me more tea or something stronger? Believing that he'd continue more directly after a sherry, I agreed.

Once the glasses had been filled, we continued.

"Where was I? Oh yes, anyway, Edmund and Alice's courtship was the talk of the village. All her friends were envious of her good catch and she enjoyed being the centre of attention, I understand.

"When he finally popped the question, in the April, and Alice accepted him of course, an engagement party was arranged to which the whole of Skelton was invited. It must have cost a small fortune and preparations were well under way, to the general joy of the populace, when something happened which changed the course of all their lives.

"The night before the engagement party, I assume in a moment of weakness and in honour of the commitment he'd made to her, Alice finally gave in to Edmund and they consummated their relationship. I believe it happened in the old church, which was particularly shocking to me when I first heard of it.

"Sadly, once he'd known her — and I use the biblical sense of the word here, Joanne — some of the shine, as they say, went off the relationship.

"I used to wonder if that might've happened with Henry VIII and Anne Boleyn if she'd submitted to him before marriage."

He paused again, taking a sip of sherry. I needed to drag him back on track again.

"So what happened next? Did he dump her?' I asked, downing the sherry, impatient to know the ending.

"No, no, indeed," he said, quite emphatically. "On the contrary, he was honourable at first and may have realised that, with his engagement being public knowledge, he couldn't simply call it off. He was still rather fond of the girl and he didn't want to blacken either of their names, so they carried on with the engagement bash and I gather a good time was had by all. The wedding date was set for the following summer and they got along nicely until harvest time, which was when the tragedy occurred."

I was wise enough not to hurry him by this time, so I offered to refill his glass, and mine.

"How are you enjoying your stay up here?" he asked, with a smile that expected a positive answer.

"Oh, I love it — but then again, I always did."

"I often say to southerners who come up, 'Don't tell everyone how beautiful it is, or they'll invade us!' Rather unkind, I know," he twinkled, "but I like to think this coastline is our secret."

Once again, when confronted with such simple goodness, I was overwhelmed with guilt for my supposed sophistication, which was really dressed-up cynicism. In a moment of gratitude, I put my hand on his and squeezed it.

"Thank you for this."

He smiled again. "It's late. Shall we get back to the story at the pub?" he asked. "I rather like to eat before 8pm, if that's okay."

We washed the various glasses and cups and walked to the Duke William. I was desperate to hear the end but wanted to buy Reverend Martin dinner before we continued the story of Alice and Edmund. I think I'd already pieced the puzzle together by then, but feared it didn't end happily.

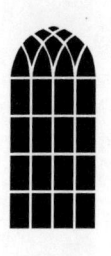

CHAPTER 19

The bar was full when we arrived. The football team plus hangers-on were out in force but I couldn't see Greg.

'Nicely tucked up with his corned beef pie and a cup of tea,' I decided. It was mean-spirited to reduce the man to that, but I was very disappointed that he was nowhere to be seen.

"No Greg?" I asked one of the lads.

"Eh? Yeah, he was here earlier. Sorting out the fixtures for next season, so he had to be." He shouted to the lumpen man at the bar, "Gary, Greg gone off, has he?"

Gary shrugged.

Reverend Martin stood patiently watching. "Did you want him to join us?" he smiled.

"Let's just go through to the dining room, shall we?" I said. "Can't wait to get to the end of the saga!"

I returned the smile and we walked through to the more sedate end of the pub.

"So, tell me how it all ended."

"Well, there was great excitement around the harvest that year, because the old scythes and hand gathering of the crops had recently been replaced by mechanisation – the Industrial Revolution, you understand."

I nodded, mentally piecing together my own puzzle.

"Alice was walking to the castle through the fields, having some wedding business to attend to. You'd have more idea than I would about that. Anyway, some of the men were quite excited about the new threshing machine and I believe her brother, Jerome, called her across to see it in action. The man in charge, keen to show off his prowess, I suppose, started it up and somehow, Alice had put herself in its path and one of the arms caught her dress and pulled her down. Once on the ground, it was the work of a moment for her hair, which she'd left loose, to become tangled in the mechanism. Of course, they switched the thing off immediately but the damage to her face, head and legs was extensive. As you can imagine, medical care was rudimentary in those times, and the doctors patched her up as best they could, but they didn't make much of a job of it and the poor girl was left with freakishly horrible scarring to much of her face."

One of the bar staff brought us our menus at that point and we had to break off momentarily to make our choices.

He then continued. "Her beautiful hair would never grow back, of course, having been ripped from her skull with such force; and she was left with a permanent limp, the right leg permanently shorter than the left... It's all written up in the castle files. I'm sure Saul will let you see them."

For a kind man, the old priest had been strangely unmoved in his retelling of Alice's tragic story. It had affected *me* much more than him. I felt as if I knew her, after seeing the apparition in the church earlier.

"As I told you, I saw her," I blurted out, "in the old church, earlier today."

He looked sad. "Yes. I have seen her many times. Him, too. It's a place of tragedy despite the many happy events which have taken place there."

There was no mention of the baby I'd seen in the stone coffin. I wondered if he knew.

A sudden noise from the other end of the Duke startled us out of our reverie.

"Here's your man," said Reverend Martin.

Greg was centre stage in the bar, giving out what I assume were the fixture lists for next season. He looked happy and handsome, smiling as the team milled around him taking their copies.

"You've played a blinder there, mate," shouted John, the man I'd met on my first night at the pub, more personable now though, and more sober.

"Brilliant," said another. The approving comments continued as the men drowned each other out.

My eyes had widened when the Reverend had called him, 'your man'.

I was half pleased that he had seen something between us, but surprised at the assumption. He wasn't my man, yet I was feeling something akin to regret that he wasn't.

Finishing our food – well, me leaving half of mine, as usual – I walked with Rev Martin through the bar to see him off to the Rectory.

When we reached the door, I said, "I take it that Edmund didn't behave well after the accident."

"I don't think he meant to be unkind, my dear. He just couldn't bear to look at the once-beautiful woman he'd loved, who had now changed beyond all recognition. I don't condemn him, but much of the village did. Initially, of course, he was attentive to her needs, summoning the best doctors and so on and he continued to play the part of the devoted fiancé, but it was too much for him. Once Alice was out of danger, he decided to go away for a while. The wedding had, of course, been postponed, but everyone knew it would never take place. What they hadn't realised was that Edmund had no intention of coming back."

We stood in the vestibule with the door half-opened and he continued. "Alice, her hopes and dreams shattered forever, became embittered and reclusive. She spent much of her time praying in church – for what, nobody knows – a miracle perhaps?"

In the ensuing pause, I thanked him as he bustled about, searching for an umbrella he was sure he'd brought with him. I was able to reassure him that he hadn't.

"Well, goodnight, my dear and thank you for dinner." He scanned the sky. "It's a clear night for a stroll. Go and join Greg before he gives up on you completely."

And with that, he was off down the lane.

I stayed in the vestibule for some time, contemplating the space where he had been and thinking about the extraordinary story he had told me, when, once again, I felt the heat of a hand on my back and a slow finger tracing my vertebrae, one by one, down the length of my spine. It stopped at my waist and lingered there, having the same effect as usual, arousing every nerve in my body.

I stood stock still for a moment then turned slowly to see Greg standing in the doorway.

"What *are* you doing?" I asked, a hint of indignation in my voice.

"I'm looking at you from a different angle," he said, leaning against the wall, head on one side. "What are *you* doing?"

As ever, I got the feeling that he was laughing at me. From where he was standing, there was no way that he'd have been able to reach my back. Then I realised at once that it must have been Edmund.

"I'm thinking."

I smiled into his handsome face.

"How's the old priest doing nowadays?" he asked, straightening up. "Must be better company than me, eh?"

It was a question I chose to ignore; otherwise I'd have been forced to admit that I hadn't *really* intended to work at all that night. Maybe I owed him an explanation, but my body was still feeling the repercussions of that ghost-caress.

"Sorry. I just thought he looked in need of a good feed."

Pathetic excuse, but he accepted it. By way of an olive branch I said, "Drink?"

He smiled slowly. "Thanks. Mine's a pint of Black Sheep. I hear you were asking where I was earlier."

"Oh yeah. Just thought you'd deserted your followers."

His eyes were a striking shade of brown; the whites almost blue in contrast.

We tried to get some service at the bar and we tried to be heard above the noise, but there were so many demands on his attention we could scarce get two sentences out. I mimed 'tired' and 'going up to sleep'; then, as he tried to settle yet another disagreement, I wrote on a piece of scrap paper: '*Greg – I'm going back down south for a couple of weeks but maybe we could have dinner when I return? Rev M and I were talking about the ghostly happenings in All Saints. Bit boring for you I expect, but fascinating to me. George has all my numbers if you want to get in touch. Best, The Blue Girl.*'

As I climbed the stairs, I really was 'the Blue Girl'.

CHAPTER 20

I admit I was tempted, as I set off for London, to stop by the church in the hope of seeing Alice Thomas again. I wanted to somehow let her know how sorry I was for all her suffering. In the end I chickened out and settled for buying some flowers, which I left on Mrs Barrington's doorstep with a note asking her to put them in the church in memory of Alice.

Probably a futile gesture but I wanted to do something.

All the way home, I thought of the impact Greg's face had had on me across the scruffy bar. His confidence and the obvious respect he commanded amongst his friends had been almost palpable. The tattoo had long since ceased to horrify me. On the contrary, I would have liked to trace it with my fingers or my tongue… but no.

"This is mad," I said aloud as I drove along the A19. I physically shook my head to get him out of it.

The motorway joined the A1(M) further along. It was a particularly busy part of the route and I admit to allowing my concentration to lapse, but as I glanced in the rear view mirror to check my make-up, I saw a very different pair of eyes staring at me.

Blue ones.

What was happening to me?

For the split second it took to register whose eyes they were, my heart had leapt into my mouth and I could feel its quickening beat all over my body. I had taken my own eyes off the road in my panic and was veering madly across two lanes of traffic, out of control and miraculously, missing two cars, whose drivers honked loudly at my stupidity.

I managed to slow down but still hit the barrier. I heard a sickening scraping noise before skidding to a halt on the hard shoulder.

What happened next felt like a slow motion film. First I froze, then I panicked. The strange presence in the car filled the whole space and there was a trace of incense in the air. I dared not look in the mirror again, but began to shake, trembling with fear and the shock of the accident. I wasn't aware of the passing of time until suddenly, a face appeared at the window.

"You alright, love?" A small man in glasses leaned in at the window, peering anxiously at my face and shouting above the roar of the speeding cars flying past just feet from the rear of mine.

"What happened? You just seemed to go careening off for no reason. Did the brakes fail?"

I looked behind him to see a woman emerging from a car which had stopped on the hard shoulder next to mine.

"I thought you'd had a heart attack or fainted or summat," the woman added.

She was carrying a flask.

"Thought you might need coffee," she said, almost embarrassed to be doing something kind. "It's nice and strong. Sugar?"

I shook my head, overwhelmed, and just accepted the cup, managing a shaky thank you as I did so.

The woman explained, "We were just moving into the slow lane, ready to get off at the next service station when you lost control. Good job you managed to stop when you did."

"So, what happened, then?" the man asked.

"I don't know. Just felt suddenly faint. Must've passed out for a second," I lied. What would've been the point in telling the truth?

He told me there was a service station half a mile up the road. "Give her a try. See if she starts. Don't carry on driving until you feel better, though," he warned.

The engine started fine. I nodded and thanked them both,

but they still hovered, anxious not to leave me unless I was okay, and still making offers of help or more coffee. Should they ring someone, they said. I pressed my trembling palms tightly together, so they couldn't see.

"I think I need to stretch my legs a bit," I said, just to get rid of them. Whatever had happened, I needed time on my own to think.

The woman scribbled her phone number and address. "In case you need witnesses later."

Then they were gone. I must've knocked my elbow when I'd hit the barrier and I could feel a bump – 'a right keggy' my dad would've said – coming up just above my eye where I'd hit my head after the jolt.

My rescuers waved cheerily as they drove past me and I managed to mouth a, 'Thank you.'

Then, taking a few deep breaths, I slid across and opened the passenger door onto the hard shoulder, thinking to avoid the motorway traffic. Even so, the fumes and dust hit me at 70mph. My legs had gone to jelly but by putting my palms along the bodywork, I managed a couple of tentative steps and breathed in the pollution for a few seconds until I felt I could drive again. Parts of my body which had felt fine before, now began to hurt.

Maybe I shouldn't have got back into the car again but I needed to make sure that I still *could* drive, and I had to get off that dangerous road to the relative safety of the services.

I thought long and hard at that motorway café. I felt... for the first time in years, I *felt* something. I was weary and sad about the ghostly girl and baby in the church. I felt afraid but almost excited about the nightmare that had turned out to be a premonition, and I was grateful because I'd survived the crash. Above all, I felt as if I needed the comfort of friends, old and new. The old who might come to help me and the new – my man in the north – who might want to help me if I'd let him in.

I got a cup of tea and a croissant and sat at one of the tables. And, there, surrounded by strangers, I began to cry. It wasn't that picturesque filmstar crying though. It was the ugly, red-eyed, blotchy, gasping crying that real people do. And, embarrassingly, it was quite loud. So, in the neutral chrome and plastic environment of a motorway service station, I broke my heart into a cardboard cup of tea.

It was the first time I'd cried since Jenny died. I was crying for her; for Alice and her child; for all the pent up, unspent emotions I had carried and denied ever since; and it was triggered off by a set of superficial injuries on a motorway. I also cried for every kind act done by strangers and friends that I hadn't acknowledged. The emotional floodgates had opened and would not be stilled.

I snivelled my way over to the counter feeling dehydrated and took a couple of thin napkins from the dispenser. My behaviour must've been making people uncomfortable. Most of them did a good job of ignoring me, but one young woman came across and asked if I was okay.

I looked at her, saying nothing for a while, then I said, "Yes, I think I am. Thank you," and it felt true.

I did realise of course, that I'd had two shocks together. The ghost sighting followed by the belief that my life was about to end – as in the recurring nightmare and then, the realisation that I was safe, had all been too much to cope with.

A young man stood at my table, carrying a small box. "Hiya," he said, in a soft, northern accent. "I'm the first-aider. You look like you need that sorting out." He indicated my forehead. "I'll put something on to stop the bleeding and protect it from infection."

With infinite care, he cleaned the cut and put a dressing on whilst I sat, feeling weak and excessively grateful.

I was about to order another cup of tea, but one of the assistants had already brought one across to me. "You look like you could use this," she smiled.

Foolishly I felt the tears well up again. "Thank you."

An hour later I was on my way back to the flat. I'd called Steve and Sylvie and everything at work was running smoothly, despite my absence.

It was time to get on with my real life and find out what was happening with 'Operation Amelia's Wedding' from the office; where I belonged.

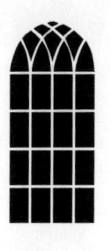

CHAPTER 21

Over the next few weeks, I got back into the routine of office life and found it comfortingly familiar and predictable. I worked harder than before and enjoyed it. Sylvie had reinstated herself as my secretary and we'd put the 'unfortunate incident' – as she insisted on calling it – behind us.

There had been no more ghostly happenings and the shadows of Skelton were fading, apart from a twinge of regret on my part about Greg.

'So, once again, thank you for your kindness,' I wrote to my kind motorway rescuer, *'and I'm happy to report that the car is once more on the road, and my mind is too!'*

I enclosed a voucher for a massage, fished about in my bag for the flask woman's address and wrote the envelope.

"Post this, Sylvie, would you?"

"First class?"

I smiled, "Oh yes, please."

We'd been getting on better than ever since my visit to her home. She'd done a lot of the wedding ordering, to be fair, the wedding being on again, for the present. She enjoyed that sort of stuff more than I did. I looked down the list, and ticked off a couple of things. Only invitations and fittings of the bridesmaids' dresses to do this week.

Lucy had been promoted to Maid of Honour since I last saw her. Amelia hadn't been in touch with me, but had arranged for Lucy to meet me some time in the week. I called her to make the necessary appointment and we met at a fancy bridal shop in Bond Street, but an hour into the fitting I finally received a text from Amelia.

'Dear Jo-Jo. Thanx for yr help. Hv chosen dresses. Go to Harrods. They will know. Ammy.x'

Lucy's face fell. It appeared that this had become a pattern – first *she* could choose the style, then Amelia spoke to her father, more money was granted, then Amelia chose what *she* wanted. Hmm. Anyway, it sounded like Amelia had forgiven me, for which I was grateful. So, we were off to Knightsbridge and to Harrods.

This was our first time in Harrods – both of us being too poor to buy anything of substance there – so we took some time to enjoy the opulence, and for Lucy to enjoy the obsequious manner of some of the staff, which I hated.

It had all been organised in advance, however, and we found ourselves in a private room, being shown the chosen dress and having it fitted and pinned prior to alteration, within ten minutes of arriving.

It was a pretty lace dress of silver grey and looked well on Lucy. Matching shoes were quickly brought, along with accessories. I didn't ask the prices. I didn't dare. Lucy was in awe of everyone and compliant enough not to raise an objection to anything.

"Would you like to see how the bridal gown will match up with this, madam?" the assistant asked.

"Well, if it's not too much trouble," said Lucy.

The assistant glided out of the dressing room and returned with a flurry of organza that would have made Cinderella look shabby at the ball. We smiled our approval and made a quick getaway, Lucy, enchanted, and me, sickened at the wastefulness of it all.

I couldn't help thinking of that shimmering fabric being dragged across the grubby flagstones of All Saints Church, and also of the shocked faces of the residents of Skelton if they ever got to see the price tag.

Then I thought of those two men. The living and the dead. It was the first time in weeks that I'd really allowed them into my head. The lovely brown eyes and the clear blue ones.

"Shall we go for a drink to celebrate?" asked the still starry-eyed Lucy.

We found a suitably starry bar and ordered champagne – her choice.

"How are things with Amelia?" I asked.

"Oh, you haven't heard from her? I thought you'd know. She's up north. Went to check out the venue again with that man; you know, the good-looking one. Trying to organise someone to clean and paint the church or something. She had this brainwave, she called it. She wants a carpet of rushes on the floor, for insulation and as a sound barrier and to keep our dresses clean." She smiled in admiration. "Amelia really thinks of everything, doesn't she?"

"Doesn't she just," I said.

CHAPTER 22

The phone rang at 7am precisely. It could only be James, who was always at his desk by 6.30 in order to make more money for his profligate daughter to waste. Still sleepy, I mumbled a hello through a mouthful of toast, feeling indignant. It was too early and I was still tired.

"About this wedding," he said. "Amelia seems to be getting too involved. She's back up there again getting that gamekeeper chappie to do more than he should be. I think he's turned her head. If we're not careful, there'll be no wedding – and I'll have spent a fortune on the arrangements for nothing. What are you going to do about it? Because she's quite headstrong, you know, and if she doesn't sort herself out, I'm minded to go up there myself to get to the bottom of things."

I wasn't able to respond immediately. On the one hand, I was horrified that my misgivings had travelled as far as James; on the other hand, hearing Greg described as 'that gamekeeper chappie' made me want to laugh out loud. What would he have made of that, I wondered. Mellors, out of 'Lady Chatterley's Lover' sprang to mind.

"Look James, I'm sure Ammy loves Robert. Greg's too old for her anyway, and I don't think he's interested. She's such a child. She's just intent on getting her own way. Apparently she wants rushes for the church floor – don't ask – and he's virtually in charge of Skelton Castle estate, so he'd be the best person to arrange that. No doubt he'll be sending you the bill, sorry."

I sounded much more confident than I felt. However, it was a plausible enough explanation, and one that James grudgingly accepted.

"I really must thank you, Joanne, for keeping Amelia straight. She does tend to get carried away sometimes, you know."

I smiled again. 'He is totally out of his depth with this, poor thing. It's the one thing he can't control and he hates it,' I thought.

"It's a pleasure, James, and it's what Caroline wanted."

There was a longer-than-usual pause.

"I still miss her, you know. Every day I think, 'If only you were here, Caro, to talk to our wayward daughter. Have I spoiled her, Joanne? It's hard for a girl to be without her mother – as, of course, you know too well. I'm sorry. I wasn't thinking. You did alright though, didn't you, without your parents?"

Not a question I wanted to respond to, so I just said, "She'll turn out alright in the end. Don't worry, James. You're doing everything you can to make her happy." I had another thought. "Would you like me to go up and check on her?"

I swear I had no ulterior motive for offering. I had plenty to do at work and I was settled again, which was worth a lot. Peace of mind is often underrated.

"Oh, would you, Joanne? Please?"

So, we'd come to the reason for his phone call.

"Yes. I'll make the arrangements. Everything is going to be alright. Trust me."

"Joanne – if you need any money…"

"No, thank you. I'll be alright. The landlord of the pub is almost my best friend. I get mates rates already."

It wasn't true, but it made him feel easier.

The rest of the day was spent making arrangements for yet another absence from work and Steve wasn't best pleased. He spent the morning 'harrumphing' around the office, getting on everyone's nerves, including mine.

These days our relationship had subsided to a distant friendship – all closeness was at an end. Since my crash last month, I had taken stock of my London life, a life in which Steve used to be important. We'd rubbed along well together for ages but we both knew it was going nowhere. He'd become more friendly with one of the buyers, Adele something. To my shame, I couldn't recall her surname. The acid test, for me, was – am I jealous – and the answer was definitely not. Which was quite a relief.

CHAPTER 23

It was with some trepidation that I sent a text message to Amelia, telling her I was coming up at her father's request, 'to see what I can do to help'. I wasn't fooling anyone with that excuse but I had a pleasant response nevertheless, with a couple of references to Greg, which intrigued me.

Amelia sent, '*Ask him why he was chucked out of the choir when he was a lad. Hilarious!*'

The use of language was interesting. 'Chucked' and 'lad' were Greg's words, not Ammy's. He must have been spending a great deal of time with her if she'd adopted his mode of speech. I checked myself and made my response suitably non-committal. '*See you tomorrow, and think about what needs doing for the wedding. I'd hate to come all that way for nothing.*'

It was early evening when I pulled up at the Duke William, fully expecting my room to be available, but George looked surprised and embarrassed when I greeted him.

"Oh, now then. I wasn't expecting you. We're fully booked."

He wasn't one for sugar-coating bad news, that's for sure. He carried on polishing the glasses with a grubby cloth.

"I asked Amelia to let you know I'd be here today."

"Aye well, *she's* stopping in your room. Has been for about a week now. Never mentioned owt about you coming back. Sorry."

"Is she up there now?" I must've sounded angry because he put down the cloth and rang the room number straight away.

Gurning at me as the seconds ticked by and the phone remained unanswered, he shrugged and said, "She must be out."

"Where?"

"Dunno. Maybe the Royal George? Or Greg's place? Or Rushpool? Maybe you should ring round…"

'Bloody hell. Are they the most likely places he could think of?' I wondered.

In the car on the way to Rushpool Hall, I tried to calm down. If the pair of them *were* in a relationship, it was time they owned it and made it official. She'd have to tell Robert. Then, on a fresh wave of indignation, I thought – and *me*. She should have told me – the wedding organiser. First.

They were sitting at a table in the bar. Neither of them noticed me, of course. They were deep in conversation and I couldn't help thinking that I'd never seen Amelia so serious or so absorbed before. The silliness seemed to have gone. Maybe Greg was good for her?

"At last," I said. "Have you been avoiding me?"

They stared, uncomprehendingly, as well they might. I was acting as if I was the important one in this scenario when in reality I was an extra, an add-on.

"Jo-Jo!" screamed Amelia, the old Amelia. "I wasn't expecting you until tomorrow. That's why I was staying at the Duke. Otherwise, of course, I'd have moved back here yesterday."

Greg was already going to the bar. "Coffee? Or something alcoholic?" he smiled.

"Oh, tea please. I'm driving."

I kept a lid on all my unworthy thoughts. After all, it was really none of my business what they did or with whom. I handed Amelia some brochures as requested by her father.

"Your dad sent these – honeymoon venues you'd been looking at, apparently. Bit pricey." I added that last bit out of spite or jealousy – not sure which, but she smiled sweetly and pounced on them, ooh-ing and aah-ing at the exotic locations.

"How are you?" Greg asked, settling back into his chair.

"I'm a bit frustrated, to be honest," I replied. He raised an eyebrow as I explained, "All this to-ing and fro-ing is ridiculous."

"Oh? I thought you expected to come back soon. Otherwise why make promises you didn't intend to keep?"

Gratified that he'd remembered, I said, "You mean our dinner date?"

No answer. I changed the subject. "So, have you two managed to get hold of some 'rushes-o'?"

He gave me a quizzical look. "Aye. They grow green hereabouts, you know."

Amelia looked up momentarily. "What?"

"It's a song. You're too young to have heard it," he answered.

There was something in his voice – a note of irritation – that made me realise that he'd definitely had enough of Ammy's company. An absurd surge of hope rose in me.

Just at that, I turned to the huge mirror behind the bar and for a fleeting second, I saw the steady, blue-eyed reflection of Edmund Winter, smiling at me, and I automatically smiled back. It was gone in an instant but the damage was done and the moment lost.

Greg was picking up his jacket. "If you need somewhere to stay tonight, I have a spare room," he said to me. Taking out his car keys, he gave Ammy an avuncular peck on the cheek. I managed to catch the end of his comment, "Just speak to Robert. Or Joanne, okay?" he said. Turning to me, he asked, "So, do I make up the bed in the spare room?"

"Yes, please. I'm house-trained so don't worry."

We smiled at each other over the sea of misunderstandings between us, then he was gone.

CHAPTER 24

I took Amelia back to the Duke William shortly after Greg had left. On the drive back, she became tearful. "Betty's dead, Jo-Jo."

It took me a while to realise it was the little dog and not a person, that had died.

"Of course I put a brave face on for strangers, but I'm so unhappy. She was like, a real person, to me."

"I'm sorry, Ammy," I said, taking her damp hand as I drove and squeezing it, "I know how much it meant to you."

"Not *it; she*," insisted Amelia.

I apologised again. This was difficult. "Is that what you were talking about when I walked in, at Rushpool?"

"No. That was something more serious," she said, screwing up a tissue. "I need to talk to you. I've done something really bad. Let's go up to my room – your room – and I'll tell you."

So, she'd slept with him. What else could it be? Funny thing was, I didn't blame her. Robert was handsome and urbane, certainly, but Greg, with all his rough edges, was earthy and charismatic… No contest, really.

What had become known as *my* room was in a state of chaos. Expensive clothes were carelessly draped everywhere. Wardrobe doors had been flung open, with trousers and dresses hanging over them. The wardrobe was surprisingly clothes-free and her open suitcase lay upside down on a chair. The floor, or floordrobe, was covered with underwear, nightwear and several pairs of ridiculously impractical shoes, and, surprisingly, a pair of floral wellies.

It even smelled different. I realised why when I noticed a small bottle lying on its side on the old-fashioned mantelpiece. It was Amelia's perfume, which usually permeated the whole space she occupied.

Oblivious to the mess, she plonked herself down on the bed, hastily scooping the chair-clothes onto the floor to make room for me.

"I've made a terrible mistake and it can't be undone. If only I'd had the time to think, Jo-Jo, I'd have changed my mind but there *was* no time. Lucy cajoled me and I couldn't talk to Daddy, of course. I needed to protect him, you see. I know I'm weak and spoiled, and sometimes a bit dim, but I just felt so alone at the time and…"

"What exactly have you done, Ammy?" I moved beside her on the messy bed and put my arm around her shoulder, the way her mother would have. "Is there anything I can do to help?"

Through her tears and sobs, she continued. "One night when I was out with the bridesmaids, we met up with the usual crew – Robert's friends from the cricket club. He was away at the time and I felt so lonely. All the others had paired off, as usual, and when I called him, he was too busy to talk for more than a minute, so I decided to have a few more drinks then I left alone. A man who'd been flirting with me – not someone I knew well but an acquaintance – followed me out and was being very kind and sympathetic, and, well, you know…"

"He raped you?" I asked, aghast.

"No, no, not at all. I started to kiss him and then we went back to his flat and had sex. That was all it was, I swear. Just sex. To fill the lonely hours, really."

I was tempted to slap her.

"Then, later, I found out I was pregnant. I couldn't have had it, of course. You know that Jo-Jo, so I…"

"It's Joanne!" I shouted. "Stop acting like a baby for once, Amelia."

She was shocked by my response. How did she expect me to react? She'd had an abortion, and she knew I'd lost my baby. So insensitive, as usual. It was always all about Amelia.

Floods of her tears punctuated the next speech.

I was so hurt and angry.

"Why did *I* need to know any of this? You know my history. You know I lost a child. You shouldn't have told me any of it. Selfish, selfish girl." I paused for breath. "You were more upset about the death of your dog than your child."

We sat together on the bed but this time not touching. My arms were around my own body now, in an attempt to separate myself from her. Nursing my grief again, I suppose.

After a few moments, the anger took hold again.

"So, the baby died to save your wedding day. Nice one."

I stood up abruptly and picked up my bag as she continued whimpering with her head bowed.

"I have to go, Amelia. I'll go and stay at Greg's tonight, unless you've got him in your sights now too?"

She jumped, genuinely shocked.

"No, no, of course not. Greg? And me? I'm marrying *Robert*. If he'll still have me. I do love him, you know, and he knows nothing about any of this. You mustn't ever tell him, Joanne. And Greg's just a friend, I swear. He's mad about you, so why would he look at me?"

"Look, you can't do anything about the past but you might get some peace if you say a couple of prayers for forgiveness, perhaps?"

I walked out of the Duke William and drove the car round to Greg's house. Apparently he was aware of Amelia's doings so maybe he could make me feel better. For now, I just needed to get away from her.

CHAPTER 25

It was with some trepidation that I knocked on Greg's door. I'd been this close before and I'd chickened out. I wondered whether the house would look as I'd imagined: neat, clean and old-fashioned. After all, men living alone don't go dashing off to IKEA or somewhere to buy the latest kitchen utensils or flat-pack cupboards, do they?

As it happened, the house was very nice. It's not a word I use often, but it summed up the overall impression of a place that had been loved. Cosy, homely, comforting – all words I'd use to describe it. He'd bought good quality furniture, but it was very practical. Cushions – that synonym for the feminine touch – were loaded onto the couches. He obviously liked his comfort. Being nosey, I went to the bookshelves. Plenty of books about agricultural methodology there, a few Andrew Martin novels about a detective working in York on the steam railways at the turn of the century and a lot of Norse and Greek Mythology. I also spotted a copy of Middlemarch on the coffee table and had the effrontery to be surprised. 'What a snob I'm becoming,' I thought. 'I don't like myself very much.'

I'd expected him to feel a bit triumphant, since I, the one who had spurned it all this time, was in need of his help, but he was perfectly at ease and welcoming.

"Cup of tea or something stronger?" That familiar offer had a charm of its own.

"Something much stronger, please." I plonked myself down

on the smaller of two voluminous settees, and sank into the cushions, as he'd indicated. I heard kitchen noises as he rattled bottles and glasses.

"What do you fancy?" He waved red wine, white wine and whisky bottles at me from the doorway.

"Ooh, red, I think, please." I could have added, "And you?" I did it silently instead.

With drinks poured, a coffee table between us, and a quiet bustle as we settled ourselves, I began to feel a bit awkward. So far we had been overly polite and decorous around each other, but there were issues to discuss. I began light-heartedly. "So, I hear you were a bad choirboy."

He laughed. "Oh, she told you that, did she?"

"She said you were thrown out of the choir for some reason."

"Yeah, well, it was summat and nowt. I just told her to cheer her up. When I was a kid, I sang at the church, but we got a new choirmaster who was a bit of a pain. One of those people who was too upright – and uptight, for my liking." He opened the door to let his dog, Flynn, out into the garden. "I had this reputation as someone who enjoyed a laugh, so I thought I'd tell the lads I was dyslexic. Then, when we had to sing the hymns, I twisted the words round. It worked well 'til old Hopey, the choir bloke, caught me singing, 'Breathe on me breath of Dog,' and showed me the door. It was a shame really, that I never got into my stride with that one. There was plenty of mileage in it, but I didn't manage to slip any more in before I got the boot. Shame."

He didn't look as if it was a shame. He was smiling about it as he filled my glass. The wine was warming and I was enjoying the surroundings and the company.

"The game got ruder after I left, an' all. They took particular pleasure in, 'I come with Joy,' as I remember."

We both laughed. I was trying to think of something equally witty to say, but couldn't. I was too busy looking at him. It suddenly struck me that there was something I wanted to know.

"Your tattoo," I said, pointing to his chest. "How long have you had it?"

Instinctively, he put up a protective hand to his neck. "Oh, I had it done when I was fifteen. Lied about my age. And I did it for Alice."

"Who?"

"Alice Thomas. Supposedly a distant relative of ours – Ma Barrington and me. Not sure of the truth of that, but she died in the church in awful circumstances, many moons ago and I'd just heard the story from one of the castle crew, so – being an adolescent – I chose to make a grand gesture. I picked a small bird because that's what she reminded me of. Helpless, tiny." He looked across at me. "A bit like you, in fact."

I couldn't speak. These were new ideas. A new way of looking at the history of Skelton. I hadn't realised that people were interrelated here, yet it made sense that they would be.

'He's related to Mrs Barrington – the dragon. How can that be?' I thought.

"Could I do you something to eat?" he asked, breaking the silence. "Sandwich? Omelette?"

"Erm, a sandwich would be good," I said, only just realising I hadn't had much to eat all day.

"Let me help."

"'S okay. I can do sandwiches," he laughed.

"You're doing enough. It's the least I can do – preparing my own tea."

"Hmm. That's the Yorkshire in you. Calling it 'tea' rather than 'dinner' or 'supper'. And there's me, thinking you were posh."

"You laughing at me?" I asked, but smiling about it. I was starting to relax in the warmth of his company. "So, how am *I* in any way 'tiny and helpless'? I'm quite tough, you know. I'm a businesswoman in London. I fend for myself. I'm independent." Realising my chin was raised in quite an aggressive way during this speech, I lowered it and laughed again, at myself.

Greg wasn't laughing. He was leaning on the kitchen counter, one hand on his chin, thinking. "You have no parents. Your child died. You're terrified of getting close to anyone, and you have such a barricade around you, an army couldn't get past it."

He turned to the cupboard behind him and asked, "Mustard on the ham?"

"Just tomatoes, please." I could feel my hand shaking slightly and picked up my wine glass to steady it. "Good wine."

"A gift from the Gillings." He paused. "For services rendered. And by that I don't mean sexual favours – I mean sorting out a brace of pheasants for special occasions. They often send me half a dozen bottles. Perks of the job."

He handed me the sandwiches and indicated the front room, as he called it. We were back on solid ground again and I could relax.

I heard the sound of rain dropping lightly on the windows. It just added to the cosiness and intimacy within.

"You know, I've asked Reverend Martin about the ghostly doings in the church, so I know the story about Edmund Winter and Alice Thomas. Have *you* ever seen anything strange in there – the old All Saints, I mean?"

He nodded. 'Yeah, the old one's awash with rumours and I know people who've talked about sightings of ghostly figures. I only ever saw one thing. The fire had been lit when no one'd been in there for weeks. I noticed it through the window and thought it was odd so I put it out. The atmosphere was always a bit weird in there, though. And birds keep getting trapped. I think they fall down the chimney. Have *you* seen something then? Or has old Reverend M been spreading his mad theories?"

"I don't think he's mad," I cried, rushing to his defence. "He tried to play it down if anything. No, Cedric Martin still has all his marbles, if you ask me."

He laughed out loud at that. "Cedric? Aw, poor sod. Who'd call a kid Cedric, eh? I mean, even in those days it must've sounded a bit precious. 'Don't go out and play with those rough boys, our Cedric.'" He fell sideways on the couch as he said this, his long legs splayed out.

I should've tried to defend the old man again but I couldn't any more. I was too charmed by Greg.

"Hey, just as well I wasn't in *his* choir, eh? Loads of jokes about his name. 'Oi, did you hear what I said, Ced?' 'What was it Ced said yesterday?'" Still half-lying on the couch, totally relaxed, his eyes twinkled as his smile faded slightly in the ensuing silence. He obviously wasn't thinking of the old vicar or the choir any longer.

I continued to smile, enjoying his eyes, all lit up and crinkly at the corners. No, he was thinking about me. What a man.

"Well, I suppose we can't help what our parents call us, eh?" he conceded.

"Oh, *you're* alright. Greg's a nice, masculine name." I laughed.

"Yeah? Trouble is, it isn't my first name. It's my surname – Gregson. I've always been known by it. The lads at footy probably don't even know my first name."

"Which is?" I asked, intrigued.

"Well, not Cedric. Now then, what are we going to do about Amelia?"

'So,' I thought, 'we're drawing a veil over that particular subject,' but I realised he was right. I needed to talk about her.

It was easier because Greg knew all the details about her sordid encounter and subsequent abortion. He also knew how much store the girl set by my advice and opinions. His was a rational assessment of the situation, with the personal history removed.

"She's too young for that responsibility and she probably recognised that. Also, Lucy emphasised her dad's reaction, and probably exaggerated it. Between them, they must've realised the need for urgent action."

I stayed quiet, unconvinced.

"Look, Joanne, that kid is going to spend a lot of her adult life filled with regret, wondering about the child she lost, what would it have looked like, what would it have done with its life, how could she have killed it? The list goes on. I know, because an ex-girlfriend of mine did the same thing in a moment of weakness. Afterwards, she was looking for a chance to get pregnant with anyone, so she could somehow make up for the mistake. She was wracked with guilt. Punishment enough, I think? And lifelong."

I sat up at the sound of a text message. It was from James asking where Amelia was. *'Can't seem to catch her anywhere. Is she with you?'*

The rain was getting stronger and pelting the windows but I didn't care. I'd just remembered something. Surely Amelia wouldn't have gone to the old church?

"I have to go out."

"Where?"

"I need to check on something at All Saints. Just to make sure Amelia's alright."

"Why the urgency? I'm beginning to think you're a bit of a drama queen on the quiet." He laughed, unaware of the danger I might have put her in.

I was in the hall picking up my coat when he put his hand on my arm, stopping me. "It's the 21st Century, Joanne. We have phones. Give her a call and stop panicking."

There was no answer to either of our calls or texts. She was probably at the pub or Rushpool, as Greg had suggested, but I couldn't get my words out of my head. What if she'd taken my advice and had gone to the church to say a prayer? It was possible, I suppose. Had I got her wrong? And, of course, she didn't see the danger, which I had only just worked out myself.

Alice Thomas was a tragic figure who'd lost a child. Amelia was a spoiled brat who had escaped motherhood… just because she could afford to. What might happen if she went to the church, tonight and alone? I had to tell Greg what I'd done and I could imagine his good opinion of me sinking fast as the details were revealed.

"It was just an innocent suggestion, but I will never forgive myself if anything happens to her." I pulled my coat from him and put it on. The rain was falling in stair-rods now but it wasn't too far to the church. Greg was a few steps behind me as we ran.

There was only the stormlight to see by when we arrived but I was relieved to find the church doors locked. Greg, however, insisted that we walk through the trees and gravestones to see whether she was there.

I was reluctant to go near Edmund Winter's memorial but when Greg shouted me over, I ran, terrified of what he'd found.

Amelia was lying unconscious across the headstone, wearing a flimsy, unsuitable dress and one shoe. Greg gently turned her over and moved the hair from her face.

"Amelia," he whispered, checking her arms and legs for cuts and bruises. "Amelia." More insistent this time.

I lifted her head, slipping my arm under her neck and said, "Ammy?"

"I think she's alright," he said. "She's had a bump on the head. Probably tripped in the dark. It doesn't look too serious but we'll go to the hospital and have it looked at."

With that, he picked her up in his arms as if she weighed nothing, and we hurried back to his cottage to get the car.

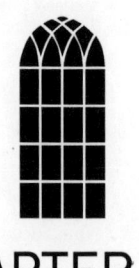

CHAPTER 26

It was 2.30am and Amelia still hadn't regained consciousness. We sat, gradually drying out and feeling miserable in the side ward, hoping for the best. This was a far cry from the evening I'd expected but I was too worried to think about that. I blamed myself for sending her to the church in the first place, but then I became angry that she'd been gallivanting around the countryside without any torch or coat, and without telling anyone at the pub where she was going.

Greg had gone for some coffee but the hospital was small and they didn't have any machines or even any food for that matter. However, one of the staff had taken pity on him and he came back with a little tray on which she'd put two mugs and some biscuits and sandwiches.

"I must've looked pathetic," he said. "This is a pity meal."

"Far from it," I responded. "Damp hair and shirt and broad shoulders? Who wouldn't feed you?"

"Well," he looked sheepish, 'I used to go out with her when we were younger, so…"

I nodded. *Of course.*

"No change?" he asked, looking anxiously at Amelia's small, pale face peeping out of the covers.

"They say there'll be nothing for a few hours. Said to go and get some sleep."

I shivered slightly and Greg came over and put an equally damp arm around me. I'd been trying to keep as still as I could, to preserve any remaining heat around my body, but the moment I moved, the cold crept back.

"You know what? I think we should do just that. We're not doing any good here. If she wakes in the next few hours, there's a network of qualified people who'll be hovering around her. We're here because you feel bad about what happened. The best thing we can do is go back, have hot baths and sleep. You could come back after breakfast and I'll join you later. Sensible?"

"Yeah. Let's go home," I said.

He threw me a grateful look. "Home it is."

An hour later, bathed and warmed, we finished off the wine and stared into the fire.

"It was nice that you called it home," he said.

"What?"

"At the hospital. You said, 'Let's go home.'"

"Oh, well, it is a lovely welcoming place. And you did make me feel at home."

I felt a bit embarrassed. It was like when you accidentally called your teacher, 'mam' and the other kids in the class laughed.

"You do think she'll be alright?" I asked.

"The hospital staff seem to think so, and they know more than we do. You must be shattered," he said as I stifled a yawn. "Shall we go to bed?"

The air was thick with implications. I refused to acknowledge them.

"Do you think I could borrow a book?" I asked. "That usually sends me off."

He recommended Thomas Hardy, 'Under the Greenwood Tree'.

"It's gentle humour with no traumas. Should be okay."

The clock said 4am when I sat bolt upright in bed in the middle of a dream. There was a rattling at the door of my room, which opened slowly when I was still trying to make out what was happening through the gloom.

At first I thought it was Greg, but the build was slighter and more elegant than muscly.

"Who's there? What's happening?" I asked, trembling.

'Oh, I think you know,' said a cultured voice – a voice I was familiar with.

"Oh, dear God!"

I felt the sheets move slowly away from my body as I scrabbled for the light switch.

"What do you want? Leave me alone," I begged as the shadowy form tried to slide in beside me. There was no substance to it and I sensed rather than touched it. The familiar heat once again penetrated my spine as I thrashed about, finally locating the lamp.

As soon as the light flooded the room, it? – he? – was gone.

I gathered my thoughts and jumped trembling out of bed, looking at the place where the form had been lying. There was no sign of anything. Of course, there was no going back to sleep any more, and I was too afraid to switch the light off, so Thomas Hardy had to get me through the remainder of the night, whilst I sat, clutching the duvet to my chest. Had I imagined the whole thing?

Soon after, I tiptoed to the window, half fearing what I might see – but what I did see was a half-hidden shadow of a man stepping lightly away from the buildings in the direction of the woods. I concluded that it was simply a trick of the moonlight but it unnerved me.

The next thing I remembered was waking up and seeing the clock. It was 10.30am and someone was knocking gently on the door. It was Greg with tea and toast on an old-fashioned tray which must've belonged to his mother once.

"Thought you'd want to get to the hospital. How did you sleep?" I noted the anxiety in his voice as he glanced at the light, still shining in the sunshine.

"I'll tell you on the way," I said, chomping on the toast.

It was probably time to tell him, but what to say? 'Oh, by the way, your house is haunted by a two hundred-year-old ghost who tried to have sex with me last night. Apart from that; great night's sleep, thanks.'

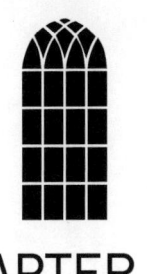

CHAPTER 27

The text arrived just as we reached Brotton Hospital. 'Good timing,' I thought.

From Steve: *'Am sick of running things alone. Need to dissolve partnership and go solo. When u coming back?'*

I was shocked. What a thing to do – and by text? It left me dumbfounded.

"Jo, you're as white as a ghost. Have you seen some more apparitions?" It was a joke. Greg was still thinking of the tale of Edmund-in-the-bedroom, which I wasn't sure he believed, but which he hadn't ridiculed at least. I simply passed the phone to him, still too surprised to speak. He read the message with a mixture of disgust and disbelief.

"How long have you worked with this bloke?" he asked as he locked the car.

"Erm, fifteen years-ish." I could feel the wobble in my voice as I spoke. "It was *my* business, initially. I only took Steve on as a partner when we expanded. What I can't understand is there's never been a hint of discontent or a suggestion that he wanted to move on until now. We've always worked well together – it worked well until…"

"You decided to cool the personal side of it?"

"Well, yeah. It looks that way. Even so, this is a bit radical. He doesn't seem to have thought it through at all."

I was thinking through the wording of the text again as I was speaking. What did he mean by 'going solo'? Did that suggest he was going to be in direct competition with me? Would he try to take my brand with it, along with everything I'd taught him? My head was reeling but I had no time to dwell on any of it because we were approaching the ward and my fears about Amelia's condition reasserted themselves.

As soon as she saw us – well, as soon as she saw Greg – it was obvious that she *had* made a full recovery.

"Hooray! At last. You took your time," she yelled. "The nurses have been *horrid*. They wouldn't even let me get out of bed. Not even for the lavatory!" She grimaced at the horror of it all. So saying, she threw open her arms to him, and as he leaned towards her in an avuncular embrace, I wondered, had he always reacted like that, but I hadn't realised until now? I was too prone to jumping to hasty conclusions of late.

I surveyed the mess on her locker and tray. There was a small feast in expensive wrappers opened on the bed, and, unbelievably, some tiny eggshells in the debris.

"Quail's eggs, Ammy? Really? Where's this lot come from?"

"Oh, I sent out for it. Well, Daddy did. The food here is just *awful*."

But I was no longer looking at the food. I was looking at a crumpled postcard-sized picture of Edmund Winter amongst the detritus of Amelia's breakfast.

She noticed my glance just as I looked away, my mind in turmoil.

"Oh, Jo-Jo, I found that picture seconds before I slipped near that gravestone in the churchyard," she said. "I'd just picked him up when I lost consciousness. In fact, he probably caused me to fall, 'cos I was too busy looking at him to see where I was going. Sooo handsome though!"

"It was in the churchyard, not the church?" I asked.

"Couldn't get in. The door was locked. I did see that dragon-woman hovering around though. She's really scary. She had a fox with her – can you believe it? Weirdo!"

Greg, who had been observing from the side of the bed, now joined the conversation.

"That 'weirdo' was old Ma Barrington. She has a pet fox called Arthur and she was probably taking him for a walk. There's no harm in her – she's just a bit… eccentric. And she has more right to be there than you, seeing as she's in charge of the church cleaning and caretaking."

"Arthur!" exploded Amelia. "I thought all foxes would be called, 'Reynard' or something. Anyway, it was a bit stinky 'cos of the rain, so what it would smell like in her house, I can't imagine."

Greg and I looked at each other. Time to get Amelia out of here before she annoyed the nursing staff any more. She, however, had other plans.

"Robert's coming up to get me later, after he's finished work, so we may as well stay at the Duke when he comes. Then, if it's too late, we can spend the night and snuggle in without disturbing anyone."

"Who might you disturb?" I asked, but she didn't answer.

All things considered, it might be better, I decided, to send her home directly from the pub. If there were any signs of concussion, she'd be cared for better by the doting father and fiancé than by me. I wasn't interested in cosseting such a spoiled darling, and Greg didn't look too keen either.

As we cleared away her mess, I picked up the postcard. What should I do with it? I was still drawn to the image; tatty and dirty as it was, the eyes drilled into me. How did it get out onto his gravestone? I distinctly remembered leaving it *inside* All Saints, and if the door was locked…

I don't know why this troubled me so much. After all, so many more bizarre incidents had happened here – the late night sleepwalks; the voice whispering in my ear; the recurring nightmares; the motorway accident; last night's attempt to… do what exactly?

The one thing that comforted me was that those sensations were all warm. I clung to the thought that ghostly apparitions were cold so it couldn't have been anything other-worldly; it must have simply been my imagination all along.

"Right, lass. We'll get you back to the pub and Joanne, you'll have to stay with me again – unless *you*," he turned to Amelia, "decide to go wandering in the churchyard any more."

"Oh, don't worry on that score. Next time I go near that church again, I'll be in my bridal finery!"

"Well, it's not long now, so get rid of that bump on your head and any other signs of your midnight wanderings, so you can look perfect on your special day."

She was smiling in anticipation when I dropped my personal bombshell.

"Oh, by the way, Steve is leaving the business, so I may not be able to spend as much time on the wedding until I can get control of things at the office."

Her eyes widened. "Steve's left?" The little face crumpled in genuine empathy. In that moment she looked so much like Caroline that I felt a pang of sadness for the loss of her mother. I rallied again.

"Oh, I'll be alright. The business is portable. I don't have to stay there, you know. I can go anywhere and rebuild it."

For once, she had nothing to say.

Then, I felt a strong, warm hand holding mine. This time it was Greg's. And this time I didn't pull away, until I had to help carry Amelia's belongings to his car.

CHAPTER 28

Mrs Barrington got in touch with me later in the day, to ask how Amelia was feeling. She'd been talking to Reverend Martin about what she called, 'health and safety issues' in the church. It transpired that what she really wanted was to close it permanently, even though it was clearly nothing to do with Amelia's accident.

"Sounds like she means business," said Greg, swigging off his mug of tea as he prepared our evening meal. I had intended to leave yesterday, once Amelia and Robert had reconciled themselves to the wedding, which was 'on' again, even though none of us had been told it was 'off' at any point! I hadn't worked out a clear strategy about the future of the business yet or, indeed, if there would still be one since Steve had defected.

"Not if we have anything to do with it," I laughed. Then, as an afterthought, "Can they though? Do you think the wedding will have to be moved if they interfere?"

"Doubtful. Pass those chops, would you?" He nodded at a parcel wrapped in greaseproof paper on the counter top. Then, "You're not a veggie or owt, are you?"

I laughed out loud. "You haven't a clue about me, have you? A veggie? Why? Where would you get such an idea?"

"Amelia said you were a fussy eater," he said unapologetically. "It just struck me that you were a bit pale. Thought you weren't getting enough red meat or summat. And you did faint at the castle that time."

"That's ludicrous." Another thought struck me out of the blue.

"Jack."

He looked startled and stopped in his tracks.

"I've just remembered. Your name *is* Jack, isn't it? When we met as kids, you introduced yourself as Jack, and I didn't remember it until now. How weird. Jack Gregson."

"Well, if we're being formal, it's Jack Edmund Gregson."

My heart lurched. "Edmund?"

It was a faint sound, that 'Edmund', as if I had no breath left in my body to speak.

"Yeah," said Greg, watching my reactions closely. "I was named after my illustrious ancestor. Hence the tattoo. To counteract the guilt over Alice Thomas. Didn't work though."

I sat down. "Well, you've really surprised me now," I said, looking down at my hands, trying to make sense of it. I just hadn't made the connection between the Winter family and Greg.

He was called Edmund.

His middle name was Edmund.

Bloody hell.

I recovered sufficiently to continue the small talk until he brought up the subject of his name again when we were sitting with a glass of wine at the table.

"I wonder why you remembered my name after all this time. Isn't the mind a strange thing?"

"I know. Suddenly, a picture came into my head from nowhere. It was of a diary I had when I was young. I'd written your name in it and decorated it with flowery things. And I recalled it was when you were talking about vegetarians, because there was an entry on the opposite page about deciding to renounce meat and live a purer life, as I think I put it. All very noble. It lasted about a week. It only took my dad making us all bacon sandwiches one Sunday morning after swimming for me to succumb again, and I haven't looked back since."

He laughed as he brought the casserole to the table.

"Can I ask you something? This is delicious. Why, when you can cook this well, do you employ – oh, I've forgotten her name. The corned beef pie woman?"

"Freda." His brow furrowed. "As a rule, I work odd hours, depending on the season. I live alone nowadays, so it's always good to have a meal in the fridge to come home to."

There was a long, embarrassing pause as we looked at each other.

"We don't know much about each other, Joanne, do we? I have to blame *you* for that. You were so stand offish when we first met in the pub. It was like you had a little circle of frost around you – to deter all-comers."

I wanted to protest but there was no denying the truth of it.

"I want to know now though. I want to know everything about you and your life here, Jack Edmund." It was out before I could stop myself.

That half-smile again, the heart-melting one, played across his lips.

"How long have you got?" he asked.

CHAPTER 29

After dinner, we went out to walk the perimeter fence around the grounds of Skelton Castle, that he and Flynn, his dog, were checking for signs of poachers, foxes and ne'er-do-wells. "The damage gets worse around Bonfire Night," he explained, "what with the Skinningrove bonfire being such a big event round here."

"Oh, is that still going on?" I asked, as the memories flooded back.

"So, you remember it?" he asked, astounded that I should know. "Were you one of the wood collectors, then?" This said with a laugh, as if it were an impossibility.

"Actually, I *was*. Of course. Didn't every kid from miles around go scavenging for old furniture and bits of wood to build the bonfire? I remember sneaking through the back gardens in Green Road, then taking bits of fallen trees and rubbish to the beach. All the gang was there, drinking cider and thinking they were really sophisticated and grown-up. The adults knew of course, but they let us keep our secrets – more fun that way."

I paused to take in the beauty of the gardens before continuing with my tale.

"One year, Caroline's dog went missing and we were beside ourselves searching for it and fearing the worst. She was hysterical, I remember, and shouted at me that it was alright for me, because I wasn't allowed to have a dog so I didn't know what it was like for her."

I could still feel the mean tone of her voice, all those years later.

A frown slid across his brow. "Why weren't you allowed a dog?"

I was reluctant to tell him. "Oh, you know, parents." I shrugged it off but he wasn't to be diverted.

"Why weren't you allowed a dog?"

"We couldn't afford one."

This time the laugh filled his whole body. "That's ridiculous. You could've got a dog for nothing in those days. What was the real reason?"

"Well, we were quite well off when I was small, but my dad was a gambler and he gradually lost all our money. One time, the worst time, he'd put a massive bet on something – I don't even know what it was 'cos my mother would never say a word against him – but we ended up losing our house. It broke her heart. I know she cried a lot and it scared me, but she just carried on as usual, getting cleaning jobs to make ends meet. My dad left soon after – probably out of shame, and we eventually rented a room above the Co-op."

I paused for a moment. This was very difficult for me. I took a deep breath.

"You can't have a dog in a room above the Co-op," I explained.

He'd stopped walking and turned to me, enveloping me in his brawny arms. I could feel the rough wool of his coat on my face, and the comforting earth-smell of it. We stayed like that for a long time, then I pulled away.

"Come on, I wasn't Little Orphan Annie, you know."

"Did your friend *know* all this?" he asked, a serious look clouding his face.

"Well, yeah, I suppose. I think the whole village knew. Why else would we be living in a poxy little room after that lovely house with a garden?"

He must have heard the bitterness in my voice.

"I know she was your friend, Jo, but she wasn't very kind, was she?"

"Oh, she was just stressed. The dog was lost and we thought it must be sniffing around under a pile of junk on the bonfire.

She wasn't usually that mean, Caroline. She was just scared that it might be burned to death, I suppose."

He looked unconvinced.

"Anyway, we found it at her house later on, not lost at all. In fact, it had been fed and was curled up on an armchair by the fire when we got back."

"What was the theme that year? I might have been there an' all?" he asked.

"Oh, it was 'Doctor Who', I think."

"Which was your favourite one?"

"Which was yours?"

"The Viking Ship," we said in unison, and smiled broadly at each other.

Flynn began scuffling around in the undergrowth at that point so I used the distraction to change the subject.

"Anyway, I've confessed all – well, one bit – of my history. Your turn."

Greg leaned in to see what Flynn was chewing at and removed a bit of dead wood from the dog's mouth. He put it in a plastic bag he'd fished from his pocket and gave the dog a look. It was enough. Flynn drooped, looking so sorry for himself that Greg took out a ball from his pocket and threw it. The dog's mood lifted immediately. Alert and happy, he bounded away in pursuit. "Splinters," he explained. "Get embedded in his mouth."

He noticed me smiling. "What?"

"I was just thinking, if only humans were as easily satisfied."

After we'd walked a little further in companionable silence, he began speaking. "Right-o. Here's a sop to satisfy your curiosity about *my* past. Where to start? I had a reasonably happy childhood. Quite strict father. Doting mother, but too weak – is that a fault? Probably," he said, answering his own question. "She was under my father's thumb and he always seemed angry, but we never really knew why. He was one of those people who felt disappointed by life, I suppose, and he wanted to control everything. Unfortunately, my mam was the only person in his power – and me, of course, when I was small, so we bore the brunt of his temper."

We'd arrived at his cottage by now and he was unlocking the door.

"Was he violent?" I asked.

"My dad? No. He didn't need to be. There are crueller ways of keeping someone down. Come through and I'll feed Flynn while you put the kettle on."

At that moment, I was happier than I'd ever been in my life. I felt part of something – a household, a friendship, call it what you will. He continued as we put out the tea things.

"I realised that he was a jealous bloke when I was about nine. He hated it when my mam was friendly with other people. He'd hear her laughter in the garden talking to neighbours then he'd punish her by sulking for the rest of the day. Whatever she did to please him was never enough. He was determined to be disappointed or disapproving of everything. There was no point in trying, but she never gave up. What a waste of a life."

"'My Last Duchess' syndrome," I said. It was then I made the mistake.

He stopped what he was doing and smiled.

"Oh, sorry," I said. "You won't know what I'm talking about. It's a poem, by a man called…"

"Aw, no. Joanne," he said, interrupting, and holding his hand out to stop me.

"What?"

"Not you an' all."

"Not me, what?"

He went into the living room to fetch a book.

"Not you… 'cos you ought to know better than to explain that to *me*. Not you… thinking you need to tell me that it's a poem 'cos, of course, living in the sticks, I wouldn't know who Browning was."

He looked more sad than angry as he continued. "Joanne, I have a mind and an education. And I happen to have a copy of that poem because I *like* Browning. Here, listen…" He sat on the kitchen chair and the book fell open at the poem. "This bit is my mother…"

He read the relevant part,

> *"She had*
> *A heart – how shall I say – too soon made glad*
> *Too easily impressed. She liked whate'er*
> *She looked on, and her looks went everywhere…*

and then he goes on to tell the listener how his jealousy ate him up and he had her killed."

He slammed the book shut and it made a dusty little 'phutt' sound as it landed back on the table.

"*My* father killed my mother but much more slowly."

The silence between us was palpable. What had been a harmonious domestic scene had become a chasm because of my crass ineptitude. His genial self had been replaced, quite rightly, by indignation. I should have known better because I'd had a taste of this arrogance myself shortly after I'd moved to London and had striven to combat it by joining in with the belittlers. And now, *I* was patronising *him*. I wanted the floor to open up and swallow me.

Was it unforgivable? The atmosphere was different now. Like a snail that had been prodded by a thumb, he'd been insulted and gone into his shell. Whatever I could have said at this juncture would've been inadequate, so I said nothing.

He made the tea in silence and placed it before me, then scooped up the book, meaning to return it to the shelf when I grasped his hand and took it from him. I tried to meet his gaze without success. He didn't hate me, he was simply disappointed – and I had been patronising, I admit it.

For the rest of the evening, I read and he did paperwork relating to the estate management. We didn't speak again except to say goodnight.

I drew the curtains in my room, thinking of Greg so close in the next room. I wondered how easy it would be to knock at his door when I saw through the window a man trying the handle of a parked car in the street below, then looking around surreptitiously. He seemed somehow familiar so I assumed he was a local boy just checking that he'd locked up properly and thought no more about it and went reluctantly to bed.

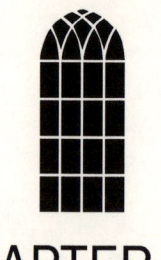

CHAPTER 30

I didn't get much sleep that night, and it was past three when I finally drifted off but it was not a sound sleep. There was too much stuff swirling round in my troubled mind.

I was awoken by a gentle tapping on my door, and someone turning the handle. Quite disoriented, at first I couldn't quite get my bearings and my first thought was that Edmund was playing his tricks again but then I heard Greg's voice.

"Tea?" he said, as he stood on the threshold holding a cup and saucer.

"Groagh," I moaned from under the duvet.

I emerged blinking into the daylight, remembering instantly the awful distance that I'd caused between us and the way things were left the night before. Luckily, it took a few minutes for me to fully return to the land of the living, during which time I tried to formulate an apology, but when I focused properly I saw that he was about to leave.

"Oh, thank you," I said, gratefully sipping the tea, whilst taking in the scene. He was wearing a countrified Tattersall checked shirt, and green cords and he carried his waxed jacket under his free arm – and he looked like a man who meant business.

"You going out?"

"Erm, yes, I have a meeting… estate business; in about fifteen minutes. I didn't want to just leave without letting you know… after last night."

He sat on the edge of the bed and, foolishly, I felt tears

stinging my eyes. It was partly sadness at how I'd misjudged him and partly from relief that he was still speaking to me, albeit with a certain stiffness of manner.

'Early days.' I told myself. 'We can make this thing right eventually.'

He looked concerned as I snuffled my way through the hot drink, finally handing me a small packet of tissues from his breast pocket.

"Here, I keep these in case I run out of sleeve," he said, half-seriously.

I got the joke but only managed an embarrassed smile. "Please, forget what I said last night. I don't know what came over me. It was thoughtless and snobbish. All the things I despise in others, in fact."

He listened without comment, then, looking at his watch said, "It's forgotten. Look, I'll have to go. Breakfast things are on the small table in the kitchen. I'm sure you'll manage. My 'corned beef pie woman' will be here about midday. Not sure when I'll be back though so I'll see you later on."

As he moved to get up, I smelled the fresh soap and toothpaste on him and was aware, all at once, of the contrast with *my* sleep-ridden grubbiness. The reference to his kind housekeeper – in inverted commas – and the ludicrous idea that he would *ever* wipe his nose on his sleeve had escaped me initially, but now, I realised that despite what he said, he still hadn't entirely forgiven me.

I struck a blow for what remained of my pride.

"I'm going back to work today anyway, so I'd best get up and be off sharpish, if I don't want to be stuck on the M1 in the rush hour. Thank you though, for letting me stay. It's been… well… lovely."

That was scary. That exposure and vulnerability.

'Haven't done that for a long time,' I thought. I wanted to say, 'I really like you and I want to kiss you as soon as I've made myself presentable' but I just put the teacup to my lips and pretended to drink instead.

He stood with his hand on the door handle, half out of the room already.

"You're welcome. Good luck in London. I lived there, you know, for a couple of years after college. Couldn't stand the air though: concrete, dirt and traffic fumes mingled with humanity? Not for me. A man could lose the will to live there."

I must've looked crestfallen because he tried to ameliorate his assessment. "Oh, *you'll* be alright. Made of sterner stuff, eh? And if you feel like you belong there…?"

With that he smiled briefly, nodded, and was gone.

I think the word was devastated. I was truly devastated when I looked at the hollow space he'd occupied on my bed. So, that was it. "Good luck in London."

And off you go.

I must admit I'd expected some expression of regret or a suggestion that I'd be missed and welcome any time in the future. I knew he'd liked me and we'd been getting closer by the day but, of course my prejudice had changed that. He'd been polite and kind but more distant and I didn't think there'd be any opportunity to get back on that intimate footing again.

After all, I couldn't keep coming up here after the wedding. I had no business being here and anyway, the Duke William now had my room available so there was no need to stay with him in future… apart from the fact that I *really* wanted to.

CHAPTER 31

The morning I said goodbye to Skelton was one of those perfect, still Autumn days, when the sun shines and yet there's still a faint half-moon fading in a blue sky. Wishing I'd never said I had to return to the Metropolis, and feeling so much dissatisfaction at the outcome, I tried to prolong my leaving (despite what I'd said to Greg), and decided to walk as far as Mrs Barrington's house. I thought if I left some money for church flowers, I could somehow make amends.

Seeking out a piece of paper to write a quick note to Greg, I felt the now-familiar weirdness that always surrounded me when I sensed Edmund Winter in the room, only this time he was in the atmosphere somewhere.

"Go away," I said. "This is very bad timing. In fact, leave me alone. I don't want to have any more problems on the motorway or anywhere else."

It worked.

The old battleaxe was at home and opened the door to me talking to myself. Feeling somewhat flustered, I stuttered out my request, fishing out a couple of notes from my wallet as I spoke. "Oh, hello. I was just about to go back to London – well – to work actually – and thought it would be nice to leave some flower money for the church. That is, if you don't mind buying them?"

She nodded once. "I've got a message for you," she said, still with that 'untouchable' demeanour.

My heart leapt. "From Greg?" I asked, eagerly.

She inclined her head towards All Saints. "From them two in the church. Crows are flying round again. It's the unquiet spirits of the dead that inhabit them."

"What? Surely that's just superstitious nonsense? Why would *you* get a message anyway?" I felt both intrigued and irritated by her tone and raised a disdainful eyebrow.

Arthur nuzzled his way past her at that point, and stood on the threshold, looking at me. I held out a palm and he sniffed it. Approvingly, I thought.

"I'm a psychic – or a 'sensitive' as we prefer to be called. That's why I get messages. It's not through choice, believe me."

"Look," I said, handing her the notes, "buy some flowers, okay. If you see Greg… well, just say I said thank you."

I saw no reason for any more discussion with this woman. 'I'd rather talk to Arthur,' I told myself. 'At least he likes me.'

At that, the fox turned away back into the house, and I went to the car. A sharp u-turn got me back into the 21st Century and from there to the motorway and back to my broken business. Sadly, I realised that something more important had been broken and wondered if that could ever be mended.

The journey back was shrouded in gloom, echoed by the worsening weather. Grey clouds scuttered overhead and matched my sad mood. I tried listening to the radio for solace, but to no avail.

What I needed was a plan. Something positive to do when I arrived home.

London looked at once smarter and shabbier than I remembered. The thing was, as I unlocked the door, it didn't feel like home anymore. I felt this longing to be back in Greg's kitchen, singing and chatting in the brightness of the day.

I sent him a text, on a mad impulse. *'Am back in the dirty air. Wishing for greenery and soft countryside. Hope yr day went well. J.'*

Then I rang Sylvie as I waited for his response. Just like I'd waited in the old days for Sammy Bridgeman to call me when I was fifteen and Caroline and I both fancied him but she won.

"Hiya, Sylv, it's me," I said in trepidation. It was probably fair enough if they all hated me. It was, after all, true that I'd lost interest in making money lately. Who cared about cosmetics anyway?

"Oh, Joanne, how lovely!" she said, falsely cheerful. "Where are you?"

"In the flat. Just got back. In fact, still taking my coat off as we speak."

"Oh, well, I'm flattered. I suppose you'll want to know all the ins and outs of the dismantling process?"

"Well, yeah. Well, first of all I want to know how *you* are, of course."

"Me? Oh, y'know. As usual. Doing the job. Going out in the evenings. Looking for a man." She laughed shortly at this last one. "Nothing changes, does it? How are your ghosts, by the way? Anyone tried to seduce you lately?"

I blushed at the memory of the phone call I'd made to her when I'd been at my most frightened, and regretted making it. Teeth gritted, I tried a light-hearted laugh, "Naww. Not this week, anyway."

Was she being catty?

"No one tried to get into bed with you again, then?"

"Sylvie. Honestly, I wish I'd never confided in you." Pause. "I hope you haven't mentioned it to anyone else in the office. They'll all think I'm going doo-lally."

A pregnant pause ensued. Oh God. She had.

"Anyway, I thought I'd check in with you to see when Steve is planning his breakaway move. Has he set a date yet? Or has he already done it? All my attempts to pin him down have come to nothing."

There was silence.

"Sylvie, you still there?"

"Yeah, oh yes, sorry, Joanne. The cat's just jumped onto a load of files. They're all over the floor."

"Cat?"

"Oh. Steve's cat. He's had it in the office for a while now. It's litter-trained," she added by way of an explanation or apology.

I sighed as my heart sank deeper.

'This situation is of my own making,' I thought. 'It's time to face Steve, have the row, then make some decisions about the future of my business.'

"How're the finances at the mo, Sylv? Are we still healthy?"

"Ah, that's not for me to say, Joanne. You'll have to see Steve about all that. The Japanese deal's still going strong though, so we're not bankrupt or anything, but if Steve's input goes, anything could happen."

I could hear the sound of a kettle boiling in the background and Sylvie appeared to be eating something. That told me everything I wanted to know, actually. It was apparent that she was on Steve's side, (although why this had turned into a battle I didn't know).

"Right Sylv, I'm gonna get something to eat and have a hot bath and an early night. See you tomorrow."

"Bye," she said, blithely.

I checked my phone. No new messages.

CHAPTER 32

The knot in my stomach just wouldn't go away. I went into my office – my one-time refuge – and it felt alien. I had planned to see Amelia and make friends with her again. Since she'd returned to her father's house, I hadn't heard from either of them, and the way I was feeling at present, I needed to speak to her again. The wedding was now weeks away and just about everything was done.

Her friend, Lucy, had texted me – something about *'releasing white doves at the end of the ceremony'*. I had, of course, chosen to ignore that piece of nonsense. It seemed particularly repellent after Mrs Barrington's odd assertion that the 'crows were back' in All Saints and up to no good. The problems were piling up on all fronts.

The hours I'd spent in the flat looking at the business accounts had been particularly unpleasant. Steve had decided to carve up the business in a way that was most advantageous to him, but took no account of my rights as originator and promoter in the early years.

"You fancy a coffee?" Sylvie poked her head around the door.

"Soon," I said. "First, could you come in and talk to me about these plans for the future of the business."

"Well, that's up to Steve, surely?" she asked.

"Why is that then?"

"Well, he's the partner, isn't he? I'm just the general dogsbody."

I indicated a seat. "Talk to me, Sylvie. What's really going on here?"

She sat and looked at me for what seemed like an age. "You know what, Joanne? Before you went off to that god-forsaken place in the arsehole of nowhere – pardon-my-French – I was completely a hundred per cent loyal to you, 'cos I thought you were committed to making things work here. But *now*..." she broke off, exasperated.

We stared at each other. I chose to ignore what she'd said about Skelton. It was a place she'd never heard of or seen and her opinion was based on the general prejudice about a fictional place called 'the north'. *Now* we were both exasperated. Her anger hung in the air, and I wasn't willing to prompt her. I was *definitely* not about to apologise to her for anything that was not her business. This imaginary slight was just that – imaginary. If there was any blame to be apportioned, surely it was to Steve? You can't just destroy a successful partnership by text, can you?

Eventually, I put it to her. "Is there any part of this dissolution that you think might be down to Steve?"

She started, an indignant look on her face. "No, there is not. *You* have to take responsibility for everything that's happened. You've been neglectful and careless of everyone in this firm."

I think she then realised what she'd just said and looked shamefaced.

"I know we were friends, Joanne, but it all seems a bit one-sided now."

I wasn't to learn until much later that Steve had already offered her a much greater role in his new company, with a hefty increase in salary.

After our interview, I took myself off to get some fresh air and thinking time. It was all pretty miserable and I wasn't used to being in such a hostile atmosphere. The funny thing was that, on reflection, I didn't blame them.

I've worked around absentee bosses before and it wasn't much fun. There was always an assumption that the boss was off somewhere at the party and the rest of us hadn't been invited.

I was having a coffee in Prêt a Porter when my phone rang.

"Jo-Jo!" tinkled the familiar voice before I could speak.

"Ammy?"

"Who else? Yeah, just catching up with you. Did Lucy tell you about the doves? Fab, isn't it? All white and symbolic as we walk out of the church. Oh, I just *love* the idea!"

"How are you?" I asked, unnecessarily. She was obviously her usual, exuberant self.

"Oh, you mean my injuries," she said, slightly more soberly. "Well, almost cleared up but still a little bit of bruising to my temple. I may have to postpone the wedding if it isn't completely gone by the day, though."

"Amelia. You can't do that, just because of a little mark? What are you thinking? Well, if you're thinking at all. What about all the arrangements? The venue, the flowers, the cake, the reception?" Pause. "The doves? Will the doves have to stay boxed up 'til the final bit of bruising has gone, too?"

This last, thrown in cunningly to appeal to the animal lover in her.

Silence.

I tried again in a more reasoned tone.

"You *know* it can't all just be postponed, Ammy. The food will have been ordered and prepared well in advance. *What are you thinking?*" I repeated.

I could almost hear the pout in her response.

"Well, Joanne, I'm thinking that I don't want to look horrible on the most important day of my life. Is that a crime?"

"Amelia, you are beautiful. You will never look horrible. But you *are* a bit spoiled and selfish. I'm sorry, but nobody else will tell you, so I have to. I love you but you exasperate me sometimes." I looked at my watch. "I can't talk now but will you please come round to see me after work tonight? Please."

She hung up.

It was a risk, telling the truth, but she needed to hear it. I knew she didn't have a resentful nature, so I was almost sure she'd turn up. I hoped so anyway.

I also wondered if she'd heard from Greg. But I didn't ask.

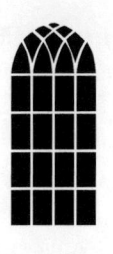

CHAPTER 33

Journal Entry: *'I think I'm running out of friends. Amelia didn't turn up last night and I'm wondering what to do now. I can't ask Steve or Sylvie because relations there are – well, shall we say 'frosty'. And of course, by far the biggest loss in all of this is Greg. He didn't respond to my text and I'm not capable of pestering anybody who doesn't want to know me anymore.'*

My heart leapt, as it always does nowadays, at the arrival of a text message. *'Dear Joanne, What do I need to know about Amelia's wedding? There seem to be a few unfinished details. Are we having doves? Stupid idea in my opinion, but then, I'm just the father-of-the-bride and as such not allowed to interfere. Haven't heard from you lately. Are you alright? Love, James.'*

I looked at the text again. I almost knew it by heart yet still hadn't responded. The reason was – I didn't know what to say in a text. I'd need to go and speak to him in person. Which I dreaded, knowing it might mean a return to Skelton. Nevertheless, later that day, I phoned to arrange the meeting.

"James? Oh hi, it's Joanne."

"Well, about time. What's happening, Jo? Amelia won't speak to me. Is she still carrying on with that man up north? She's there again, I think."

"No, James. She *can't* be. Did she say she was going? I haven't heard from her for some time now. I'll speak to Lucy and find out what's happening. Got to go, 'bye."

I didn't have to go. I had nowhere to go. I could try work

again but the atmosphere there was poisonous. Seemingly, Steve and Sylvie had moved in together. Most of the other office staff were mildly disapproving of the arrangement but as long as their salaries were paid – who cared?

When I tried to pick up the threads, they deliberately blocked me using half-truths to stop me from taking control again. I imagined Greg saying, 'What's up with you? You can get in where a draught can't! Don't let them do this. Take control, lass.'

Trouble was, I didn't care enough to do it. Everything seemed not worth the effort and I was sinking into a sea of self-pity.

'Lucy is the key to everything,' I decided. 'I'd better see her.'

Then I did nothing of the sort.

I ached to talk to Greg. I wanted his voice to warm me and make me comfortable again. Let's be honest, it wasn't just his voice I wanted. The man had hooked me and I was floundering comfortless, like a fish on the riverbank, without him.

After wandering the streets of the city for hours, buying stuff I didn't need or want, I called into a posh off-license and bought a bottle of Bombay Sapphire. Even as I was paying for it, I was shocked at myself.

'What the hell do you think this is going to solve?' my inner voice asked. And the answer came back, 'It'll take the edge off.'

I held it like a comfort blanket all the way home.

Luckily, my best laid plans – the ones that 'gang aft aglae' according to Burns – were thwarted.

Sitting on the floor outside my flat, huddled together in a flurry of faux-fur were two blonde heads. One belonged to Amelia, the other to Lucy. Beside them were a wicker basket and a huge carrier bag with the words 'Fortnum and Mason' emblazoned on the side.

I can't say I was sorry to see them. In fact, I was relieved that Ammy hadn't gone northwards. So, with genuine pleasure, I invited them in. Lucy smiled but Ammy grabbed me in a fierce, furry embrace with many exclamations about how *simply wonderful* it was to see me again. I was sufficiently grateful for their company to accept her effusions with good grace.

"Do you realise, young lady, that your father is worried to death about you?" I asked in a mock-serious tone.

"Oh, Jo-Jo, is he?" she breathed. "I love him, you know, but he can be horrid sometimes. He was really angry with me about the doves. That's why I brought them *here!*"

There was some movement within the wicker basket and suddenly all became clear. She'd brought the bloody doves round for me to look after.

'Unbelievable – even for her,' I thought.

"I take it these are they?"

"What?"

"These are the doves? Please tell me that these are *not* the doves, Ammy."

Lucy interjected. "'I told you Ammy,' I said to her, 'leave them with the shop 'til nearer the date.' But she wouldn't."

Poor Lucy's voice trailed off, defeated.

"Ah, yes, but you don't understand," said Amelia, in an ever more excited tone. "Dear Jo-Jo, if we hadn't brought them with us, the man was going to sell them to another couple whose wedding was on the same day as ours. Then where would we have been?"

Before I could speak, she put a finger on my lips.

"Sshh. Just listen, Jo-Jo. Robert's coming round tomorrow, I swear it. He'll take them and look after them. Then, on the day of the wedding, we'll release them at the door of the church and they can be free again, and everything?"

Her voice went up at the end of the sentence as if she were an actress in an Aussie soap and her arms did the 'releasing doves' action to accompany the speech.

Lucy smiled indulgently at her.

A child.

She was behaving like a spoiled child again and my wise words had made no impression.

"Bring 'em in," I said, giving up. I walked to the kitchen and opened the gin.

CHAPTER 34

The girls ended up sleeping on the sofas for the night, having seen off most of the alcohol in the flat. I must also admit to polishing off a great deal of the G&T myself, and managing to fall into bed and into a deep, coma-like sleep for the first few hours of the night. I was feeling relaxed and cosy, now I was not alone in the flat. Generally, I don't miss company but with friendships dissolving all around me, the girls' presence was comforting. Even their initial exuberance hadn't fazed me. Once that had subsided, and a gentler mood took over, the subject turned to Caroline, Amelia's mother.

"I wish I could remember more about mummy. I miss her so much," she said, sliding across the carpet, drink in hand, and leaning her head on my knee. "I bet you got into all kinds of scrapes when you were younger?"

It was an invitation to reminisce.

"Well, did she ever tell you about the Blood Sisters Episode?"

She sobered up suddenly, eager to hear. "No! No. Tell me."

"I can't remember all the details – it was a long time ago and I'm old, you know."

They both gave squeals of protest.

"Your mother was always keen to have a sister but it had never happened, so she decided that we two should be blood sisters, which just seemed to consist of us cutting ourselves and mingling our blood. She'd read about it in some girls' adventure magazine and liked the idea. Trouble was, I was horrified about cutting my wrist to do this blood-letting thing, so eventually we agreed that if – or more likely, when – I fell over and scraped my knee or cut my finger accidentally, I'd let her know quickly and she could do the necessary and we'd become sisters."

They were full of questions which tumbled out all at once.

"So, did you?"

"How long did you have to wait?"

"Where did it happen?"

I held up a hand. "Hang on." I slipped out to the kitchen to fill up my glass – with water this time, and continued. "Well, as it happened, I would have been better off agreeing to a small cut at the time but of course, hindsight and all that. The Skinningrove bonfire was in full swing, I remember, and we were daring each other to throw bits of wood onto it – unauthorised of course – when I fell over onto a piece of glass and gashed my shin. I can remember the pain even now. It was quite deep and near the bone and I had to go to Brotton hospital to have it looked at, but your mother wouldn't let me. 'Not until we've mingled,' she said. What made it worse was that by now, sand and salt from the beach had got into the cut, so it hurt like hell. I took my sock off to stem the flow but she kept pulling it away while she searched for the piece of glass so she could make a cut for herself. Anyway, some paramedics carted us both off and we had our wounds dressed and then your mother decided she had a massive crush… her words, on the junior doctor who attended us. Typical. For ages after, she kept trying to break a finger or something so she could go back and 'gaze into his eyes again.' Hmm. Melodrama was always her speciality."

"*You* take after her," declared Lucy to Amelia, pointing a shaky finger at Amelia and slurring her words somewhat, but Ammy was enchanted.

"How wonderful! I wish I'd been there," she said.

"Idiot," exclaimed Lucy. "Are you drunk, Ammy?"

"Course I am." But by then, Ammy was curled up in a heap of cushions and was drifting off, with a smile on her face.

Feeling non-too-clever myself, I stumbled to my room and

fell into bed, falling asleep to the sound of the 'coocru-ing' of a dozen white doves which had miraculously been deposited in *my* bedroom. ("Ooh, I will *never* fall asleep if I have to listen to *that* all night!" had declared the half-asleep Ammy, as she slid the basket into my room with her little foot.)

It often happens that when you've let your guard down for a moment, the forces of the universe decide to punish you. Well, alright, that's a bit melodramatic, but somewhere in the deeps of that night I awoke suddenly with the knowledge that I was not alone.

As I surfaced from some dream-state, I told myself that the presence was probably one of the girls going to the kitchen or loo, or the doves shifting gently in their basket, and tried to turn over and go back to sleep, but it was not to be.

I felt the now-familiar heat of the ghost of Edmund Winter lift the duvet from my bed and insinuate himself next to me. And before anyone decides I was too drunk to know fantasy from reality, I have to say I have no doubt about that entity – or whatever you want to call it – being an almost physical presence in the room. I could also smell the faint, familiar odour of incense on the stilled air that took me back to the church.

I tried to sit bolt upright and reach for the light, but this time I found myself unable to move – as if a weight were pressing down on my chest.

This paralysis was frightening. A light movement of the air around my face told me it – whatever it was – was coming closer, then a soft touch of lips on my ear breathed the words, "There was no child.'

As I lay there, terrified, the same message was repeated, 'There was no child; there was no child.'

And I must have passed out at that point because when I awoke, the duvet had been tucked in around me and daylight was streaming through the margins of the window blinds.

All was quiet and calm in the flat so both girls must've been sleeping still, so who had tucked me so neatly in my bed?

I didn't move for some time, feeling the need to understand what had happened last night. There had been some sort of 'visitation' I suppose you could call it. I also wondered if that was the message that Edmund had wanted to convey when I was at Greg's house. Maybe I was still guarded at that point, having just fallen out of favour with Greg and unable to fully relax and that was how I had thwarted him? Why was this happening? And why just to me?

And, I thought again, who could I confide in? Certainly not the two sleepover girls.

Nor Sylvie and Steve.

James?

Mrs Barrington?

I avoided *his* name because I had already discounted him from the list. However, there was one person who wouldn't think I was an idiot for believing in the supernatural, and certainly wouldn't feed off it like Mrs Barrington would.

Dear Reverend Martin. Cedric Martin.

'I need you, Ced,' I thought, smiling sentimentally at the memory of that conversation with Greg. There I'd said his name – albeit only in my thoughts.

Shaking him out of my mind, I jumped out of bed and headed for the shower.

When I was feeling fresher, I decided I'd ring the old priest and talk him through the events of the night. I needed clarification about Alice Thomas's state when she was finally found in the church. If it was true that, 'There was no child', what exactly had I seen? And was this all just a figment of my unbalanced imagination? I wondered if perhaps I should see a doctor...

By the time we'd all taken our personal hangover remedies and the girls had arranged their make-up, appointments and dove-collections, we all trooped out of the flat.

"Where are you off today then, Ammy?" I asked by way of goodbye.

"We-ell, I thought I might slip up to Rushpool Hall again. I just want to see our first-night room arrangements are all in place," she said, slyly.

"But you *know* they're all organised." Once again I was exasperated. "Anyway, you can speak to the staff – or ring George at the Duke. He'll know someone who'll know someone who can do it for you."

"Or Greg?" she suggested. "I could always ask Greg. Trouble is, he's lost his phone. Been lost for ages now, but he won't give up on it 'cos it's got all his data on – personal and business, apparently. Doesn't think he can get it back unless he writes to everybody – which will make him look foolish."

"How do you know all this?" I asked, breathlessly. She always had the ability to shock me.

"They've got Skype at the castle. Saul Gilling collared him one morning when I just happened to be trying to see how the flowers were coming on."

"You witch!" I said. "You *know* I've sorted the flowers. There's nothing left to do."

"Ah, but Saul Gilling doesn't have a clue about that, does he?"

I looked at her face. What was she up to?

Initially, Lucy had gasped at Amelia's ability to tell lies. They fell 'trippingly off the tongue', as some poet once said. Then, with a fresh understanding, she declared, "You're interfering again, Ammy."

I couldn't resist the question. "So, how was he?"

"Gorgeous as ever. You know, someone should snap him up asap," she said, with a look in my direction.

I'd had enough. "Bye then, you two. Come and get drunk with me again sometime. But give me a chance to sober up after this binge first." I smiled. "And get rid of those bloody doves before I get home from work."

But I had no work.

CHAPTER 35

After a couple of weeks of worrying abut the ghostly happenings at the church and the problems they might cause at Amelia's wedding if left unchecked, I decided I had to do something and contacted Reverend Martin. He sounded very surprised to hear from me at first, then, with his customary grace, he inquired after my health.

"You sound tired, Joanna," he said, in a tired voice.

"Do I? Oh, I'm fine, Reverend Martin. Just a couple of sleepless nights, that's all. How are you?"

"I'm always the same, my dear. Bit of lumbago, but otherwise, booling along quite comfortably."

I smiled at the idea of the Rev 'booling'. There was the awkward pause then, as he probably wondered what I wanted but was too polite to ask outright.

"Erm, are you down south still? Or did you come up here to see your young friend again? She's taking a great interest in the doings at the castle, from what I hear. I've not seen her at church though…" His voice trailed off in a disappointed sigh. I imagined his life was filled with disappointed sighs nowadays – either because of his recalcitrant flock or the sheer energy needed to get on with his day to day duties.

I decided to get straight to the point.

"No, I'm at home – that is – I'm in London. I haven't seen Amelia for a couple of weeks so I didn't know she was in Skelton. I'm calling you, Reverend Martin because I need to ask you for some information." I paused to let it sink in. "It's about the business with Edmund Winter and his fiancée. I don't know where to begin but he's still troubling me."

Silence.

"When I say, troubling me, I mean, he has visited me in the flat. I felt his presence stronger than ever and he whispered something that's been bothering me ever since. When you told me the story about Alice Thomas, I got the impression that she was pregnant at the time of the fire. Was that true?"

There, it was out.

"Ooh dear me... now, did I say that? Pregnant? Well, that would certainly explain a lot, wouldn't it?"

I waited to see if he'd say any more.

"You know, you'd be better off asking Mrs Barrington or your young man, Joanna."

"Ah, well, that's a bit difficult," I said, hoping not to have to explain why.

"Would you like me to make some enquiries on your behalf?" he asked. "If it would be of any help, I'd be happy to do so."

Realising that this was the best I'd get from the conversation, I accepted.

Then things took a surprising turn. There was a scuffling, nuzzling noise and a door opening. After a pause of some minutes, the Reverend said, "Hang on a minute, my dear. Here," he said, presumably to someone in the room, "It's your friend. She wants to speak to you."

Then, the old familiar tightening of my lungs and the sharp intake of my breath when I heard Greg's voice on the end of the line.

"Hello?"

"Hello," I breathed, in a tiny voice, before I started to make excuses. "Well, this is embarrassing. I didn't ask to speak to you. It was just Ced who said I did."

The lazy laugh turned my heart over. "So, you don't want to speak to me? And he's forcing you to! How awkward." The smile was in his voice still. "Now that I am here, is there something you want me to tell Amelia, perhaps?"

Mortified, I said no, there was not. After another prolonged pause, just as he was saying, "Bye then," in a puzzled tone, I stopped him. "No, don't hang up. This is what I wanted to ask the Reverend, it's why I called. When there was a fire in the old church, was Alice Thomas pregnant?"

"Oh." He sounded somewhat taken aback. "Still brooding about that? Well, as far as I know, village gossip said she was but medical reports said she wasn't. I'll ask Ma B and get back to you, if you want?" Then as an afterthought, "Joanne, are you alright? You still having those Edmund Winter dreams?"

"I'd really appreciate it if you'd ask around, Greg, please. I'm okay. Just out of work and fed up." I tried to lighten the tone in that last sentence but it didn't wash.

"Look," he said, "I'm coming down to an Estates conference in Berkshire next week. I could call and see you, if you like. We can talk face to face then and I'll get as much info as I can in the meantime."

How wonderful. How marvellous, I wanted to say. What I did say was, "Oh, yes, please. That's really kind."

"Oh, hearts of gold, us Northerners. Didn't you know?"

"Please don't, Greg. I can't apologise any more. And, do you know what? I'm not going to. Lessons learned and that's an end to it. Truce?"

With a voice as smooth as velvet and filled with affection, he agreed, "Hah, truce."

When I heard him close the door, Reverend Martin's quiet voice asked me, "Was that satisfactory, Joanna?"

I smiled at the name he was still calling me but didn't correct him. I got straight to the point of my phone call. "Who's able to do exorcisms hereabouts?"

He explained very patiently that his friend, Father John, 'a Catholic, but a good man nonetheless' would be willing to conduct a ceremony if I wished it.

"He used to be a prize fighter in his younger days; before he was called to the priesthood I mean. I'm becoming frailer by the day, and I'd prefer to have someone with his physical strength on our side in such a case as this. I'll contact him tonight and discuss it with him, then I'll let you know."

When I put the phone down, I felt reassured that this, at least, was going to be done properly.

CHAPTER 36

How odd it is that your mood can change in an instant. Before that phone call I was despondent and quite depressed. I can own it now. I had become careless of how I looked and hadn't bothered to keep the flat clean and tidy. I'm told it's a classic symptom. It's because you feel worthless and can't be bothered, apparently.

As soon as I put the phone down, in fact, I was filled with a new energy. I had a goal – to make everything tidy and fresh again. I was my old self – and my present self was glad of it.

I looked at the calendar. There was a month to go until the wedding. It had been postponed by madam because of what she called the horrendous scarring of her face – which was simply a tiny indentation in her brow and a slight discolouration on her perfect cheek. I thought, wryly, of how Ammy would have reacted had she been involved in the sort of accident Alice Thomas had endured.

No doubt Daddy would have had to shell out *thousands* on plastic surgery and implants.

No. I was not going down that route. Today was about getting my old self back. For the first time in over a month, I scoured my business contracts and agreements, contacting the solicitor who was acting on my behalf. I'd been stupid to accept the terms Steve had dictated and it was about time I joined the battle and fought on my own behalf.

The day passed in a flurry of phone calls and appointments.

I arranged meetings with the concerned parties and rejected proposals that didn't have my interests at heart.

Sylvie called me when she got wind of this, and muttered sympathetic platitudes down the phone, but I wouldn't let her dupe me again and I was brisk and business-like in my dealings with her. No word from Steve though. Typically.

So, Greg was coming to see me. He was coming to see me.

My heart fluttered. I must make him welcome, and I must take him to some lovely places – restaurants, coffee shops – maybe even fitting in a theatre visit? I tried in vain to remember what we'd said – what arrangements had been made. Would he be staying here or in Berkshire? Where in Berkshire? How long was this conference? How long could he stay? And would he kiss me? This last one sneaked itself in. I badly wanted him to kiss me, and in this day and age it sounded impossibly old-fashioned – a kiss. It was like I was in a film from the nineteen forties. The hero lays the lips on the heroine in the final reel. Ridiculous.

At this point I gave up on the speculation and decided to calm down.

The solicitor arranged a meeting for October 25th. She suggested some changes which would give both of us part of what we wanted without either losing face. I had a lot of reading and decision making to do before the deadline but it struck me that I was very tired of the cut and thrust of the corporate world. It seemed to me now to be false and shallow. It was also obvious that with our newly-negotiated terms, I was free to set up in the same business anywhere in the country. I'd done it once: I could do it again. And I've always liked a challenge – did I say?

I was in the middle of these life-changing ideas when I had a phone call from Amelia.

"Jo-Jo!" she trilled. "It's me! Oh, you won't believe this, but I wanted *you* to be the first to know... I'm pregnant. I know, I know. It's too marvellous. And I feel absolutely fine. No morning sickness or anything yet! Can you believe it? And I've actually *given up* the booze, darling! Well, what do you think?"

Astounded, I asked, "Have you told your father?"

"Oh, Jo-Jo, trust you to be practical! But, tell me, honestly, how do you feel about it? Oh, and I want you to be godmother. And I want Greg to be godfather – well if Robert doesn't mind. I still haven't decided on names yet…"

I cut her off in mid-sentence. "Ammy, how far gone are you?"

"Well… about three weeks, but I dooo feel pregnant, Jo, I really do. My boobs are tender and everything. Aren't you pleased for me?"

Of course, I had to tell her how happy I was at the news. It was true to a certain extent. If that was what they both wanted, who was I to put a damper on their happiness? I didn't dare ask if it was Robert's.

"How does Robert feel about it?"

"Oh, he's just thrilled to bits. Keeps walking around in a daze saying, 'I'm gonna be a father.' Then kissing and kissing me. I swear, if he smoked, he'd already be handing out the cigars! It's wonderful, isn't it? And Jo, I won't do anything stupid this time, you know." There was a serious tone in this last sentence which rang true.

"Oh, yes, Amelia, it *is* wonderful," I answered in wholehearted agreement. It might be just the thing to anchor her. She was very much like Caroline and motherhood could be the making of her too. On the whole, I decided, it was a very good thing for them all. I couldn't resist speculating about how spoilt this child would be though.

I went back to the mound of papers before me and began to speculate about my own future, now that Amelia had hers all mapped out.

"Where do I want to be in five years?" I asked myself.

Then I was too scared to answer.

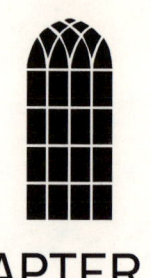

CHAPTER 37

'I've had a letter. It was handwritten, with a stamp on. A proper, old-fashioned letter. The hand was masculine and definite. Just the kind of handwriting I'd expect of him. And I can't believe I've examined it so closely, desperate for clues of some sort? About what, I don't know. His character, perhaps? But I know enough about that already.

Hm, business-like and to the point, it details everything about his visit – times and length of stay – apparently he has to get back to keep an eye on the Skinningrove lads and their bonfire shenanigans.

And the most surprising thing of all – he's booked a table for us at his favourite London restaurant – someplace called 'Sticks 'n' Sushi' in Covent Garden. Being pathetic, I looked it up immediately and the food looks marvellous. I now feel doubly ashamed when I remember my assumptions after the 'designer' bread and olive oil concoction I shared with Steve, before he stuck the knife into our business. Since then, I've had a necessary and humbling lesson about judging people.'

That was the diary entry I'd written, in anticipation of his visit, but in the light of subsequent events, it proved optimistic, to say the least.

The day before our 'date' – was it a date? I didn't know, but I was ridiculously excited and nervous.

Much as I liked the idea of being wined and dined, I had hoped to have him over to eat at my place. I wanted to recreate that time at his house where I felt so much part of his life, although, looking round at this place, it was more like a hotel stopover than a home.

I called in at the deli round the corner and bought some ingredients, then took the bull by the horns and sent a text.

'Why don't you let me cook for you tonight? Can't promise George's standards but will do my best? Jo.x'

After I'd sent it, I wanted to scrub out the x but it was too late.

I kept looking anxiously for a response but nothing came so I just went ahead anyway. The food could be frozen for another day if he didn't turn up or hadn't read the text.

For the first time in ages, I made an effort with my appearance, which I realised anew, had gone steadily awry since I finished working.

The main style I had nowadays could be described as 'comfortable-and-loose-fitting-for-the-older-woman' tops and trousers. Ugly and shapeless – but that's how I felt. Shoving them all to the back of the wardrobe, I chose something more stylish – a white cotton sweater and some well-cut grey trousers. The white gave my face a bit of colour and the clothes showed that I had a figure somewhere among the dun-coloured dross that was my usual garb.

I dressed quickly, as soon as I'd decided on the outfit, and was putting the finishing touches to my make-up when the text arrived.

'Oh dear. Hd invited Bill Stevens to join us for dinner – before I got a better offer. He's on his own. Shd I cancel or bring him with me? Sorry. X'

"Bugger, bugger, bugger!" I shouted at the wall. "No-ooo!" I may have even done a little angry foot-stamping.

I responded, of course – saying, 'Of course', when I wanted to say, 'You are the most infuriating man I've ever met and no, don't bring bloody Bill Stevens – whoever he is.'

After an hour or so, I'd calmed, relented and was gracious enough to welcome them when they arrived at my door.

Greg looked fabulous. He apologised for not having had the

time to change since the conference, but that meant I got to see him in a dark business suit complete with white shirt and tie.

Bill turned out to be affable and brought a few bottles of good claret and some flowers. I think he realised that he was cast in the role of gooseberry, quite early on in the proceedings.

"Do you mind if I…?" Greg asked, loosening his tie and removing his jacket before he'd even sat down.

I couldn't help smiling. He looked good, but obviously didn't feel comfortable as a city slicker.

I plied them with drinks, hoping it would take the edge off *my* nerves too.

"So, this is the London pad," he said with an appreciative sweep of the sitting room. "Now when I picture you, I can see you in your natural setting."

I scrutinised the handsome face. Was he being sarcastic? Did he often 'picture me'?

"It's great to see you, Joanne."

It was so honest and straightforward that I was immediately disarmed.

'Let's just play this straight,' I told myself. 'Two friends spending a little time together and helping a third one to feel at home.'

I realised there would be no chance of taking the relationship further tonight and in a way, it was quite liberating.

"Where are you staying?" I asked.

It was one of those big, corporate affairs with a thousand rooms and a never-ending buffet breakfast thrown in.

"It'll do," he said.

The meal went down well. They were an appreciative audience. It turned out that Bill was in charge of a huge estate in North Somerset, no more than ten miles from where he was born. He was quite new to the job and had been asking Greg's advice on a range of management issues. I decided to let them have some time together whilst I cleared away.

"Where's your pinny?"

Greg stood in the doorway, leaning in his old familiar way, head on one side and smiling at me.

As I turned, he moved towards me in one long stride and put his arm around my waist. I could feel his heat as he brought his head close, resting his forehead on mine. Our eyes met and held together for what seemed like an age.

"You've been brilliant about this, Jo," he whispered. "I'm so sorry. I'd planned something very different for us, you know."

I put my hand to his cheek and pulled him closer. 'Do it now,' I thought. 'Now or never.'

It was never. Bill stood at the threshold with a couple of empty wine bottles.

"Where's your recycling bin?" he asked.

We pulled apart and I began to laugh.

"Good timing, Billy-boy," Greg said, with a note of irritation in his voice.

"I'm sorry." Bill glanced at his watch. "Look, I hope you don't mind, but I arranged for a cab to pick us up in twenty minutes. I have a lot to do before tomorrow's session and I must get on with it."

We both stared at him.

"Of course, if you'd like us to stay a bit longer, I can always cancel it?"

Bowing to the inevitable, I said, "No, of course, Bill. Greg and I can catch up some other time."

Reluctantly Greg agreed, but as he turned his back on Bill, he gave me a meaningful, wide-eyed, 'I-could-kill-him' stare.

As they were collecting their coats, Greg kissed me gently on the mouth and said, urgently, "Come to Skinningrove – to the bonfire? This year's theme is 'Fishing-grove' and they're just putting the finishing touches to this massive fishing smack with giant fish tails sticking out at all angles at the back. It's not a Viking ship, I know, but it'd be marvellous to watch it together… and I'll buy the fish and chips?" he added, sealing the deal.

When they'd gone and the silence followed me round the room, I found a scarf which belonged to him, hidden down the side of his chair. I put it around my neck and sniffed it every now and then as I tidied and washed the dishes.

There was a promise in the air that night, and I meant to fulfil it.

CHAPTER 38

Greg and I had exchanged texts almost daily since the ill-fated dinner party, but they were on a practical, everyday level. In the middle of my walk (an early New Year's Resolution to keep my fitness levels up), I asked him what news he had on the Alice Thomas front but he simply said, "Could we save that until I see you again?"

I suppose it made more sense that way. Whatever he'd found out, there was nothing we could do about it now, anyway. People who had lived ages ago shouldn't have any effect on our present day lives, I decided.

"And in what way could it possibly pertain to me anyway?" I asked the Jack Russell terrier tied up outside the convenience shop. He couldn't answer either.

When should I go up to Skelton again? I didn't want to make it too soon but then, I wanted to see him for as long as I could stretch it out.

'Don't bring another Bill Stevens, though,' I told myself, shuddering slightly, then instantly regretting the mean thought. I'd had a lovely 'Thank you' card from the poor man - and *he* hadn't realised what he was getting into that night. He was exonerated.

I went on line to book the Duke William. Seemingly, George had been dragged into the 21st Century by his new barman and was in the middle of refurbishing the bedrooms with en suite facilities. Wonderful.

I hadn't heard from Amelia since the gush of excitement

surrounding her pregnancy died down. I thought of her situation often, and worried that if she put too much weight on too quickly she'd find another excuse to postpone the wedding. No. Surely not. Her mind was probably on the baby rather than how she looked. Probably…

I checked my calendar. Only three weeks to go.

It had been an interesting year for all of us.

I was almost looking forward to the wedding, but I was determined to organise a ceremony of exorcism before it went ahead; this would be private, of course, between the Rev and me. Everyone else would think I'd gone batty, and perhaps I had, but I wanted the church to be somehow 'cleansed' of all the horror and sadness associated with it in the past.

From the first moment I'd crossed the threshold, I had felt a – a something – in the very stones of the building. The smells of incense which shouldn't have been there, the bibles being turned over by nobody. Edmund's overwhelming presence. And my growing attraction to him which might have continued had I not fallen in love with Greg.

I'd have to see the old priest as soon as I arrived and make an arrangement with him to get it out of the way quickly. On a personal level, I had been genuinely scared by the latest manifestation in my flat, when I couldn't move or breathe because of Edmund Winter's visitation. That couldn't happen again. He had to be stopped and I was determined to work out why he had targeted me for these visitations and what it was he wanted me to do.

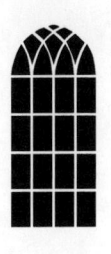

CHAPTER 39

Even at this early hour, the exciting smell of cordite filled the air. I arrived at the Duke William just as the evening light was fading. A mizzly rain had been falling sporadically through the day and try as it might, the sun failed to break through the grey, dense cover of a sky full of heavy clouds.

'What a shame,' I thought. Everyone had hoped for fair weather – well, at least, dry and clear weather – enough to get the bonfire ablaze.

For myself, nothing could dampen my spirits and hopes tonight. I had booked in to the Duke but hoped to be resting my head at Greg's house that night. I wished, momentarily, that we British were more relaxed about these things. Why shouldn't I have assumed that our odd little relationship would soon become more intimate? All the indications were there. And yet, and yet... I hesitated; afraid of presuming too much, I suppose.

Greg had arranged to meet me for a drink in the pub, after which we would trek (his word) down past Carlin Howe to the beach at Skinningrove. He'd found times out and planned for us to get the famous fish and chip supper at the wooden shack that was Skinningrove Fish Shop.

Best laid plans, then.

I dressed for the weather in boots and parka, but wore something more feminine beneath – just in case.

He arrived in good time and took my hand in both of his.

"Thank you. This is such a long way to come for what could

be a washout." He indicated the lowering skies with a wry smile.

"Well, I come determined to be delighted," I said. "This is a trip down memory lane for me and I'm gonna make the most of it." We clinked our glasses and the world took on a rosier glow.

"I'll take the car," he conceded, looking at the grey weather. "Did you bring gloves?"

'No, why?'

"Sparklers," he explained, pulling a packet from the inside of his coat.

"You big kid," I laughed.

"You can wear mine. I'll be noble and suffer third degree burns for your sake."

"And they say chivalry is dead," I laughed, walking out of the bar.

We had got as far as Brotton High Street when we realised our plans had to change. The crowds heading to the beach would make parking impossible. We realised that the bonfire had become more famous since we were children, and people had travelled for miles to see it.

Greg parked in a cul-de-sac and we set off to walk, torches in hand. He took me through a small, wooded area where a path led directly from the High Street and down past a series of farm buildings and fields. Damp but undeterred, I was gloriously happy, but then, suddenly, Greg stopped and turned to me, a serious expression on his face.

"By the way, you do realise where we are?" he asked, lifting my chin gently up into the glow of the torchlight.

I looked around. It was the field. *The* field. The one where, a lifetime ago, two children met for the first time – the one in the blue dress and the one with the punctured tyre.

"Oh. This is it?" I looked around. "Of course. The Queen Anne's lace is long gone, but the sea's still rolling and I recognise that old farmhouse."

He kissed my damp forehead and said quietly, "I've thought of doing this for a long time. Since we first met, in fact. It just seems like the perfect place."

I couldn't catch my breath but managed to say, stupidly, as it turned out, "I never thought of you as sentimental, Greg."

He drew closer, an intense look in his eyes. "I'm *not* sentimental. I have to kill birds and animals in my work sometimes and I take it all in my stride. If I'd been there when Mrs B broke the crow's neck, I would have said she did the right thing to give it a quick, clean death. No, the townies are the sentimental ones. We know better."

What a surprise. The mood was broken instantly and it left me feeling a little afraid. He took my hand and in a lighter tone said, "Not sentimental then, Jo. I'm something much more dangerous. I'm a romantic."

"Dangerous?"

"Yeah. Come on or we'll miss it."

Still holding my hand, he steered me down the path past the farm to the gravelled steps leading to the beach. Nothing more was said, as we lit the way across the dunes and tried not to lose our footing, but my mind was busy trying to interpret his words. 'Dangerous,' I thought, 'how could that be?'

When we reached the magnificent blazing 'ship', there was no time to talk. The flames licked their way across the wooden fish tails in the painted boat to great effect, and even though I knew it was just a mock-up of a real fishing smack, I still found it impressive and suspended my disbelief.

Shortly after our arrival, the lads from the footie team found Greg and grouped around us, all talking at once, offering us beers – John taking fish and chip orders from the team, so we hadn't much time together but then, to my utter horror, Robert and Amelia stood before us.

"What the hell are you doing here?" I asked her. "Shouldn't you be avoiding danger instead of courting it?"

"Jo! Hooray! I *told* Rob I'd find you. We've been collecting wood – just like you and my mother used to. I'm going to throw it on later – once the fire's cooled down a bit, I mean – and guess what? Daddy has *bought a helicopter!* It got us here in half an hour! Honestly, it's marvellous. He said he didn't want anything to happen on the journey up and he's offered to send it to collect us tomorrow." She looked shamefaced for a second or two. "And yes, I know how lucky I am, before you say it. Brilliant though, eh?"

"A helicopter," said an expressionless Greg, shaking his head. "Where's it parked?"

"Oh, it's on the beach – rather, it *was*, then it took off again and now – who knows? Very exciting though, isn't it?" she asked, turning her face to the orange glow.

Ah, incorrigible Ammy.

"Look, take care not to go anywhere near the fire. Give one of the lads your wood to put on it, please, Ammy," then I added, just for good measure, "It's what your mother would have said to you."

With a big hug, she dashed off again and I didn't see her for the rest of the evening.

Sadly, I didn't see much of Greg either, as he was waiting in an interminable queue for food. Eventually, we walked to a more deserted part of the beach and sat on driftwood seats to eat it. Delicious.

"Open air food always tastes better," I told him, trying to catch a stray dribble of vinegar on my chin.

"You see, that's why I love you. When you say something like that. Like when you called those women in the pub 'fat lasses' without a hint of malice. You never cease to surprise me."

"Well, as Oscar Wilde told me 'one should always be a little improbable,' so I took it as my motto. It's my defence against becoming predictable."

"Oh, right. You knew him then, did you? Old Oscar?"

"Oh, yeah. Bezzie mates, me and him."

There was no mistaking the message in his eyes this time.

"Shall we go back to mine?" he asked.

CHAPTER 40

"No," I said, in what I thought was a decisive voice.

"What?"

"Before we go back to yours, and before I break the mood again, I need to ask you who or what made you so angry or touchy, or whatever you'd like to call it? I mean, I can't believe we had such a daft falling-out at your house because I made a mistake about how literate you were. And just then, on the beach, I called you 'sentimental' and your hackles rose. Was it me or was it your own hang-ups? You won't talk about stuff and I don't want to walk on eggshells all the time."

He took my hand as we walked and after a short silence said, "We're neither of us in the first flush of youth, so it follows that we've both had relationships. My first serious, long-term one was with a local girl called Anna Millbank. After a couple of years, we got engaged – because that's what people do, right?"

I nodded.

"Problem was, she wanted to move away to London for a while and try her luck in the city, so off she went, with my blessing, and landed a job in a bank. After a few months, I worried that we were growing apart and I decided to join her. I arranged an interview with one of the big land agents thereabouts and went down, thinking to surprise her once I'd got the job – bit presumptuous, I suppose, but then that's me."

He gave a wry smile as he made the joke, and squeezed my hand.

He paused, the expression on his face changing. Looking out to sea, he said, "Ha. 'The crowd' were polite but one bloke insisted on repeating whatever I'd said, but in a parody of my accent. I ignored him at first, mainly because he was a little, weedy sort of lad with a thin neck and even thinner hair. If I'd taken a swing at him, it would have been like one of those cartoon punches that sends the victim clean across the room."

He smiled at the thought momentarily before continuing.

"I looked pointedly at Anna, in the hope that she'd see how he was trying to belittle me – then we could leave and be alone somewhere, but she joined in. She bloody joined in! She was good at it too. Well, being from the same village an' all, she would be."

"How could she *do* that?" I asked, horrified.

He shrugged. "I finally got the message. She'd nailed her colours to the wrong mast and I was proving to be an embarrassment. I decided that I wouldn't let her show me up in front of her new friends. I said I had to go, and the daft thing was, as I walked out, the weedy lad, Joel, his name was, came after me and apologised. Said how he *loved* my accent – something about me being a 'real man'. I think he was gay. Anyway, he shook my hand before I left – seems like he had better manners than Anna. So, that was that as far as our relationship went. She sent the ring back and said something about how sorry she was and that we'd 'grown apart' – all the usual bull, you know."

"So you never saw her again?" I asked.

"No. If I'd been sentimental, I could've played a few daft songs and cried into my beer and it would have gone away, but I'm not. I'd believed we had a future together, and I'd invested a lot in this relationship. I didn't know how to deal with it all, so I just got on with work and pretended to be okay. Which I wasn't. Which I'm not. No, I mean, I wasn't until the Blue Girl came back into my life."

As we reached the car, I continued the conversation.

"And that's what you were saying about being a romantic?" I asked, fully aware of the compliment he'd just paid me but unable to acknowledge it.

"Sentimental is shallow and romantic is deep – and much more hurtful."

We'd reached the house by this point and he set about opening a bottle of wine and pulling back a snowy white cloth from the kitchen table, under which was a cold collation. I recognised Freda's hand in that but was still unable to speak after I'd heard his story.

"Aw," he said with a mixture of sadness and gratitude, taking in the scene. "I told her not to bother. I'm stuffed – how about you?"

It was time to be practical.

"Well, yeah, but it'll be easy to put all this food in containers in the fridge. It won't go to waste – we can eat it tomorrow, can't we?"

He nodded agreement and poured the wine. "Before we have a drink, there's something I want to play for you." Pressing a button, he said, "This is my favourite of all the Beatles' songs. And it's for you." He led me into the sitting room, and held me close to him.

Paul McCartney's mellow voice surrounded us as we moved slowly to the rhythm.

The words echoed our mood exactly, saying how the singer had loved someone for such a long time and he always would. Even if it meant waiting all his life, he'd wait for her.

By then, I just wanted him to kiss me but he had more to confess. We stopped the shuffling excuse for a dance and he said, "I didn't answer that question, about when I first recognised you because it was about a second after I saw you in the pub – being so ridiculously efficient and stand-offish. You can't imagine how good it was to see you again, but I didn't say anything because it was too soon."

I couldn't contain myself any longer.

"Why haven't you kissed me yet?"

Holding me at arms length, he fixed the warmth of his brown eyes on me for what seemed like an age, searching my face. Finally he spoke. "Because it was too important to get wrong," he said, looking steadily into my eyes.

I lifted my head up to him and he touched my cheek then cupped my face gently in his hands, eyes still open and intense.

I looked back at him. Leaning towards my face, he kissed my eyes closed, then, searching for my mouth, he traced the tip of his tongue around my lips, hesitantly at first, but then with increasing pressure and intensity, kissing every part of my face and neck until I could hardly breathe. My whole body was aroused by the passion in that kiss. His lips and tongue probed and caressed my mouth urgently, as a longed-for and long-denied desire was finally released. Our bodies responded, pressing together in mutual yearning – thigh to thigh, feeling the need to come together at last.

The music had long faded by this time. In the silence, all that existed was our wanting.

Hastily unfastening his shirt, I buried my face in his chest and smelled the woodsmoke that still lingered on our clothes and our bodies. It was time to take this further. But as we made our way upstairs, an urgent knocking on the front door echoed our own urgent needs.

"Greg! Joanne!"

We froze momentarily, not believing this could happen.

"Good timing," Greg muttered, hastily re-buttoning his shirt as he reluctantly left me and hurried down to answer whoever it was and probably hating them.

I stood there, numb with disappointment and longing. Why did these things keep happening to us?

I was brought up short, however, when Robert tumbled in – soaked to the skin and in a terrible state.

"She's disappeared," he shouted. "Amelia. First she was there. Then she'd disappeared. We were at the water's edge at first. Then we walked away but then, suddenly, she'd gone. Where could she have gone? It was only seconds. I looked away and she'd vanished." His panic was palpable.

We made him sit down, of course, and tell us more calmly what he thought had happened. Greg was already phoning the police and the organisers of the bonfire. We hastily put on our outdoor things as he related the tale again, more slowly this time.

"Come on. The police are sending someone to the beach to meet us," said Greg – probably sounding steadier than he felt.

To my shame, I confess to being really annoyed with Amelia. Of course I was worried. Of course. But the girl was a liability. She was not a stupid person but she gave a good impression of one sometimes. I also wondered if Robert was over-reacting. I mean, it wasn't that long since we arrived back at the house. She'd probably gone off in search of hot dogs or something. She was very good at looking after number one was Ammy. I couldn't see her putting herself in harm's way.

The blaze of the bonfire was beginning to die down when we arrived. Rain was pouring down and had dampened spirits – compounded by the police presence.

They tried to be discreet and not to spoil the occasion but it was inevitable that they would. The drummers, tired and cold now, were packing all their kit away, fearful that the wet weather would affect their drum skins. The fish shop queue had dwindled to nothing and the scene had that forlorn, end-of-the-party look about it. Spent firework casings were strewn about the beach.

We were all questioned about where we'd last seen Amelia and why we hadn't stayed together, and at that point the officers went off to scour the beach. After about fifteen minutes, one of them came back with something which, on closer inspection, was a handbag. I recognised the expensive leather at once and identified it as Amelia's.

Robert began to panic at that point.

"You don't understand," he told a detective. "She's pregnant. We need more people here to search. Please, get reinforcements." He hadn't grasped the fact that we were in a tiny village in East Cleveland and we didn't have the resources of the Met.

"If anything has happened to her…" he trailed off, hopelessly, leaving the sentence unfinished.

"Sir, this isn't really helpful," said one of the constables, obviously irritated by his panic-stricken tones, and the underlying threat implied.

A sea-fret had now begun to settle in, making visibility almost impossible.

"Why don't you go and wait somewhere warm and leave all this to us?" he said in a more concerned tone.

We urged him to come away, and after giving our details, we returned to Greg's house, and – I'm ashamed to say – I fell asleep, snuggled under a woolly blanket on the settee. When I woke, the others were at the kitchen table, Robert, slumped over and snoring after finishing off a bottle of brandy and Greg just waiting for the dawn. There had been no news from the police and it was six hours since Amelia's disappearance.

When I made waking-up noises, Greg prepared tea and toast for me and said, "Could you follow me after breakfast? I'm going to see what's happening at the beach."

Then, with a whistle to the ever-alert Flynn, he was gone.

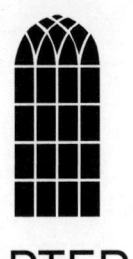

CHAPTER 41

The beach that morning had a definite 'morning-after-the-party' feel about it, despite the army of workers on clean-up duty. The miserable atmosphere was added to by a police presence which forbade most of the cleaners from doing anything much until the investigators had thoroughly examined the evidence.

'Evidence of what?' I wondered, but the people we spoke to were as bemused as we were.

Greg found me as soon as I set foot on the beach, and, gratifyingly, held me close to his side at once.

"Have they found anything?" I asked, feeling like a spare part.

"I don't think they quite know what to do. They're taking photos of the scene but then one of them said the search would have to continue around the village and then they'll be interviewing residents."

We wandered aimlessly for a while, letting Flynn have a sniff about. He got quite interested in a few bits of discarded food and longed to go into the freezing North Sea but was called back quickly. I stroked his head in a preoccupied way then, for want of something to say, I asked Greg, "Why did you call him Flynn?"

He laughed. "You sure you want me to tell you?"

Intrigued now, I said, "Yeah, 'course."

"Well, remember Errol Flynn, the film star?"

I nodded.

"And what *he* was famous for?"

I threw a puzzled look his way.

"That enormous tackle?"

I laughed and instinctively looked down at the dog's nether regions.

"No point in doing that now," he said, chuckling. "Errol Flynn, it seems, was a great liar about his love life and his 'endowments'. Well, as soon as Flynn had the chop, so was he. Poor sod, eh?"

"Don't laugh, you!" I said, poking him in the ribs, and smiling. "Not funny."

"Ah, well, he's pretty happy – and now there's no chance of him fathering another brood of pups."

I looked up.

"Yeah, I did let him father one lot. I'm not the brute you take me for, you know."

It was incongruous, I know, to be in this situation with Greg's eyes twinkling with mischief, but oh, how I loved it. The softness of the brown and the almost blue of the whites – coupled with the way he looked at me – filled me with happiness. I was unable to deny myself the few moments of pleasure, even in the midst of Ammy's disappearance.

A constable came across to talk to us.

"Where's the other bloke?" he asked.

"Who, Robert? He's at mine, sobering up right now," Greg told him. "I expect him any minute though. He's not allowed to drive until he's had a few pints of water."

Unexpectedly, the policeman understood. "Quite right too, sir," he said, nodding for emphasis. "Haven't you any idea where she might have gone?" he asked yet again.

"No. Normally she'd have gone off to Rushpool Hall or Skelton Castle – anywhere for a bit of luxury, but not without telling her fiancé first. And she'd never have left her bag behind. I can't understand it."

He looked at me for too long, with no expression on his face.

I felt uncomfortable and added, "And she doesn't know anyone else hereabouts."

"Well, miss, all I can suggest is that *you* need to be at home, in case she returns."

He turned his attention to Greg. "Does the dog know her, sir?"

"Not sure," he said. 'Probably." Then he suggested to the policeman, "Would it be better if we had something of hers that he could sniff – maybe track her down then?"

"Oh, but I have her scarf," I said. "Would that do? She left it behind last time we met up – people do that all the time, don't they?" I looked at Greg. We were both remembering 'the Bill Stevens night' as I now called it in my head.

I fished around in my bag and brought out the flimsy piece of silk that served as Amelia's scarf. Flynn was on to it immediately and we were all starting to feel hopeful again.

Greg and the policeman followed the dog and I decided to drive back and check on Robert.

On the way back, the enormity of the situation hit me. A missing girl on a deserted beach could easily have got lost, but with the bonfire's light to guide her, surely she could have followed the noise and got safely back? All the horrors that could have befallen her crowded into my consciousness.

What if they never found her? On the brink of a new life, pregnant, with a lovely man and a wedding to look forward to, surely she wouldn't have put herself in danger?

I glanced automatically in the rear view mirror and, once again, a pair of blue eyes stared back. Could *he* have had anything to do with this? When I blinked again, he was gone.

"Get a grip!" I told myself. "This is no time to think about phantoms."

But that's exactly what I *was* thinking about.

Could Edmund Winter have anything to do with Amelia's disappearance?

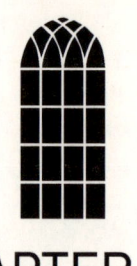

CHAPTER 42

They say, 'no news is good news', but it isn't true. Robert and I must've had a small-talk marathon that afternoon. We skirted admirably around Amelia, the elephant in the room, and instead went over all the minutiae of the wedding preparations and the pregnancy news along with the police and their game plan, but we didn't discuss the possibilities that her continuing absence might signify that something dreadful could have happened.

I mulled them over in my mind. Could she have drowned? The tides and currents were not mild in November and could easily have knocked her off her feet if she stood too close to the sea's margin. The dunes had been searched but how thoroughly? And in daylight?

Could she have walked in the wrong direction and lost her bearings? That would've sent her straight to Saltburn – tides permitting.

"Another cuppa?" I asked a despairing Robert, wishing desperately that Greg would phone with some news.

The ticking clock measured out the slow minutes until the light began to fade. Nobody had any stomach for food but I offered Robert some, thinking to involve him in preparing veg and chopping salad to distract him from his own misery.

Around four, a police car drew up at the house, and almost simultaneously, Greg arrived with Flynn in tow. They smelled of the fresh, salt air and had that energy about them which we indoor-waiters lacked.

"Anything?" Greg asked, as we looked to the door in case Amelia was walking behind. A vain hope, I know.

"What's happening?" Robert shouted. "Why haven't they found her yet?"

Nobody had anything to say in reply, because there was a knock on the door at that moment, and a very young-looking police constable poked his head round into the sitting room and said, "Which one of you is Robert?"

He bounded in from the kitchen immediately. "That's me. Have you found Amelia?"

"Yes, she's safe, sir. We have her outside in the car. She was found wandering about in a distressed state in Carlin How. She seems to have had a rough night, didn't have any ID and had no idea where she was." said the officer. "See for yourself."

We all rushed out, leaving the poor constable talking to the dog. We brought Amelia into the warmth of the house. She clung to Robert, tearfully, and was led to the sofa, cushions being heaped behind her and blankets draped across her legs.

"You sure she's alright? She's pregnant, you know," said an anxious Robert, looking at the pale, drawn face of the exhausted girl.

Robert was on tenterhooks all through this. I just hoped she was still carrying the baby. I couldn't cope with any more tragedy.

I told Ammy it might be best if we got her to the hospital to check on the baby as soon as possible.

"Not yet," said Amelia, decisively. "First I want to tell you all what happened last night. I owe you that much." She turned to Robert, held his hand and began. "Remember we were standing looking at the sea? Well, I needed to find a lavatory but I didn't want to spoil the mood so I went across to the sand dunes and thought I could just hide behind one of them and, well, you know... do it there. I put my bag down on the beach, and shouted to you, but you can't have heard me, darling, above the crowds and the waves. Well, when I'd finished, I was looking everywhere for my bag. Of course, I couldn't find it. You know, I always used to get lost when I was paddling in the sea as a child. You sort of drift along the beach a bit and lose your parents, don't you? Anyway, You'd gone, and my bag was nowhere to be seen – and as *you'll* know," she turned to me, now, "my whole life is in that bag – keys, phone, money, make-up and well, everything!"

Greg said in a serious voice, "Do you realise the trouble you've caused? And over a bloody silly handbag? Why didn't you just follow the sound and the lights back to the bonfire? Robert was terrified that something awful had happened to you. We all were."

Amelia held up her hand to silence him. "Hear me out!"

We sat on the edge of the sofa as Amelia continued. I couldn't help feeling that this wasn't going to be good.

"I was just going to do exactly that, Greg, when the mist came down and it felt darker and colder. I was on the other side of the beach and I couldn't see the fire at all from there. I stood on something and reached down to touch it. Too late I realised it was some sort of bird. It was big, but it was cold so it must've died some time ago. I think it was a seagull. Horrible! I felt around on the beach for a while then, as if out of nowhere, he was there, this figure of a man emerging from the fog. He didn't say anything, just came close and indicated the way. All I could see were these lovely, blue eyes, and I remember thinking, well, anyone who looks *that* kind can't be wishing me harm. So I followed him."

The others looked shocked and made little sounds of protest, but I, who knew what was coming, kept silent.

"We seemed to be climbing up a steep, stony path and by then you couldn't see your hand in front of you and I was so very cold, Jo-Jo, and crying because I was really, really tired. Then a funny thing happened. He disappeared just as we reached the road, but I felt a warm hand on my back and just as I was feeling safe again, another smaller hand pushed me out into the traffic, and I heard someone whisper, 'Look after the baby,' as I struggled to get up."

She paused for breath and continued, "But I keep thinking, who would do such a thing, and what if there'd been a car coming at that moment? I could've been dead! As it was, my knees were cut and my elbow hurt from the impact. I still won't believe it was the man with the eyes, because I'm sure there were two people there. I was quite shaken up by it all."

Robert held her closer at that.

"We found her sitting on a doorstep," said the policeman who couldn't keep quiet any longer.

I interrupted him. "I think she's still very tired. We'd better take her to the hospital now. Thank you so much for bringing her back."

After a tearful, grateful goodbye, Amelia and the policeman parted. Only then, in the daylight, did I realise just how pale and ill she looked.

"Actually," said Amelia as soon as he'd gone, "it was a young lad who first found me. It wasn't the police. This blond boy saw me sitting on someone's step. He never said much, just texted the police and said, 'You'll be okay now. Just stay there,' and patted my shoulder. Then he was off. It was like he didn't want to be thanked. Funny but I remember thinking he smelled like the church at the time."

So many questions crowded into my consciousness. Was it Edmund who had rescued her? And if so, who had pushed her? And why?

On later reflection, I suddenly thought, 'The baby. Edmund told her to look after the baby.'

It was *always* about the baby.

What did it mean? Why was he guiding her, if only to put her in danger?

And was it Alice who shoved her into the road?

I needed answers but there was nobody to ask.

CHAPTER 43

Back at the house, with Amelia and Robert waiting at Rushpool for transport home to London, where it was hoped she'd fully recover from her ghostly assault, I pondered over the future. The medical check-up had proved positive and although we were all tired, we carried on a veneer of bonhomie which disguised our own private concerns.

James, in a typical rush of excess, had arranged to send his new toy, the helicopter, to pick up the pair from the grounds of Skelton Castle, close to the lake. The Gilling brothers had complied with this request, leading me to think that some kind of business deal was in the offing.

I was becoming more cynical and didn't like it.

After they'd gone, with promises to 'see you at the wedding', Greg disappeared upstairs to wash and change. After all, we must've all looked and smelled the worse for wear after the interrupted night and the running around we'd done after the bonfire.

I heard water gushing out of the upstairs pipes in a gurgling rush and waited a few minutes before, inhibitions conquered, I quietly took the stairs two-at-a-time and began to strip off. The bathroom door wasn't locked so I opened it a crack and saw Greg's outline in the steamy glass of the shower. Even through the misted-over door, I could tell from the shape of the man that he was very fit. I waited a minute then opened the shower door and slipped in.

To his credit, the unexpected intimacy of the moment didn't faze him. He turned his back on the stream of steaming water, a half-smile on his lips, and took me in his arms, his warm, wet body touching mine from feet to face.

"Fancy seeing you here," he smiled, brushing a damp curl from his eyes, picking up a bottle of shower gel and slowly soaping my shoulders and neck as if it were the most natural thing in the world. I could feel all my senses responding in harmony, could hardly contain the pounding in my heart. 'What a result,' I told myself, gasping for air with the long-awaited nearness of the man.

I responded in kind and soon we were half-sponging and half-caressing each other's bodies, giving and taking pleasure from the wet kisses, stroking and enjoying the contact at last.

I had a chance to appreciate his splendid body too: muscular and taut – more so than I had imagined. It was a pleasure to run my hands from the bird tattoo beneath the curve of his throat, to the broad chest and around the well defined muscles in his buttocks, arms and legs. I hadn't thought he would be such a confident, sensual lover. An unexpected surprise. I also admit to having felt the familiar pang of anxiety, hoping *my* body hadn't disappointed *him*.

The telephone rang but this time we ignored it. I heard the answer machine click in downstairs and a female speaking, followed by an older-sounding male voice.

'Who cares?' I thought.

Later, satisfied and sleepy, we lay, still not quite dry, wrapped in towels, then slid beneath the sheets in Greg's rumpled bed, careless of the day and the world.

Those lazy, languid hours were lovely, and were to be the last we'd have for a while. Dozing and dreaming together, we roused ourselves and made love once again, then, spent and happy, Greg slipped on a bathrobe and with an easy lope, made his way to the kitchen to make tea. I stretched my naked body, comfortably, ecstatically happy.

I daydreamed about the future – about our deepening familiarity, now physical, and our compatibility, one with the other. Flexing my toes and lifting my arms above my head, I awaited his return, a worm of doubt creeping into the idyll as I wondered what *I* must look like, and scanned the room for a mirror.

Downstairs, I could hear the muffled message of the answer machine dragging him back to the real world. In hindsight, it was the worst possible way to surface from our delight in each other. However, we didn't know what was to come, so I lingered on in ignorance, awaiting his return.

"Was the message important?" I asked when I saw his expression.

"Depends what's important to you." His voice was toneless.

"Why? Who was it?" A creeping dread filled my heart as I felt my muscles tighten.

"The priest, and then Mrs Barrington. They were talking about the arrangements for an exorcism. Of course, I knew nothing about it – seeing as I wasn't privy to your arrangements."

He raised a questioning eyebrow, giving me an old-fashioned look as he lowered the tray onto the bed.

By this time I had sprung up, a guilty pang sending my heartbeat soaring once again.

"I thought you knew I was going to have the church exorcised before the wedding? You agreed to speak to Mrs B. It was after I'd left last time, do you remember? But then Bill Stevens happened and we didn't get a chance to talk. After that, I assumed you'd know about the plan – or that there was nothing for her to report – of a supernatural nature anyway. That's why I never bothered to mention it again."

We looked at each other for a long minute.

"I'm really sorry."

My clumsy stumbling didn't make sense. It was all sorted ages ago, in my memory anyway. I stuck to my guns; and I still thought, especially in the light of Amelia's experiences, that even if it didn't do any good, at least it couldn't do any harm.

I pulled my blouse on over my shoulders and scanned the room for something to wear. I felt at a distinct disadvantage having this conversation half naked.

Greg found another bathrobe and handed it to me, automatically, but the mood had changed.

"So, it's going ahead, is it? This nonsense?"

"Well, obviously. Did they give you times? Who will be doing it – there has to be a designated priest in any diocese but the Reverend was going to make inquiries. Did he say?"

"I asked him to speak to you later. Said I didn't know anything about it. Drink your tea before it gets cold," he smiled, softening slightly when he saw my distress.

"I'm sorry it doesn't meet with your approval," I said, gulping the rapidly cooling liquid, without tasting it, "but I have to do this. Too many odd things have happened. Remember, one of these… entities… tried to get into bed with me! No, it has to be done before Amelia sets foot in that church. It's the only way to ensure her safety."

He looked resigned. "Oh, and Ma Barrington wants to see you. Apparently she has a message – probably be Jack the Ripper asking you on a date or something. Don't meddle with something you don't understand, Jo. Please."

At that, the alarm went off and he had to go to work. "These poachers don't catch themselves, you know," he said in an attempt at flippancy.

I sat and stared at the wall for some time after, wondering what to do.

CHAPTER 44

I sat for the next hour watching rubbishy telly. A presenter had people competing against each other for a thousand pound prize. They had to decide which of the exhibits was a masterpiece. The objects were on cloth-covered plinths ghostly in their white cloths. Contestants had to sieve the wheat from the chaff. I didn't give them very good odds. Two out of the three teams didn't know what 'alabaster' was.

I stared into space again, wondering whether it was worth continuing with the exorcism in the light of Greg's opposition. On the one hand, it all sounded like superstitious nonsense and was likely to cause my lovely new relationship to founder. However, if we didn't get it done and something went wrong, I'd never forgive myself.

These ghosts meant business and were encroaching on my life, my friendships and now my relationship with Greg, not to mention poor Amelia and her unborn child. That was a recurring theme in these hauntings. My poor lost baby, Ammy's abortion, and her present pregnancy were all somehow bound up with the doings in All Saints Church and Skelton Castle. But why and how?

I glanced back at the television screen. One of the teams had chosen a stool and one, a baby's shawl as their 'alabaster' object. Somewhere in the back of my mind, and not for the first time, I marvelled at the general stupidity of people.

Then I went to see the Rev.

Arrangements were finalised. Reverend Martin and another priest arranged to meet me at the church.

"This must be a secret. I don't want anyone else to know," I told them, trying to look stern instead of scared. Both nodded in unison, understanding. After all, it was an important part of their job to keep other peoples' secrets.

Two o'clock was agreed. Two tomorrow. I sorted out the necessary items, to which Reverend Martin added a rosary. Seeing the questioning look in my eyes, he explained, "I know we are not of the Roman persuasion, my dear, but it can't do any harm to protect ourselves with anything that speaks of goodness and of Jesus."

I accepted dumbly. After all, what did *I* know of any of this?

Before the ceremony – I assume you'd call it a 'ceremony' – I decided to pay Mrs Barrington a visit, and knew instinctively that I'd rather call well before dusk. Accordingly, I stepped uncertainly up to the cottage door and knocked softly. I wandered round the side to look at the garden as I waited.

I could hear Arthur snuffling at the bottom of the gate and imagined his tail beating against the wall in his eagerness to see his visitor. Nobody answered and I was reluctantly retreating when she appeared, peering over the garden wall.

"Hello." I forced a smile. "I understand you have something to tell me?"

I stared at her hands as she spoke. She was pulling off a pair of gardening gloves and I noticed that they were very white, the fingers long and thin with knobbled joints. 'Arthritic,' I thought. 'Must be painful.' Maybe I was trying too hard to be kind.

"Oh, yes. I have a message for you."

"Who sent it?" I asked.

She disappeared into the fox-scented living room and I waited outside. Arthur, now released, snuffled round my legs and feet. I stroked him, apprehensively. After all, he was only doing what normal animals would do. On her return, the fox scuttled indoors, as if stung.

Mrs Barrington held a crumpled-up piece of paper in her hand.

It struck me that her skin was the perfect colour of alabaster. Wordlessly, she passed the note to me.

My whole body froze.

'Jenny's cold. She's crying for her mother,' it said.

A stiffness paralysed my joints and my brain burned. Utter confusion befuddled my head as I tried to make any kind of sense of this cruel joke, if that was what it was.

"Why have you done this?" I asked, my voice sounding like a stranger's voice, slow and far away.

She seemed genuinely confused. "Done what? I simply gave you a message."

"But who's it from?"

"Well, I'm not sure. Sometimes I don't hear a *voice*, just something pushed into my head at night. It was either Alice Thomas or Edmund Winter, I believe, but I have no idea who 'Jenny' is."

I recovered my senses. "You are a very cruel woman," I announced, turning on my heel and hurrying towards the church.

It was five past two by the clock in the church tower.

"And you are a very foolish one, meddling in things you don't understand," she shouted after me. *"Don't* go into the church. There's danger there."

I paused for breath at the church door.

Nobody was around.

Where were the priests?

My head ached and clamoured for an explanation – or at least for somebody to tell, someone who could make sense of the inexplicable, or Greg, with his infinite sense of the absurd, to diminish the madness and make it go away.

With my hands in my pockets, clutching the rosary and the holy water, I opened the church door.

Immediately, I knew they were in there.

Both of them.

Their scent filled my nostrils. Their dust entered my lungs. At the far end, the holy end, the tiny stone coffin sat, where my baby was supposedly in need of comfort. I ached to go to her but

I *knew* she wasn't there. I knew she was dead and no mumbo-jumbo could conjure her back to me. No spells and potions could assuage my grief.

No sign of the priests, still.

"Where are you both?" I shouted, then was scared of the ensuing silence and the echo of my voice reverberating around the old building.

In a blind panic, I dashed for the door and reached out to grab the handle, but to my horror, I touched – although there was nothing there – something soft and yielding. A body? Yet I could see nothing. *I could see nothing.*

Logic desperately tried to help me. I'd withdrawn instantly, repelled by the touch of heat and flesh, but had shaken off the fear because I could not make sense of it.

'So how can it be? And who can it be?' My head ached with unanswerable questions.

I reached again, this time with the cold dread of anticipation, but my hand was unable to reach the door at all. Someone – or something barred the way. And that someone was not of my world.

Knowing that I had to leave before anything really bad happened, I made a move towards the other exit, a glass-panelled door near the altar, but before I could reach it, a loud screeching and flapping filled the air, as if a flock of frightened birds were fleeing from something that had terrified them. At the same time, the massive bible was lifted and flung from its place on the topmost pulpit. It flew directly at my head but I couldn't move. I heard the shrieking reach a crescendo before it found its target then I fell to the ground in pain, hitting my head on the cold, flagstone floor, and lost consciousness.

CHAPTER 45

It was almost dark when I finally opened my eyes and felt the searing pain on the back of my head, presumably where the bible had struck me, and on my cheek where I had hit the stone flags head-on. I couldn't move, and my eyes could only see the ancient wood, which had shrunk away from the flooring in Pew 13. I remember thinking, 'You could easily catch your ankle in that gap and knock your head on those heavy flags. You could really do yourself some damage there.' A stupid thought in a dreadful situation.

Slowly and painfully, I dragged my poor body up, managing to grasp the edge of a pew and bring myself to a semi-standing position, but immediately threw up and sat back down, slowly, slowly, gasping for air and trying to recover some energy. I reached for a tissue to wipe my face.

I know not how long I sat in that church. I was frozen to the spot for some time, then edged backwards not daring to turn away from the pulpit until I hit the edge of the nearest pew. I slid the ancient catch and on opening the door really slowly – the way you move so as not to scare a small bird – sank down onto the wooden bench.

At least now my back was protected by the box that made up the pew. It was colder now and I was trembling with fear in the chill air.

As soon as I dared, I glanced at the phone in my pocket. It was dead. I couldn't even call for help. My watch told five – an hour before the darkness would be complete. I realised I must avoid the dark at all costs, but I was too afraid to try for the door again.

Summoning up all my resolve, I decided on desperate action, to crawl and drag myself along the floor, which would mean passing the dreaded pulpit, in order to reach the long window and make my escape, when I felt the heat again, only this time it felt like something to welcome rather than dread.

A strong hand – or so it seemed to me – took hold of mine and guided me gently to my feet. It felt as though permission had been given, but to do what? As I rose, the door slowly swung open about three inches. The pressure on my hand ceased and I stumbled to freedom, stiff, cold and terrified.

How strange it was that there to greet me were Reverend Martin and Father John, the exorcist priest. I almost fell onto them in my relief.

"Sorry we're late. We must go back in there. This thing must be confronted before it can do any more harm," said Father John, a formidable person, more stocky and robust than dear Reverend Martin, and one who made me feel more secure. At that moment, Mrs Barrington tiptoed into the vestibule and stood in wait.

I recoiled at the idea of returning, but was helped by Reverend Martin, who looked seriously worried, and by Mrs Barrington, who had brought something that smelled like old-fashioned liniment, which she was dabbing on the back of my head. Dismissing her, Reverend Martin nodded to us and we went back into that dark place once more.

Father John began to intone:

'May the cross of the son of God,
Which is mightier than all the hosts of Satan,
And more glorious than all the hosts of heaven.
Abide with you in your going out and your coming in
By day and by night; at morning and at evening,
At all times and in all places may it protect and defend you
From the assaults of evil spirits
From foes visible and invisible, from the wrath of evil-doers

From the snares of the devil,
From all passions that beguile the soul and body;
May it guard, protect and deliver you.'

I was staring down at my fingernails, which had taken on a purple hue, when my whole body began to tremble and I saw horrible things, souls in torment and the fires of hell, whether real or hallucinatory I don't know. They felt all too real to me at the time and I started to scream.

From behind us came a hissing, flapping sound of birds' wings, newly released from captivity. I turned to look but Father John instructed me to face east and whatever happened next, to stay where I was, in the darkened pews.

"Safer there," he said.

He continued the ritual sprinkling of holy water where the birds were now circling above us in a black profusion. Their cries at first sounded like, 'Caw, caw,' as they clawed at his head, then slowly it changed to, 'Whore! Whore!' as they came closer to me, flying directly at my hair and face.

A cacophony of discordant sounds joined in, seeming to emanate from the gallery as Father John walked to the centre pew, the Winters' pew, holding a shining crucifix aloft, his lips moving constantly in a whispered prayer.

When he reached the fireplace and turned towards the pulpit, a fire sprang to life in the centre grate and the birds flew as one towards it, singeing their wings in the flames. The air was filled with their unbearable high-pitched screams as they did so, then they circled again, filling the air with smoke and the acrid smell of burning flesh as they caught alight.

Father John sprinkled the holy water directly onto the now-blazing flames but to no avail.

Reverend Martin, until now a silent observer, sprang into action at this. He flung the heavy lid from the font at the rear of the church, to the floor, and took up the stone vessel beside it. Scooping up water he rushed across and threw it onto the fire, then hurried back for more. I had my bottle of water in my hand and wanted to pass it to him to help, as he neared me, but there was nothing I could do. Rooted to the ground as I was, I was unable to move. It felt as if I were being held by tight bands across my chest and legs, which stifled my lungs and sucked more of the breath from my body, the more I struggled to be free.

Reverend Martin was by this time at the altar, also praying. I believed he was safe until a bird dived directly at his eyes. I watched him drop to the ground and tried to shout, "Father John!" but could not speak. Reverend Martin recovered somewhat and returned to the font for more water when I noticed a stray spark from the fire catch at the hem of Father John's robes. I watched, horrified. The dry air ignited his body in seconds.

Reverend Martin rushed back to him and tried to stifle the flames before they could take hold, but it was hopeless. Both priests fought valiantly against the fire enveloping John, but soon his screams subsided and he lay inert, the heavy gold crucifix in his hand clanging to the ground, the sound echoing all around as the birds, sensing weakness, clustered about him, plucking and pecking, even as they burned.

At last he lay still and silent on the flagstones, defeated, the scorched carcasses of the crows and ravens piled deep around him, the air filled with the acrid stench of death and evil.

And that was when, unable to breathe any longer, the searing pain in my head took over and I passed out again.

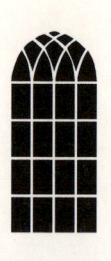

CHAPTER 46

Journal Entry: *'I have been ill for more than a month now, during which time I've been keeping a diary, simply to help me stay sane. It seems that the doctors are happy for me to go home and James has arranged transport and some help – in the form of Lucy, Ammy's friend. She'll stay for a short while and make sure I don't do anything silly. I have no idea what 'anything silly' might be but all I want is to be fit and well again and to be rid of the nightmares which haunt my dreams.*

After the 'accident' in the church (that's what they're all calling it) I was rushed for an x-ray and it was found that I'd fractured my skull, probably a combination of the fall and the blow to my head. These old bibles can pack some heft. I am writing a diary to try and get things into perspective. I was told that Father John had died and that was the most difficult thing to come to terms with.

It's hard to look back now at my first diary entries, that I wrote a few days into treatment...'

Entry No 1: *'I can't trust anybody. I keep hearing them plotting. That nice nurse – what's she up to standing at the end of the bed whispering to the doctors? And what's this stuff they're injecting me with? I think they're trying to make me go gradually blind – or mad. Oh, they're clever alright. Nobody believes me, but then, I think they're all in it together. I must speak to Greg. He'll sort it out and take me back to his house. I'll be safe there.*

My head aches with all this medication. I can't even think of how to escape. I'm too weak.'

Entry No 2: *'The old woman opposite me in here – she's in on it. Keeps offering me sweets but I won't take any – I know they're poisoned. I daren't eat anything they prepare. They know I know that Edmund and Alice have been kidnapped. That's what they won't admit. That's what worries me.*

Greg's concerned, or so he says. But what's all that about? He's watched them sticking needles in me. Why doesn't he stop them? He says he loves me. If he loves me, why's he on their side? I daren't relax and I'm not allowed to move my head. It's torture.'

Entry No 3: *'A breakthrough today. The fat nurse with the dark hair has agreed to help me escape. She wouldn't let them put any more needles in me today and when she took me for an x-ray, she ran with the trolley and brought my bag on top of it, so I think she was trying to get me out.*

It didn't work but at least now I know she's on my side.'

Entry No 4: *'They're putting insects in my bed now. I don't know why. Edmund seems to think it's like leeches – in his day that's what they used, he said. I know he loves me and is trying to help. Together we've been killing them, the insects. Today it was ants. They're marching along my shins in neat columns then they go into the sheets, but where? I don't know how they escape. However many we kill, they keep coming back.*

Greg's still pretending he's on my side but he keeps encouraging me to take the poison pills, so I don't believe him. Oh, and they've moved my friend – the nurse who was going to get me out of here. They say she's 'away on holiday'. Oh, very convenient. They've banned her from seeing me because she knows the truth. I can't trust anybody.'

Entry No 5: *'Unbelievable. The nurses are on some sort of mission now. Because I've complained about all the insects in my mattress, they've started 'physio' on me. That's supposed to 'keep my limbs working' but in truth, all they're doing is mashing up the ants and using a cream to rub them into my legs. That can't be right. The doctor says I'm getting better but slower than they thought. Ha. Maybe if they stopped the poison pills I'd be okay. I've started putting them under my tongue and then spitting them out when the staff nurse leaves. I'd rather be in pain than take any more.*

And another thing: I wish Greg would stop turning into Edmund each time he kisses me. Although, to be fair, Edmund has told me that he's dodging in between us, so that he's the one who gets my kiss. It's a pity he can't show himself to everyone but he has to keep it secret or they'd ban him from the ward.

Still no sign of the dark haired nurse. I fear the worst.'

'I can smile about it now, but it's the scariest thing in the world when you genuinely believe everybody is against you. Nonsense, of course. I must have been on very strong medication. The doctors told me I was hallucinating at one point. The worry is that it'll happen again, and the worst of it is – every time Greg kisses me, I can see his face changing.

He becomes Edmund Winter. The softness in the eyes changes to a blue, brittle stare and the curls become blond waves. The first time it happened, I thought I was out of my wits. Since then, it's happened a few times – I'm kissing two men at the same time and one of them is dead. I find it repellent but how can I tell the man I love? When I draw back, I see the hurt look in his face, so I make an excuse, that my head hurts, or my neck is still painful, but I know he isn't fooled. I don't know how long I can use these evasive tactics.

I'm hoping that James will send for me soon, so that I can get some space to think and recover. I realise now that Edmund's presence wasn't real, just a side-effect of the drugs. And, of course, that Greg was always on my side – though there weren't any sides, except in my skewed imagination.

I love him to distraction but I'm afraid I'm losing him. I fear he'll give up on me. The thing is, to go away and find myself again. My body and mind have been through the mill and need a change and a rest. I just hope he doesn't forget me.

God bless Amelia, too. She's postponed the wedding until spring in the hope that I'll be able to attend.

'Christmas went by in a blur for you, poor darling Jo-Jo. We *simply must have you at our wedding. I'll have my dress altered especially, to accommodate the bump!' she enthused.*

I was really affected by what would have been a massive sacrifice for her – and an expensive one.

The only thing that bothers me is the absence of Rev Martin. I haven't heard anything of him since that fateful day and it's out of character. Mrs Barrington seems to think he's been quite poorly since the exorcism. She visited me one afternoon in full, doom-laden mode to tell me how he wasn't a well man and that the excitement had been too much for him – her words. I do hope he'll recover enough to see me before I leave.'

CHAPTER 47

When I finally arrived back home to my flat and slid the key in the lock, my sense of relief was also tinged with an odd feeling of anti-climax. I pushed open the inner door where the air had a strange still, stale smell like the inside of a recently-opened cardboard box. I watched the motes of dust dancing in the slim shaft of sunlight escaping through a gap in the window blinds and felt like crying.

It felt as if something had been disturbed, but it was not necessarily an unwelcome interruption.

'Oh, it's you,' the place seemed to say. 'You were missed.'

A thin layer of dusty residue had settled across every surface, the vacant chairs, the kitchen counters, the bed. Strangely, a vivid sense of Greg came flooding back to me. The memorable catastrophe of that night I'd wanted him to stay and the subsequent ruins of my plan: his much-treasured discarded scarf I'd worn almost with reverence as a substitute for the flesh and blood object of worship I thought I'd lost.

And the whispered, 'I love you' to the empty room which had echoed in my head for ages after.

I wandered around, touching random things, remembering them, their familiar shapes and textures. I looked again at my bookshelves, thinking of the hours I'd spent in hospital longing for some volume of poetry or a much-loved novel instead of the trashy magazines I'd been offered.

So now, this was the future. It was something I didn't recognise, and I was scared. Did I really want to continue with my business? Cosmetics just seemed so unimportant – playing on the vanity of weak women – offering unattainable perfection, 'if only you'll buy this cream or that lipstick'. Was that really what I wanted now? I felt much older and wiser than before and yet, what else could I do? I had to make some sort of living for myself but I needed time to think about it. Something meaningful had to come from all of this, which meant massive changes to my way of thinking and my way of living.

Exhausted, I sank down in my favourite chair beside the fire and switched on the radio.

The sound filled the empty space… It was Paul McCartney singing about loving someone forever, with all his heart, no matter whether they were together or not. It was Greg's favourite Beatles song, 'I Will'.

At the flick of a switch, the sound stopped.

That song.

My first thought was that someone was playing tricks on me. The very song that Greg had played at his house when he'd first kissed me, and here it had come to torment me again. No ghosts here though, not now. They'd all been disposed of. The atmosphere had lightened and I had no expectation of Edmund, Alice or anyone else coming to haunt me again.

And yet, and yet…

The light had faded to purple when I awoke. Probably the exhausting journey had finished off my last reserves of energy and my heavy eyelids had drooped without my realising that I was drifting into a silent sleep.

I shifted in the chair and stretched my aching limbs. Rising uncertainly and feeling the strain on neck and back as I walked to the kitchen, I realised that I needed to keep active and went out to the nearby shops to buy some essentials for tea.

James and Ammy were coming tomorrow with Lucy and probably, with a shedload of food, but tonight I wanted, needed, peace and quiet and my own company. I wanted my own, albeit dusty, bed and possibly a bit of rubbishy telly as background noise.

I dragged my cases into the kitchen to unload into the washing machine when a few get-well cards fell out onto the floor. One, still unopened, was written in that familiar hand. Why hadn't I looked at it? How was I feeling about Greg nowadays? It was almost like a sign – this card – telling me... what?

I took it into the bedroom and held it, wanting to open it but not daring to in case all my hopes were dashed in an instant. I had to read it. I started to lift the corner of the envelope when there was a sudden discordant clanging from the kitchen. The washing machine sounded like it was about to fall through the floor. That was all I needed. I dropped the card and ran to rescue the situation.

Routine is a good place in which to seek refuge and that is what I established in those next few weeks. I met up with old friends and business associates, but the hollow feeling about my meaningless working life persisted.

I went to familiar haunts – restaurants, pavement cafes and such – and this seems stupid, looking back – but the air was as stale and polluted as that in my flat. I longed for green spaces and took to walking in parks and the grounds of stately homes where I could feel temporarily refreshed.

Amelia was blooming in that restrained way that slim young women seem to have in pregnancy. She had a neat, small swelling in her belly and her hair looked more lustrous, but these were the only indicators of her condition.

The first visit she made to my flat was full of surprises because she brought me a massive sackful of belated Christmas presents. I was taken aback that the festive season had so completely passed me by and I felt cheated. I had nothing to give in return, of course, but she didn't care.

"Oh, Jo-Jo, darling, of *course* you couldn't have bought presents. You poor thing, you weren't in your right mind! I like to think of it as your druggie period, ha ha!" then, more seriously, with a smothering hug, "Oh, I'm sooo glad you're better; and I'm *dying* to have the wedding and I want us to go dress shopping for you as soon as you're ready!"

I exclaimed in all the right places. Everyone had been very generous and soon the floor was covered in spangly wrapping paper and boxes containing cashmere sweaters, jewellery and the like.

There was nothing from Greg. I'd searched all over the flat for the get-well card from him that I'd been too scared to open but to no avail, it had vanished in the wake of the washing machine disaster. There was no card, even, from Rev Martin, and I didn't dare ask about them both.

And so the spring gradually crept in. The winds gave way to showers, the days grew longer and I grew idle – a woman without motivation. Because the days were so similar, their pattern entrenched in routine, time seemed to pass more quickly and I was almost surprised to see the first day of April on my calendar.

It was then that I received a letter from the Reverend Martin, asking if he could come and visit me, *'on a matter of some importance,'* it said.

CHAPTER 48

I was at a loss to imagine why the elderly priest would come all the way to London to see me, especially in view of his failing health. I spent a couple of sleepless nights thinking about it. What was so vital that he couldn't phone or write the news? I now understood him to have been rather ill after the exorcism, but since I hadn't been in my right mind at that time, I had no idea about the seriousness or otherwise of his illness. It had been a vague background detail and I now felt the guilt that came from my neglect of him. So selfish.

I'd made careful preparations for his visit. I would be picking him up at King's Cross station and bringing him home, where I'd prepared a comforting meal and a comfortable bed to follow. I meant to make up for my earlier lack of interest during his illness. A tiny part of me was hoping that there'd be a message from Greg but I pushed that to the back of my mind for the present.

Reverend Martin looked very frail when I met him. I could hardly pick him out from the crush of commuters at the station and I recalled the hurried goodbyes at our first meeting when he'd rushed off the train double-quick and almost missed his stop. I couldn't imagine him hurrying anywhere nowadays and I slowed my pace to match his as we walked to the car.

"My dear girl," he said in those beautifully modulated tones, "how very kind you are to put me up in your home. I would have stayed with my cousin Albert, you know, if you hadn't insisted, but I'm sure it will be much pleasanter staying with you. Albert's ancient rectory is draughty and full of extremely old furniture – rickety and uncomfortable if the truth be told. A bit like me." The twinkle returned.

He then went into reminiscing mode again so we stayed silent until we arrived at the flat.

Tea, gallons of it, were consumed through the afternoon during which time he regaled me with stories of Skelton at Christmas and the things I'd missed during my stay in hospital.

It wasn't anywhere near as difficult as I'd expected because he was an interesting companion and, like many people who live alone, he took pleasure in company. It was good for me to have company too and I realised how much I'd missed other people, despite my new found independence.

After we'd eaten, I got out the brandy – his favourite tipple – and asked the question.

"Why did it seem so important to see me in person, Reverend? I've been at a loss to work out why it should be."

He stared at me for a minute and then asked, "Isn't there anybody you'd like to ask me about first?"

"Sorry, I should've checked on how everyone's getting on, but you pretty much covered it... didn't you?"

"Well, Joanne, since you were wondering, your young man is pretty miserable at present. I wonder why that could be. He's taken himself off to Majorca – a cycling holiday no less – with a few of the football team and assorted wives and girlfriends."

I felt a pang of panic.

"Has he got a new girlfriend?" I said in heart-stopping mode.

"I have no idea." He wasn't going to let me off the hook that easily.

"Well, who was going? Anyone I know?"

"Once again, I have no idea. I don't know who you know, apart from Jack Gregson, that is."

Ooh, wily old fox. Using the full name for extra effect. Not so frail, then, after all. Not mentally, anyway. I cut my losses. We could reopen that can of worms later.

"So, was that what you came all this way to tell me, Reverend?

That Greg's gone off on a jolly which may or may not include another woman?" Oh no. It was impossible to keep the emotion out of my voice. A bitter edge had crept in, whether I wanted it to or not. "I hope he has a lovely time. Was there something else I needed to know, then? Because, if not, I'm getting pretty tired and I'm sure you're ready for another brandy, then bed?" I managed a weak smile.

His reaction surprised me. "No, no. I need to do this before bed, my dear. There's something of importance that I discovered – well, that I and the Gillings found out." He struggled to his feet and looked anxiously around for his battered leather briefcase. "I know how you were plagued with those hauntings in the church so I asked if I could look at the archive which is stored at the castle. There was something that made no sense – about Alice Thomas and Edmund Winter. It's been nagging at me, right at the back of my mind for months now."

My stomach started to churn. What could he possibly have wanted to tell me and did I really want to know?

"The received wisdom," he said, "is that Alice set fire to the church in her despair about the accident and possibly about the baby, but I couldn't bring myself to believe it. The two ghosts and their odd behaviour troubled me. How would Alice, a bright young woman, be so careless as to let herself be caught up in farm machinery? She was a farmer's daughter, for goodness sake. She'd be used to keeping her distance from the plough horses and the other mechanical innovations used regularly on the farm. What had distracted her this time? Then I thought about the people there at the scene of the accident that day. Jerome, Alice's brother, was above suspicion, of course, but who was the man operating the thresher? Did Alice know him?"

I was really interested but could only mutter sounds of encouragement, shaking my head in sympathy and not knowing how to respond.

He continued, "Then there was Edmund's behaviour. He adored Alice. He was about to marry her. If he'd been responsible for her pregnancy, it would have been easy to go ahead with the wedding and await the 'premature' birth of the child, surely? He had power and wealth. Nobody would dare question him. Besides, this was a small village in the country. These things were happening all the time. No. It didn't make any sense that he would reject her, even with her injuries. In fact, being seen to do the right thing would have earned him the respect and honour he craved."

He paused but, again, I didn't speak.

"I also thought," he said, "about the behaviour of the ghostly beings towards you. Why you? At first, I wondered if it might be because of your own sad loss – that some fellow-feeling might have been there, but if so, why was Alice so full of hate? It was as though she sought to punish you in some way. None of it made sense. Edmund's palpable attraction to you, we both know about. And, this is no disrespect to you, my dear, you are a very attractive woman, but *plenty* of women go to All Saints on sightseeing tours. Why would he only pick *you* out? He seemed almost to have become your protector. Why?"

During this speech, Reverend Martin looked agitated and excited but also seemed younger in some way. His colour was higher than usual (the brandy?) and he was breathing heavily. Altogether he had the demeanour of a sleuth on the trail of a notorious criminal, ludicrous as that may seem.

I asked him to pause for a minute and take some tea or a glass of cold water before we continued, but he would have none of it.

"No, no. Very kind, but no thank you. I need to tell you everything now."

He opened his briefcase and brought out a battered book the size of an old foolscap ledger, with various scrappy pieces of yellowing paper sticking out from it at odd angles.

"This helped to answer some of my questions. Well, at least it proved my theory. The key to the whole mystery lay in the identity of the farm worker who was operating the thresher at the time that Alice had her accident." He broke off abruptly at this point and asked, "Have you researched your family tree at all?"

"What?"

"It's definitely relevant. Trust me."

"Well, no I haven't – especially on my dad's side anyway. I know more about my mother's family, 'cos she stuck around and brought me up. Why on earth are you asking about this? Continue with the story, please."

He fumbled with his old man's hands, pulling out various bits of crumpled paper and card then turned to one of the markers and opened the page. "Here, you see, where the list of workers and their wages are noted each week." The gnarled finger traced a particular entry. "Look."

It was a name.

"Alan Monner?"

"Yes." He moved across the page. "Now, look there. See his position on the farm?"

"Thresher? Does that mean he operated the machine or was this when the threshing was done manually?"

"The date, Joanna. Look at the date. It's a fortnight before Alice's accident. Now, look at this."

He pulled out a smaller piece of paper – it appeared to be some sort of certificate of competence with the thresher's name on it.

"This proves that he was trained in some rudimentary way to operate the machinery. You'll see that the other threshers didn't have that training. Later on in the ledger, they each manage to get the qualification – or whatever it was called."

"Sorry to sound like someone in an Agatha Christie novel, Reverend, but I don't understand why all this is relevant. What's it got to do with Alice's accident?"

"All in good time, my dear. Give me a moment, would you?"

And he toddled off to the bathroom.

My mind was racing. Alan Monner? It didn't sound like a local name, but then, people were more mobile than we think at that time. They had few possessions to carry with them and they were used to walking miles to find work, so he may have been an itinerant farm worker when he fetched up at Skelton Castle. I smiled at the unconscious use of the Yorkshire phrase. Greg would've enjoyed that.

"So sorry. I'm very old now. I have to look after my bladder." He chuckled to himself as he sat down. "Now where were we? Ah, yes."

He skipped back a few pages in the ledger, six months earlier than the first entry – to a page again marked with a small bookmark – and pointed to another name.

"Alain Le Monnier," I read. "Is this the same man?"

"Yes. He's changed it to fit in. Remember, we were at war with the French, on and off, for hundreds of years. People didn't take kindly to Frenchmen. Remember, they hanged a monkey not too many miles away from Skelton because they said he was a 'frenchie'?"

There was the twinkle again. He was enjoying the joke. I, however, was becoming frustrated with the interruptions.

"So, tell me, Reverend, what has this Alain Le Monnier to do with Edmund Winter and Alice Thomas? And me, for that matter?"

"Ah, well, that's where it gets interesting…"

CHAPTER 49

We settled down to our brandy then, because the old man was starting to get tired and it showed in his face. Although I was desperate to carry on, it seemed cruel to press him any further.

Then, out of the blue he asked, "What was your father's name?"

"Erm, the same as mine, Logan."

"I only ask because according to this research, your grandfather five times removed, born in 1760 was one 'Alan Monner' – aka Alain le Monnier. It's all recorded in the old All Saints parish records of the time."

I couldn't take it in.

"Grandfather five times…? So, how does that pertain to me, Reverend?" I asked, bemused.

"Well, this might help to explain why the connection is relevant, my dear," he said, handing me yet another piece of paper. It was a photocopy of an old letter whose signature was almost illegible.

"The man who wrote this, Father John O'Donnell, was coincidentally, a parish priest at the Catholic church at the time of Alice Thomas's death. Now, I know about the sanctity of the confessional and all that stuff, but the poor man must have had the weight of this knowledge on his shoulders for many years, and he decided to leave a letter hidden in the leaves of his journal, unburdening himself to his friend Father Monsell – who had the neighbouring parish of Brotton at the time."

I looked at the copied document.

'Dear Patrick,' it read, *'I can no longer keep to myself the shocking secret I am about to unfold to you. You will know that I have been ill for some months and I fear that I now have only a few weeks left on earth. If God is kind, he will forgive me for breaking the sanctity of the confessional. If not, then maybe I will not want to spend eternity with such a God.*

'A young woman by the name of Alice Thomas was buried in All Saints Church many years ago. The grave is unmarked – with good reason. At the time it was thought that she had committed suicide; but this sin was compounded by her condition. When she was examined, it was found that she was with child and that the child had died with her.

'It was a tragedy which affected the whole of the village, but most of all it affected the young man who was to have married her. He left home soon after and became involved once more with a disreputable sect called the 'Demoniacs' whose principle desire seems to have been the pursuit of selfish pleasures with scant regard to the welfare of others.'

I cried out at that. Edmund's downfall *was* because of Alice's death, then.

I passed the letter back to Reverend Martin. My mind was in turmoil, but he wouldn't let me off the hook yet.

He continued to read.

'Some time ago, I gave absolution in the confessional to a young man, at the time unnamed, who told me about his nightmares – a direct result of heinous sins he had committed against that very woman, Alice Thomas. I was so disturbed by his words that I wrote them down, the better to digest them.

"I took her against her will, Father, God forgive me. I wasn't thinking straight. My needs got the better of me. She was so beautiful – too good for me, and I knew it – and I planned to find her one night as the sun was setting and take her: with or without her consent. I know that was bad, Father but I was driven mad with the constant thinking about her. Every minute she was in my thoughts. I had such dreams, such dreams, Father..."

We looked at each other, not really wanting to make any comment until everything was finished. Reverend Martin continued reading.

'Of course, I was not able to tell a living soul at the time. The girl was sent away to stay with her cousins in Kent and returned some months later without a child. I have no idea what happened to the child but rumour had it that she was sent to an orphanage somewhere.'

"Would you excuse me for a minute, Reverend Martin?" I said. I suddenly felt nauseous and needed some fresh air.

I had already worked out that the child was, somewhere along the line, related to me. The product of a rape. Poor little thing. I couldn't bear any more, yet there *was* more. "Maybe we should leave it there?" I planned to say.

I went back in and found the vicar snoring on the settee.

'Good,' I thought. I wrapped his frail form in a woollen blanket, left him a note, and switched out the light, even though I knew there would be no sleep for me that night.

CHAPTER 50

Having spent most of the night trying to close my eyes, to no avail, I crept downstairs at dawn, planning to sneak the bundle of documents from the ledger up to my room to read again. I wanted to make sense of some of this stuff. It appeared that my ancestors were Alice, and the Frenchman Alain Le Monnier. Aka Alan Monner, rapist. No wonder he changed his name. How would he dare to stay and brazen it out, I wondered? And *this* man was my blood relation? It made my blood run cold.

I soon realised that I would never be able to piece together the missing parts of the story without Reverend Martin's help. He must've woken up and gone to his room because the sofa was empty and the rug neatly folded when I finally went downstairs again. I made some tea, as quietly as I could, and returned to bed, intending to think things over, but falling into a sound sleep within minutes.

It was just after ten when I woke to a loud banging on the front door. My head ached badly and I was in that grumpy-lack-of-sleep mode which didn't bode well for the visitor – whoever it might be.

A bulky shape loomed large through the frosted glass of the door with a slighter shape beside it. I was apprehensive opening the door, but James and Amelia stood smiling before me, fragrant and clean, awaiting a warm welcome – which was their due, really, after rescuing and caring for me since Skelton. I probably managed a wan smile and nodded them in.

"Oh, God, I must look a mess," I said by way of apology, pushing my unruly mop off my face. This was met with polite murmurings as I rushed to the kitchen to make some coffee for them.

"We wondered if you were feeling well enough for a wedding, Jo?" shouted James from the sofa.

"And please, please say you are, *lovely* Jo-Jo!" This from Amelia, who was clutching a large leather satchel (which was gorgeous – just like the one in John Lewis's window that I'd been lusting after for months) which I guessed was filled with wedding paraphernalia.

"Everything's ready, you know. It's going to be fabulous and I *daren't* wait much longer 'cos I'm sure I'm just about to *burst!*"

She patted a tiny, tiny protruding baby bump on her abdomen – about the size of my normal stomach.

"Nonsense," I said, laughing. "I bet you'll still fit into the pre-preg dress – it's sickening."

She looked gratified but returned to the subject of getting-her-own-way.

"No, but Jo-Jo, *will* you be able to travel north soon?" She lowered her head and looked up through her eyelashes.

'She flirts with everyone,' I thought.

"I won't get married without you, you know."

"But, have you got the church and the minister on stand-by? Not to mention the doves?"

They smiled in unison.

James spoke first. "Everything awaits your pleasure, m'lady," he smiled, with a courtly little bow. "Although, best not to mention the doves."

"Then in that case, you'd better get on with it."

Fragrant coffee aromas began to permeate the apartment and a little birdlike sound came from the kitchen doorway.

"Good morning, Joanne," said the Reverend. "I trust you slept as well as I did."

Then, abruptly changing his tone, as he saw the visitors, he began to apologise and I began to explain his presence;

at the same time as great surprise was being expressed by James and Amelia – the latter flinging her arms around him as if he were a long-lost relative – or should I say *another* long-lost relative?

Over breakfast, all was revealed to the new guests, who were intrigued in a detached way – after all, it was nothing to do with *their* ancestors. It is easy to dismiss shameful events when you are not sullied by direct connection with them.

Amelia drew me aside as we cleared the breakfast pots.

"Sooo...? Any news from that delicious man of yours?" she asked with mock-lasciviousness. "I got a postcard – from Majorca, of all places," she continued. "He's with that cycling crowd – and that awful bleached blonde tarty piece. I can't remember her name. Janet something?"

As I shook my head, she became serious.

"Really? Nothing? Does he have your address, though?"

"You making excuses for him, Ammy?"

I emptied the coffee grounds and whispered this last in her ear as she leaned against the sink. "He's been here in person. He has my address alright," I explained, noticing the crestfallen expression.

In an attempt to make her feel better, I said, "It doesn't matter. All that seems a lifetime ago to me. I really was horrible to him during my illness, you know. Thought he was plotting to kill me." I smiled. "You can't blame him for not wanting anything more to do with me. Probably still thinks I'm a nutter."

I was filling the dishwasher with our breakfast things when James asked for more coffee.

"I always need a few hits of caffeine before I go to work," he said.

Amelia was not to be deflected. Her pretty face crumpled. "Well, you want to know what I think?"

"You're going to tell me, aren't you?"

"I think you are the most stubborn, unyielding pair I've ever met. Hell, Jo, write to him! Tell him you're sorry and you're well now! Bloody hell, I can't believe all this stupid pride!"

The old priest was standing on the threshold and heard most of the conversation.

"I must say, I agree with you, Amelia, my dear," he said.

She managed to look contrite.

"Ooh, sorry Father – about the swearing! I don't normally do that but it makes me so angry, the way they're both ignoring the obvious."

He nodded wisely and paused before saying, "You know, you can't control anyone else, Amelia. Not even *you* can make *everyone* do what you want. It's not good for you anyway – too much getting your own way. Now then, am I still conducting this wedding ceremony?"

He was setting out more coffee cups and saucers as he spoke.

I never bother with cups and saucers normally, just mugs, but I was glad he was busying himself, so I let him carry on. Besides, what he said made sense. James, hearing it all from the sitting room, nodded his approval in perfect synchronisation with his daughter.

"Of *course!* That would be marvellous, Father Martin, if you would," Ammy cooed, filling the cups again with a second serving of coffee.

The pair left soon after and alone with the Reverend, I was able to find out a bit more of the story at last.

"Reverend Martin," I began, "I'm puzzled by the way Alan Monner was able to return to Skelton without any penance being exacted from him. I mean, he rapes the daughter of a respectable farmer – and one engaged to be married to the son of the principal family in the village. It looks like everyone covers up for them both and she has the baby at the other end of the country. She comes back and there he is working at the same place again. Why? Why would that happen, I wonder?"

Cedric Martin turned again to the bundle of notes in the ledger. Leafing through them, he came up with an inner package, smaller than the rest, in the same handwriting as the Frenchman's confession.

"Read these," was all he said.

'These' turned out to be a series of love letters from Alan Monner to Alice Thomas, and some of her responses.

Once I had read them, everything became clearer.

"So, she was in love with Monner all the time?" I asked.

He checked his watch before replying, and began to collect his things together ready for departure, as he continued. "Seemingly. They'd made an agreement to part because of the trouble it had caused with her family, who were very much against the match – not least because the farm belonged to the Winters and was only leased by them to the farmer. Looking at it in that light, it was in everybody's interest that she marry Edmund Winter and secure the family's future living. Girls who brought shame on the family name were outcasts in those days. It would have taken a much stronger-willed girl than Alice to bear such dishonour. The rape story was concocted to defend the girl from gossip." He paused to reflect a moment. "...and when you think about it, it was quite a noble gesture from Monner. He went through a mock-confession and was reviled in the village when the rumours inevitably spread. From a Christian point of view, he put his immortal soul in danger too. He left soon after."

I couldn't bring myself to comment about the immortal souls nonsense so I said nothing. We carried the old man's luggage to the car and he continued as we set off to the station.

"Later, when Alice returned, the plan had been to run away together, but of course, by then, she had decided that she fancied being Mrs Winter after all, and she may have thought Monner had forgotten her. Alain was recalled to the estate because he was trained in the use of the new mechanised equipment, and the family had found out about the cover-up by now, but *she* didn't know he was back. Consequently, her shock at seeing him caused the momentary lapse of concentration which led to that terrible accident."

Once in the station waiting room, I read a couple of the letters. They were full of tenderness and love on Alain's part and fancy expressions of regret on Alice's.

I tried to put myself in their places – first Alice, which was hard to do, then my ancestor, Alain. A French national in a foreign country who had allowed himself to lose this woman he loved, his home, his job and his good name. All for love. It was so sad.

"Please, my dear," the old man said, "don't distress yourself. Here's one last piece of the puzzle before I have to leave. You may keep it if you wish."

He handed me an important-looking letter written on thick parchment. The seal had been broken but the paper was still pristine.

'*My darling Alice,*

I write with a heavy heart, knowing that you still refuse to meet me or to discuss our forthcoming wedding.

Please, think again about your decision to renounce all claims to my heart. You have it now and always will, my dearest love. What care I about your scars? I love them, because they are part of you. They will fade, over time.

If you believe that beauty is only skin deep, then you wrong me by thinking that I only loved your outward appearance. I love everything about you, my dearest girl; your kind nature, your sweet face, your grace and compassion.

Marry me!

I will wait until you change your mind. I shall be steadfast in this.

All my truest love,

Your Edmund.'

When I'd cried enough, I turned to Reverend Martin and said, "If only she'd believed him! Please, will you take this and show it to Greg? He once told me he was related to Alice Thomas. He should read it."

As the train pulled out of the station, I felt an overwhelming sense of relief about Alain's redemption, coupled with sadness about the wasted lives of people I felt I knew as well as I know myself.

CHAPTER 51

It took some time for the shocking truth to hit me. I had been busy shopping for the wedding and making arrangements about accommodation (which would be at Rushpool, apparently) and with only a matter of days to go, I was, I admit, preoccupied with the idea of seeing Greg again.

I worried about how to behave around him. On the one hand, I ached to touch him, to hold him again. On the other, I feared that his manner towards me would be stiff and formal after all those stupid, unfounded accusations. I knew him to be a kind, affable sort of man, but everyone has his breaking point and after all, he hadn't been in touch since I came home. There was also the sore point of his dashing off abroad for that cycling holiday. An attractive man like Greg wouldn't be alone for long, of that I was sure.

That 'shocking truth' though was the biggest stumbling block of all.

When the Reverend Martin left and I had had time to digest the latest developments, I'd worked out that Greg and I were related. Not closely, but enough to put a spanner in the works – if he chose to let it.

Loads of other women out there, I told Lucy and Amelia at our final dress fitting.

"Oh, but not like *you*, Jo-Jo!" Lucy protested.

I let the 'Jo-Jo' go. (You can only correct someone so many times before you raise the white flag.) I decided it was a sign of affection rather than affectation and accepted it in the right spirit.

"Well, let me see now... he thinks I'm a nutter who hates him. And now it turns out that we have the same DNA – give or take a generation or two. Apart from that..." I trailed off with a hopeless shrug.

The girls were kind and high-pitched in their refusal to accept this assessment.

I was surveying the floor of the apartment, which was littered with girly wedding paraphernalia, when the phone rang. I dashed across to the telephone, stabbing my foot with a pin in the process. Accordingly, I answered with a loud, "Ouch!"

"Is that Joanne Logan?" the voice asked.

I recognised it at once as being Mrs Barrington – still the buttoned-up unfriendly tone I knew so well.

"Mrs Barrington?"

"Yes. Are you free to talk?" The girls, hearing the speakerphone, nodded vigorously.

"Yeah, I think so." I was less confident than I sounded. This woman and I had never really been able to communicate very well.

"It's about Jack Gregson," she said.

I think she must've heard a giggle from one of the girls then, because she clammed up immediately.

"What about him?" I was eager for any tiny scrap of information. "Is he alright?"

"Yes, of course." Then, as she heard the silly background whispering, she changed her tone. "Look, I'll speak to you when you come up for this wedding. It's obviously not appropriate at the present time." Click. The phone went dead.

"Oh, bugger," I said, looking accusingly at the pair of them. "She's annoyed with me. Now I'll never get the message. It might have been from Greg – it was *about* him anyway."

My heart went back to beating normally despite the tiny bore hole in it. What was the problem? Was it a problem? Was he bringing a new partner to the do? Who?

I picked up the phone and took it outside, pressing the redial button. I couldn't wait until the wedding. If he had another woman, I needed time to prepare myself.

There was no answer, even though I knew she was there. "Oh, you really know how to turn the screw, Mrs B," I muttered, feeling huge bitterness towards the woman.

The day dragged on and Ammy and Lucy were still fussing over details. I was cajoled into showing my wedding outfit to them and was secretly pleased at their approval – accompanied by cooing and aahh-ing as I twirled around.

The amount of time it had taken me to find this particular dress was ludicrous, but I had really wanted a particular shade of blue in a light, floaty fabric. The fit was flattering too, which the girls eagerly pointed out.

"OOhh Jo-Jo, that's perfect!" cooed Ammy.

"It's really sleek. Shows your figure off to perfection," added a more pragmatic Lucy.

I was pleased with their reaction and hoped the man I wanted to please would feel the same.

I couldn't stop thinking about the message from Mrs Barrington, regretting that the conversation had come to an abrupt end. There was no time to mend relations though, because Amelia and James were taking us out to dinner at some posh, expensive restaurant – in lieu of a hen night. In her advanced state of pregnancy, Ammy couldn't have gone on a traditional hen do.

I was seeing a change for the better in her, of late. Robert's influence and the fact that she would shortly become a mother had given her a new sense of responsibility, and I welcomed it wholeheartedly.

After we'd had coffee, it was Amelia's turn. She danced lightly around the room in her wedding regalia, awaiting the compliments.

"You look very beautiful," I told her sadly, "and so much like your mother."

Her eyes glittered momentarily with unshed tears as she said, "Thank you for that," and stopped dancing, then, with a strange expression on her face asked, "And do you think Edmund will approve?"

I felt the fear shoot up from my toes. "What?"

"I said, 'Do you think Robert will approve?'"

Her expression changed back in an instant to one of openness: the straightforward Amelia I knew and loved.

Lucy who had also frozen, moved across the room and put her arm protectively around my shoulders as I realised I was trembling, but Amelia, unaware, was once more admiring the fine lace fabric of her dress.

"Oh, I do love him *sooo* much!'" she exclaimed, spinning around again and holding her bump affectionately. Things slowly went back to normal, then, but the incident had unnerved me, nevertheless.

Later as we drank a non-alcoholic toast to the marriage, the conversation turned to the night of the Skinningrove Bonfire.

"What do you remember of that night?" Lucy had not been there and was curious about Ammy's disappearance. "Did you ever meet that mystery man again? The one on the beach?"

Amelia was dismissive. "Oh, him. No, I've forgotten what he even looked like," she declared, "apart from his eyes."

Lucy prompted her again. "What were his eyes like?"

"Oh, I don't know. Just sort of – compelling. That's the word. Compelling."

"What colour?" I asked, although I already knew the answer.

"A beautiful sea-blue," she answered but she had gone into a reverie and seemed to be somewhere else.

There was a lull in the conversation then, until Lucy prompted, "Tea?" removing a cloth from the pre-prepared hamper they'd brought with them.

I sneaked a look at the packaging, now carelessly discarded on the living room floor. 'Harrods' it declared.

'Oh, of course,' I thought. 'Typical.'

Amelia came back to us then. "Ooh, yummy!" she cried. "I'm starving. Eating for two nowadays, you know!"

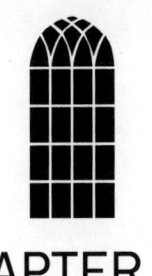

CHAPTER 52

After a few unsettled nights of overthinking and a few days of not connecting with Mrs Barrington, I realised that the only way of speaking to her was in person. I knew this obstinacy was about her refusal to be mocked by silly children when she was on one of her 'missions' and I didn't really blame her.

In fact, I'd've felt the same. I worried that she might never forgive me – thinking perhaps that I'd colluded in that stupid, schoolyard game. I just hoped she'd forget or forgive us before the wedding. Although, if the call was to warn me off Greg because he'd moved on, I probably didn't want to hear it.

If that was the reason, it diminished Greg somehow.

Which left me in limbo.

As the day drew nearer, I became more and more morose about the whole affair.

The worst thing was, I'd brought it upon myself. The exorcism was a massive misjudgement. The illness then compounded my estrangement from Greg, and now having heard nothing from the north, it seemed that the people at the Duke had slipped away too.

News in London was no more encouraging. Apparently, Steve and Sylvie had moved away to cheaper premises and given up any rights to the company name of 'Pleasure First Cosmetics' which should have made me happy, but didn't.

To be honest, I'd lost interest in the whole thing and nowadays could see how shallow and unnecessary it all was. Why had

I wasted so much of my life on trivial, ego-driven people and their need to cover their faces and bodies with so-called miracle creams and lotions?

In short, my priorities had changed. I needed something, shall I say, more 'real'? I wanted to do something that didn't have to make a shedload of money to give me a *raison d'être*.

On the other hand, I had to have money to survive. Whenever I thought about this stuff, my head began to hurt. I mean, physically hurt.

The strategy then had been to do a Scarlet O'Hara and 'think about it tomorrow'.

After finally deciding to be positive and tackle my finances and with my future head on, I called to see the accountants who had taken care of all my business dealings since the split with Steve and Sylvie. That left me feeling better – at least I was solvent, or even 'comfortable' as I was told at the meeting.

"What should I do now though, Miss Bentham?" I asked the accountant, hoping for some words of wisdom from her.

A happy career woman, she advised me to invest in a different kind of business. "If you've done it well once, it usually follows that you can make a success of anything as long as you know the product and are willing to promote it." She put her head on one side and smiled, meaning to be encouraging, but it felt patronising and false to me.

"Might I ask you, Miss Logan, do you intend to live in London or are you contemplating a move to the north?"

I was taken aback. "Why would you think such a thing?" I asked.

"Well, you *have* been spending a great deal of time up there, so I assumed that you were planning a new business venture, what with property prices and labour costs being so much lower...?" She stopped in mid-sentence, a tentative note rising up in her speech. Seeing my expression, she quickly recovered and became brisk once more. "Ah, well, whatever you decide, Miss Logan, you can be sure that we will be available every step of the way to advise and help you," then after an awkward pause, "Always a pleasure." She smiled, in full control now as she proffered her hand to signal an end to the meeting.

On my journey home, my head was full of contradictions and possibilities.

Someone said if you were tired of London, you were tired of life. Well, since my illness, I had realised I *was* tired of London. The air was stale and polluted, the noise and bustle no longer suited me – I'd long since sought respite in the green spaces around me – and I missed the sea. Even the gossip of friends had a shallow, 'who cares' feel to it lately.

Now the possibility of a move had been suggested by Miss Bentham, it had become lodged in my head. Not to the north, I decided. Well, certainly not anywhere near Skelton…

I took out the map as soon as I arrived home, and studied it between making a pot of tea and checking house prices to find out what the flat was worth.

I'd almost decided on North Somerset when I made the phone call.

"James!" I cried in a fever of anticipation, "How much would someone pay for this place? Or could I rent it out? And if so, what could I ask – per month?"

A calm voice at the other end smiled, "Ah, I wondered how long it would take you."

I paused until he was forced to speak again.

"Dear Jo, I think you knew all along that you'd go back up there once the wedding was over. Well, *we* all did, anyway."

Again, I didn't speak.

"You won't need to worry about the flat. It will always retain its value – but you'd get more rent money if you called it an, 'executive apartment'." His hearty laugh reverberated through the phone and I couldn't be affronted any more. "Shall we speak about it after the wedding? Unless there's some kind of emergency funding you need? Not pregnant, are you?"

I could still hear the chuckle in his voice as I responded. "No, James, no hurry."

CHAPTER 53

Two sayings sprang to mind on the day before the wedding. The first one was, 'Be careful what you wish for – it may come true.'

I'd arrived late that afternoon. The weather was an echo of the first day – the day I saw All Saints for the first time. Gentle breeze, green buds springing into hushed life and the promise of hope in the air.

This time, however, I didn't stop in Church Lane and I didn't look at the newly-cleared churchyard, bedecked as it was, with posies of early cowslips and primroses tied with purple velvet ribbons, which led the way down the bridal path to the church.

'Sufficient unto the day is the evil thereof,' I thought as I bypassed the lane and came to a stop outside the Duke William public house. I had no desire to hurry on the moment when I'd have to confront my fears once again.

I admit to having felt quite proud of Ammy when she told me of the floral arrangements for this momentous occasion. It was all understated and natural. She'd gone for tasteful, rather than garish and vulgar.

"No doubt the London mob will supply that aplenty when they arrive in their flash cars with matching outfits and voices," I decided, surprised at my own cynicism.

Initially, I had booked a room at Rushpool Hall, but James had begged me to help find 'suitable accommodation' (big and flashy) for his friends, and by the time it had been organised, Rushpool had been filled to the rafters with them, so, as a noble gesture, I had given up my room – yet in truth, this was no hardship because I knew I'd be more at home at the Duke, anyway.

"Hello George!" The enthusiastic greeting was genuine. Just seeing the cheery face of the landlord gave me a feeling of coming home.

The familiar is always welcome in these circumstances. It was just the circumstances that were awkward and I felt as though I was being watched by the world and his wife – even though there was hardly anyone in the pub so early in the evening.

George emerged from behind the bar and gave me a bear hug. He smelled of the slightly beery cloths he used to clean the counters at the end of the night – in fact, I noticed one draped across his shoulder – handy in case he needed to mop up spills on his glass-collecting rounds.

Taking my shoulders in his hands, he held me at arms length and stared into my face – no doubt looking for signs of madness.

"How are you, Jo?"

Artificially bright, I answered, "I'm very well, George. How hell you?"

He guffawed into the stale air, delighted at our familiar joke. "Oh, me? I'm fine – as always." Then with an anxious half-glance back at me as he walked over to get my drink, he asked, "You all better then?"

I knew I'd have to get used to this kind of tentative questioning. After all, it had been a long time since I was there and I'd left under difficult circumstances. People who'd had my best interests at heart had been snubbed – and one in particular had been rejected during my temporary madness.

"You been to have a look at yon church, yet?" he asked, busily polishing already-clean glasses and waving one in the general direction of All Saints.

"I'm saving it as a surprise," I found myself saying, even though it made no sense.

"Right." A pause. "Right…"

We both felt awkward as the silence between us grew, then in a whisper, "They're all gone now, y'know. All the dead people. No need to fear 'em anymore."

I simply smiled.

"Could I take my stuff up to the room now, George, d'you think?"

At that, he dashed out to the car as if he'd committed a major faux-pas for not thinking of it himself.

He followed me upstairs and with a parting, "Good to see you again, love," and was gone.

Safe in my room, I tried to decide on my next move. I knew there was to be a pre-wedding dinner at Rushpool and I sort of knew that Greg would be there… and why shouldn't he be? I also knew that I wasn't ready to see him yet. It would be better to put that particular meeting off until the wedding itself, where nothing intimate could be said.

Yet, although I dreaded it, I knew, that intimacy was what I most longed for.

Busying myself with unpacking and laying out my wedding outfit for the big day, I realised that a long bath, and all the ritual cleansing, moisturising and nail painting that go with it, was all I had the energy to do. I slipped into a nightie and dressing gown and lay on the bed, watching the sky darken overhead through the grubby window; only then did I realise how bone tired I felt.

In a replay of that other fateful night, I woke just past midnight to the sound of a dog barking outside. Feeling disoriented for a few moments, I froze, then, remembering where I was, I began to relax. However, now that the surge of adrenaline had woken me, I knew sleep would be a long time coming.

The long watches of the night lay ahead of me and I needed to move about rather than lie stiffly, wide awake with a turmoil of ideas flitting in and out of my head like so many butterflies, so I rose slowly from the bed, almost re-enacting the scene of my former encounter with Greg, only this time I was not feeling any force dictating my movements; I was in sole control.

The night air surprised me with its mildness. I stood outside the rear entrance of the pub, looking at the tarmacked car park and the dark of the woods beyond. Should I risk a walk into the glow of the streetlights? Might I see someone or something again? I was too afraid. I couldn't just meet him by accident. I needed to prepare.

Meekly turning back into the shadows, disappointed yet relieved, I felt myself being grabbed roughly by the shoulder.

"What *you* looking for then, love?"

I felt hands touching me and a smell of unwashed hair and dirty clothes envelop me, mingled with traces of incense on my attacker's skin, before I had the sense to fight back. The man's face was buried in my shoulder and I could smell drink on his breath.

Kicking this person in the groin with all the force I could muster, and punching him in his chest, I managed to free myself moments before the dog bounded up, teeth bared in a snarl, and seized the miscreant by the arm.

Whoever he was, he screamed in pain for some time before the dog would release him, then he limped off dripping spots of blood from his wounds.

I turned to my canine saviour and saw who it was.

"Flynn!" I cried, as he turned to me, tail now wagging and licking my hand as I tried to stroke him. I crouched down, cuddling his neck and crying into it, before bringing him into the pub.

What he was doing there, and where his master was, I could not know. Suffice to say that I was never so grateful in my life to anyone or anything. The creeping dread of what might have happened, that comes over victims after such an attack, was softened by the knowledge that he had been looking after me. I gave him a drink, wishing I could keep him in my room for the rest of the night so I could feel safe, but a clattering down the steep stairs signalled a half-asleep and grumpy George.

"What the bloody…" He stopped in mid-sentence when he saw us.

"What's *he* doing here?" he pointed at Flynn. "*You're* supposed to be keeping an eye out for poachers," he admonished. The dog didn't move.

"How come you're out of bed, love?" he asked in a somewhat gentler tone. "Not seen any ghosts or owt, have you?"

I looked at him for signs of amusement but there was only a little frown between his eyebrows.

I shook my head. "I couldn't sleep so I went for a breath of fresh air out the back. Some roughneck grabbed me. Then Flynn grabbed *him*. I think he got the worst of it. Flynn's trained as a guard dog." I kept on stroking the thick coat, to comfort myself more than anything else.

"Did you see who it was?" he asked, pouring us both a large brandy. "We've been having terrible trouble with poachers and burglars in the castle grounds lately. That's why Greg left him here. Got a kennel out the back 'specially – at least 'til the wedding guests have left."

"I only caught a glimpse of him," I said, "intense blue eyes. I smelt him though. A strange mixture of smells. I'd recognise him again just by that. And he'll need that wound dressing, and a tetanus injection, so he might go to the hospital," I added.

George was on to it immediately. I sat in the silence with the lovely dog at my feet. Had Greg left him to look after me? That was probably wishful thinking. At that point, George returned.

"Patrol car on the way. Won't trouble us for tonight though. I told them you weren't up to an interview so they'll come round in t'morning. Another?" he asked, indicating the brandy.

"No thanks. I think I'll sleep now. Could he...?"

"Aye, take him with you, lass. You'll sleep better then."

As we all climbed the stairs, suddenly grown much steeper to my exhausted limbs, I had a strange feeling about the poacher. There was something so familiar about his stance. I was sure I'd seen him before somewhere.

I pushed it out of my head for now. With Flynn settled at the foot of my bed, we both soon fell into a sound, dreamless sleep.

CHAPTER 54

The morning sounds of the pub woke us, me still tired, Flynn restless and making small indignant sounds as he shifted into a more comfortable position on the floor beneath me. Unfamiliar voices rose from the bar and among them, George, bustling about with the new coffee machine.

They were sitting at the bar chatting together when I walked in. Two fairly young constables and George, eating what smelt like bacon sandwiches.

"This is Miss Logan," said George in what must have been his 'official' voice. "These two want you to identify someone they picked up last night."

The police station was quite a forbidding place which smelled of stale food and dirty bodies.

The man from the night before – 'the suspect' as they called him – was sitting on a narrow bench, knees clasped to his chest and head bowed, when we entered the cell.

"Is this him, Miss?"

At that, he lifted his head and the dirty blond curls shook slightly, wafting a familiar scent, one that I recognised instantly from yesterday evening. Then he looked directly at me – into my eyes – and it was the face of Edmund Winter, making me question my own sanity.

I turned away, unable to think, unable to speak. How could this be?

After what seemed an age, I turned to the constable and asked, "Who is he? What's his name?"

"Max Barrington, Miss," was the whispered response. "Used to live on the Skelton estate as a kid till he was done for thieving – habitual criminal. So... do you recognise him?"

The man stood up, still looking at me but with a softened expression in the blue eyes.

"No, constable, I'm afraid I don't."

Their surprise was plain to see. "Look again, Miss. Was that where the dog bit him?"

The bandaged arm stood out, clean and newly-dressed against the dirty rolled-up sleeve of the miscreant. Of course it was him. And of course I recognised him, both living and dead.

"I'm really sorry, but I can't identify him. It was very dark and I only saw the man for a moment."

He knew the lie, and a shadow of a smile lifted his features.

They were flummoxed. "We could get Jack Gregson in to identify him?" suggested one of them.

The man's expression changed immediately he heard the name. "Ha, Gregson? Put him in the same room as me and see what happens," he shouted, then, turning to me as if he wanted to explain the outburst. "He's got my birthright and my life."

I wanted to question him further but now wasn't the time or place. I contented myself by asking if he was related to Mrs Barrington but he just smiled and returned to his earlier pose, hugging his knees again.

"If you can't identify him, Miss, we'll have to let him go," the constable said in a low voice into my ear. He was desperate to convict the man, yet I still couldn't bring myself to blame him. I couldn't have explained why to anyone. I shook my head regretfully. But I felt a strange, inexplicable sense of triumph as I left the police station.

I had a great deal to do before the wedding. The most important was to see Amelia and wait on her in what would be her special day. Lucy would do her best, of course, and James and Robert would be hovering in the background, Robert, I suspect, under strict instructions not to leave his room for fear of seeing the bride until the ceremony.

I sent a text to James to check on progress and find out how urgently I was needed. Within minutes came the response, *'All under cntrl, J. Best if you stay away. A doesn't need more excuses to create mayhem.xx'*

It was what I'd hoped to hear. I had something to do and it couldn't wait.

Mrs Barrington's cottage had an incongruously gay feeling to it when I arrived in Church Lane, with floral bunting of pale yellow around the door. She'd obviously made an effort for the celebrations, which surprised me. I knocked tentatively, not sure what I wanted to ask or to hear in answer to my questions, but I definitely needed answers.

I was unceremoniously ushered in and seated at the kitchen table. Her latest foray was into scones and their scent filled the room.

"I hate to disturb you, Mrs Barrington," I said, "but did you have a message for me?"

"That was ages ago and it wasn't important," she said, brushing it off.

"Oh," I said, non-plussed by her attitude. I let it go and continued with the business of the moment. "I need to ask you about a young man who may be related to you."

She cocked her head slightly to one side, expressionless as usual.

I continued. "His name is…"

"It's Maxie, isn't it? What's he been up to this time?"

"Oh, so you know him, then?"

"Well, the name gives it away, doesn't it?" A look of contempt flitted across her features then resolved itself.

"So, is he… family?"

She sat heavily on the kitchen chair and sighed. "What do you want, Miss Logan. I'm very busy." She indicated the rolling pin, the floury mess on the work surfaces and a jar of currants.

"Yes, as I said, I am sorry to bother you. I've just been to the police station." I explained about the assault, Flynn, the encounter and my denial as a witness. "So, I'm wondering how he's related to you. He looks very like Edmund Winter. Is there any family connection?"

She poured some home-made lemonade from a large glass jug as she spoke. "Max Barrington is no relation to me. I found him."

Whatever I was expecting, it wasn't that. She opened a drawer and fished out some photos.

"This is Maxie – he's about two there, I think. He was so beautiful then. I found him in the doorway of the church when I went in to clean, early one Saturday morning. Newborn baby. Just left on the floor." She held the picture to her chest. "Nobody knew where he'd come from, of course. No one would take responsibility for him, but *I* knew what had happened. The family at the castle have always taken advantage of the young village girls. He must have been a result of the Winters sowing wild oats too close to home – yet again. You saw the resemblance at once, of course. The features are unmistakable. He looks like his ancestor, doesn't he? That's why I offered to foster him. A beautiful child. You always hope, rather than expect, that he will turn out alright. That goodness and innocence won't be corrupted, but then it is, and there's nothing you can do about it."

I took a gulp of the acidic lemonade and had a coughing fit.

Mrs Barrington patted my back. "That's it. Cough it up." She hastily returned the pictures to the drawer. "By the age of ten he'd become quite wild. I tried my best – got him Saturday work at the castle, helping with the livestock – with Jack Gregson, who'd been apprenticed to the estate manager in his teens. He was much older than him and I thought he'd be a good influence, but I could see even then that Maxie hated Greg. Told me once that he was angry that Greg, who had no blood ties with the estate, should be favoured over, 'someone with the blood of the Winters flowing through his veins'. I had no idea where he'd got that from. It's not the words of a ten-year-old, is it? I tried to calm him. Told him that *Greg* had been adopted but that *he'd* made the best of it. But it was no good. He was on self-destruct by then.

He's been in and out of prisons ever since. Never stays in one place for long, but when he does come back, he won't stay with me. He lives rough and drinks."

Mrs Barrington looked exhausted. By this time, my head was reeling. I felt so sad for her and for Max, eaten up by anger and jealousy. But there was something else that I needed to find out about.

"You say that Greg was adopted?"

"He doesn't know, Miss Logan, so please don't speak to him about it. It was arranged by the church. I was privy to it, as the church warden at the time." She paused for a moment deep in thought. "I should never have told Maxie but I can't undo it now. And to be fair, he's never used it against Greg." As an afterthought, she added, "Maxie was the one who saved Arthur from the hunt."

She smiled sadly, seeing some grain of goodness in her foster-son.

I needed to get away from there so I gulped the remaining lemonade and, thanking her, I took my leave, mind in turmoil and unable to fix on anything else as I walked back to the Duke to put on my wedding finery.

CHAPTER 55

I thought I had plenty of time when I finally went up to my room at the Duke William. Time to wash, dress and check my hair and make-up in the inadequate bathroom mirror. However, the whole day was becoming one long panic when I realised I had ten minutes in which to get to the church. A quick glance outside told me that a fine drizzle had begun – just in time to make my hair frizz up. Thank you, God.

On reflection, I *had* had plenty of time to get organised. I'd been to the police station and Mrs Barrington's then back having coffee at the pub by eleven. The wedding was at two o'clock. No need to rush then. Or so I'd thought.

My problem was that I had to get my teeming thoughts into some sort of order before I faced the blushing bride and the congregation. And by 'the congregation' of course, I meant Greg.

The original plan of arriving first and looking calm and gorgeous had gone out of the window. I dashed around throwing my dress on over unbrushed hair, smearing a slick of lipstick across my mouth and looking as if I'd had a hot flush when I finally descended the stairs two-at-a-time in the almighty rush for the front door of the pub.

George thrust a scruffy umbrella into my hand as I was about to leave.

Not for the first time, I regretted calmly proposing that I'd walk to the church.

"After all," I'd smiled, "there won't be much room for all those massive cars, and it's only up the road." The smug words came back to bite me on the bum as I hurried, in a lather, up the bank.

It was Max Barrington, of course, who had taken up the whole of my thoughts since I first looked at him properly in that police cell. The fleeting shadow of a smile when I lied for him haunted me now. I still had no idea why I'd done that. Law-abiding me. Upholder of the status quo? I'd shocked myself.

'And now, what happens next?' I wondered. 'What if he does something worse as a result of my lie? What if someone gets hurt — or worse, killed?'

I had always been so sure of myself. My ideas, opinions, future plans, all set in stone. I'd never had anyone to please but me and I'd kept all my emotions in check — that is, until I came to Skelton: to Edmund Winter's grave, to Jack Gregson's bed.

"Oh, they've really messed with my head," I said aloud, then, looking behind me, checked to see if anyone had heard.

Turning the corner into Church Lane, I realised I needn't have worried. Nobody was in any hurry to go into the church. I noticed Mrs Barrington with Arthur (looking foxy with a blue spotted handkerchief around his neck), watching the guests.

They stood in small, gossipy groups, wafting clouds of expensive perfume about them, teetering on too-high heels and wearing too-tight dresses. The old comic routine came back to me: 'and that was just the men!' and despite everything, I had to laugh.

Then something happened to wipe the smile off my face.

Walking towards me, in a small group of friends, looking unfeasibly handsome, was Greg.

I saw him before he saw me — I was hidden behind the tall teeterers at that point. His head was thrown back in a hearty laugh and my heart slid to my feet when I noticed that the blonde girl he'd been with on holiday was linking his arm, as if they were a couple. She was doing that false, tinkly laugh that slightly plump 'kittenish' women do when they want to captivate a man. I know it often works, but I've never understood how or why.

Feeling suddenly shy, I moved round to the side of the church and stood behind a particularly tall gravestone, watching in horrified fascination as she did all the flirty moves she could think of.

Was he responding? I had to know. Peeping from behind the overhanging branches of a tree, I had a cautious look.

He was gone.

How had that happened? He was there a moment ago and seemed to have disappeared instantly.

Deciding to be bold, I pulled my smaller heels out of the mud they'd sunk into and re-found the pathway, when a voice I recognised said from behind me, "You can't go in there looking like that."

All at once, I felt the sun begin to shine inside me. He thought I looked a mess. But he was speaking to me, at least. The heat from his nearness warmed me right to the bone as I turned slowly to look at him.

"You look stunning!" he said, taking my hands and holding me at arms length, head on one side, to see me more clearly. His face was serious. "Here's what's missing, Blue Girl," he said, reaching out and pinning a tiny corsage of Queen Anne's lace and cornflowers to it. They were an exact match with the blue organza of my dress. "Perfect."

The ready smile irradiated me – I must've been glowing both inside and out.

He continued in a business-like manner. "I now need to do this before I escort you into the church – and also to ask how you feel about going in there again, after all the bad memories?"

"I'm okay... it's okay," I protested.

He drew me to him and kissed me gently on my mouth, and I felt the strength and safety of his arms around me once again.

"Where's your girlfriend?"

"What girlfriend? This one here?"

I laughed.

"I saw you with the Majorca girl earlier, flirting and laughing So, isn't she your girlfriend, then?"

He gave me an old-fashioned look. "I've been besotted with you since we were ten-ish. I'm not gonna give up now, lass."

He pulled me closer and walked me to the church door, as the flashiest of cars drew to a halt beside us.

"Hurry up. We can't steal her thunder," he said, feigning fear as we rushed in.

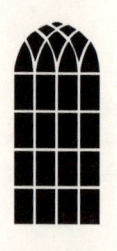

CHAPTER 56

Inside, the church was crammed to the rafters with people up on the balcony, standing at the sides, and crushed into the pews. When Robert's best man saw us, he quickly found a couple of chairs and placed them to the left, almost level with where the bride and groom would stand to make their vows. Ordinarily, being squashed up next to someone would have been uncomfortably intimate, but of course, this was Greg, so it was wonderful.

I only had time for a cursory glance at the guests and the groom, before Reverend Martin indicated that we should all stand and the music began.

Robert couldn't resist turning to see his bride and we were all rewarded by the radiance of her smile as she turned her head encompassing everyone in her happiness.

I was struck by how she looked at him, at this great outpouring of love. 'So, she truly does love him, then,' I thought, my fears dissolving instantly.

The beautiful couple began to make their vows.

"I, Robert William… take thee Amelia Caroline… to be my lawful wedded wife…"

It struck me then how sad it was that Caroline could not be here to see her daughter so happy and I looked at James, always beset with doubts about his parenting skills, who must have been thinking the same.

"Repeat after me," intoned Reverend Martin, continuing with the ceremony. Then it happened.

"I, Amelia Caroline," she said, "take thee Edmund..." There was a hushed pause, a gasp from all the guests, and then, "erm... *Robert* William," and staring at the window to her right, she stumbled slightly and lost her footing on the rush-covered floor.

A collective "Oh..." came from the congregation as they leaned forward in unison to catch her, but Robert's arm was there instantly and Ammy recovered herself, but not before throwing a horrified glance my way.

"The window!" she mouthed, panic-stricken.

To the east end of the church, just before the ancient sarcophagi, there was a clear glass door and leaning on it, to one side, stood Max Barrington, hands cupped around his eyes, the better to see the proceedings.

A general air of embarrassed relief suffused the guests as things got back to normal and Reverend Martin took control once more. The ceremony continued, but as soon as I could, I slipped out quietly to confront the culprit.

Thankful for the fresh air, I breathed deeply and walked across to where Mrs Barrington stood. Max was squatting beside her, arms around Arthur, fondling the thick fur of his neck and speaking endearments in his foxy ear. When he saw me, he lifted his eyes for a minute and the intimacy and insolence of that look took my breath away momentarily.

"What do you think you're doing?" I demanded.

She'd obviously cleaned him up and given him a decent dinner because he looked so much better than at the police station, yet still there was that faint scent of incense about his skin.

Mrs Barrington answered for him. "He didn't mean any harm," she said, immediately defensive of her son. "He just saw her get out of the car and went to have a look. Nothing like this ever happens round here. He was just looking." Then she stared out into the distance. "Anyway, he won't bother anyone again 'cos he's leaving tonight," she said, with a haunted, faraway look in her eyes.

I looked at the young man. "Why don't you try to get a decent job and stop doing this to your mother? Isn't it time to settle down?"

That smile – Edmund's smile, again.

Mrs Barrington protested. "He wants to. He's going to see about working in Nottingham; do some labouring on a farm down there. He's not a bad person. Helps me out whenever he comes home, and he was really good with the animals when he worked in the castle – until he was sacked by the Gillings. He was the one who rescued Arthur from the hounds," she insisted, repeating his one redeeming feature.

I watched her face soften as she tried to prove this foster son was capable of nobler feelings. In response, he held his hand up to her affectionately, embracing the nuzzling fox.

"Why not ask at the castle again – see if they could give you an apprenticeship or something?" I suggested – not holding out much hope.

"He won't. Not as long as Jack Gregson's there."

I gave up on them. I had more immediate concerns at that moment.

The strains of Mendelssohn's Wedding March flowed out through the open door of the church as the wedding party spilled into the sunlight, the new Mrs Amelia Belfort and her handsome husband at the head of the procession in a flurry of confetti and noisy cheers. My first thought was to move Max and his mother from the vicinity, but he'd already gone and she stood rigidly bereft, the fox, steadfast at her side.

CHAPTER 57

I must admit I felt a bit guilty leaving Mrs Barrington alone at the church as I went back to congratulate the happy couple... and to become part of another one with Greg, but there was really nothing I could do for her. However, spotting Reverend Martin, shaking hands as the congregation continued to wander out, I thought I might ask him to speak to her and offer some comfort before he joined us all at Rushpool Hall for the flashy reception.

"I really hate all this fuss and palaver," I said as I met up with Greg at the church door.

"Couldn't agree more," he said. "It's just an excuse to parade their wealth and power." He relented then and said, "I'm sorry. I know they're your friends, but I don't have anything in common with them – apart from Robert, of course."

I stared at him. "You and Robert? How so? I never saw *you* as friends."

"Nah, but we're both in love and deliriously happy." The twinkle and smile appeared again in his eyes.

I realised it was a wind-up but this was a special day so I went along with the joke. "So-o, I suppose that makes me have a lot in common with Ammy, then?"

His response was to squeeze my hand and lead me in the wrong direction – away from cars, guests and problems and back to his house.

"I've really missed you." There was that warmth of familiarity in his voice again as he opened the door and ushered me in. We were about to make up for wasted time.

Much later, when all the nonsense of photographs and reception – with guests swapping place cards and vying for the most auspicious spots – had finished, we rejoined the wedding party, relaxed and fulfilled.

The champagne – and it *was* champagne – flowed until I felt anxious about the bill for James but I needn't have worried. He had plenty of spare money. He had a *helicopter* for God's sake and a stud farm near Winchester, not to mention houses, investments and land. And only one daughter. Who else would he spend it on?

Much as I hated weddings, I decided to try and enjoy this one. I allowed the silly jokes and speeches to go over my head, along with the nonsense of the first dance and cutting of the huge, extravagant cake, and instead, I spent some time reflecting on the happy outcome for Ammy and Robert.

I kept sneaking glances at Greg who was sitting beside me, and thinking how lucky we both were to have found each other. After the formal bit, I saw him talking to a group of women in the smaller of the bars, throwing his head back and laughing in that familiar way and I didn't feel jealous in the least.

I watched him deep in conversation with Robert, unconsciously tugging at his tie and sliding it to one side, and knowing that the tiny bird tattoo would just be visible at his neck. I longed to touch it, recalling our first meeting when it had repelled me. Now it was deeply sexy and a cherished part of him.

As the evening drew on, I managed a few words with Ammy.

"Well? Aren't you going to tell me how fabulous I look?"

"Do I need to?" I asked, smiling at her.

"Oh, Jo-Jo, I'm so happy I could just burst! And…" she grabbed my hand and placed it on her tiny stomach, '…feel that!"

'That' was the baby in her womb. I was meant to feel a kick but in truth I could feel nothing.

"How wonderful, Ammy. I'm so pleased for you both."

"Well, I think I'm just about to *burst* with joy!" she exclaimed, hugging me to her chest and blowing a kiss across the room to Robert at the same time.

"Your dad looks very happy too."

"Aw, he's fine now the deed is done. He's talking business again. On about opening a new stud locally – now he's sussed the price of land hereabouts. Half the cost of the Winchester one. Can you believe that?"

She made me laugh with her naivety about money matters.

"Yes, of course I can believe it! Everything is cheaper outside the South East. Surely you knew that?"

But of course, by then she had shifted that butterfly mind to a different topic.

"Oh, but Jo-Jo, thank you so much for helping me in the church. I really, really thought it was the ghost of Edmund Winter, looking in on our celebrations! I was so shocked! I honestly thought I was going to go into labour right there on the rush floor!"

I laughed out loud. "Oh, Ammy, how very biblical. All that 'born in a stable' stuff, come to life at your wedding? You're priceless." I hugged her fondly – and it was then that it struck me. James was nowhere to be seen.

"Where's your dad?" I asked.

"Ooh, last time I looked he was in discussions with one of the landowners. Setting up that business deal, no doubt. Why?"

"I just need a minute of his time, that's all."

Before she fired a barrage of questions at me, I was off on a mission. It had just struck me that James, with all his money and influence, could easily help someone less fortunate than himself… and it was as if the scales had fallen from my eyes as I finally realised what Edmund Winter wanted from me.

As the evening drew to a sleepy close and all the guests had drifted off, replete with good food and drink, Greg found me again and suggested a slow walk back to his cottage.

"There's just one thing I need to do first," I said, heading for the table where the now-ruined remains of the wedding cake sat. I asked the serving staff to cut me a couple of large pieces and to pack them safely in napkins so that I could take them with me.

Greg looked puzzled. "A doggy bag?" he laughed. "You do know James has arranged that all the leftover food will be distributed to the village via the pub tomorrow?"

"Ah, yes. This is special though," I told him. "It's to gain me access in the morning to a person who'd normally be too proud to accept it."

I kissed his mouth to stop him from asking any more questions for now. I had remembered what an exciting lover he was, and I wanted to get back to his house without further ado to revisit our earlier, unfinished business.

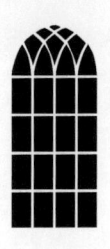

CHAPTER 58

After a lazy morning, I trundled up Church Lane, wedding cake packed into a small gift bag and knocked on the Barringtons' door. Generally, Mrs B would have been in the garden, but when there was no answer, I headed for the church.

As I approached the entrance, my eyes were drawn to the white-painted sundial on the wall, which bore the inscription, 'Even GOD cannot change the past.'

"Maybe not," I murmured, "but this is the present."

Mrs B was a conscientious caretaker and would no doubt be clearing the well-heeled debris left inside by the equally well-heeled guests.

I admit to having hesitated at the door, fearing some unknown horror inside, but I talked myself out of it and after a few deep breaths, I marched in.

She was there, of course. Having swept the confetti and spent tissues into heaps, she was shovelling them onto the fire in the central pew, opposite the pulpit. I also noticed the readings (which I had not heard, being engaged with the Barringtons outside at the time) discarded alongside the beautifully gilded orders of service, printed with the chosen hymns.

"Hello."

She turned her head vaguely to look at me. "Was it a good service?" she asked.

"Well, I only heard the end of it, so I wouldn't know, would I?" That sounded a bit churlish, so I said, "I was very pleased that

Amelia chose the traditional Wagner for the Wedding March and the Mendelssohn for the walking out bit."

"Yes. I was surprised about that. And about the floral arrangements. Thought they'd have gone over the top flouting their money – but no. Surprisingly good taste, actually."

I smiled. "Well, I think they saved that for the reception, actually. Talk about OTT."

She stopped what she was doing and turned to me. "I feel bad about Max, interrupting the ceremony like that, but he hadn't realised how clearly she would see him. Tell her I'm sorry, will you. Doubt if I'll see her again up in these parts."

"They've gone on their honeymoon. Dominican Republic."

She nodded, unsurprised. It was just as she would have expected.

We looked at each other awkwardly, until I remembered why I had come.

"Oh, I've brought you this," proffering the bag of wedding cake. "I thought you and Max could enjoy it with a cup of coffee or something... if he's still around?"

I sensed that she felt rather than heard the note of anxiety in my voice.

"Oh, he'll be gone soon enough. That's his way. A wanderer, he is. Can't settle anywhere."

"Well, I'm sorry to hear that, because I've been doing some digging behind the scenes, so to speak, and I have something for him."

It was the first time I've ever seen her unsure of how to react. A small frown had appeared between her brows and her head tipped slightly forward, the better to hear me.

She leaned on the broom beside the now-defunct rushes, stooping and eager. I felt slightly embarrassed about this. It's always the same when I do a good turn for someone. I started to gabble.

"Well, last night – at the reception – I heard that Amelia's father was planning to set up a business here – to say truth – a stud farm, you know, horses and all that kind of stuff. Anyway, you know Amelia's expecting and I said to her father, 'How would it be if she left the baby on the front step of a church and walked away from it?'

"Of course, he was horrified. I told him that, of course, nothing bad like that could happen to his grand-child, but that others were not so lucky..." I trailed off as I glanced up at her face. It was a closed book once again.

"Look, it wasn't up to me to plead for Max but I just thought he needed a chance in life – and now he can have one. James is prepared to fund an apprenticeship for him and to employ him to work with the horses as soon as the building work has been done. It won't be immediately, but it's going to happen, soon. Here's his business card. And here's some money for his fare to attend an interview at the agricultural college James will be using."

The silence could be cut with a knife, and it seemed to last forever. Then, the air was rent with great, heaving sobs, as Mrs Barrington gave way to all that pent-up emotion and fear, for what may have been the first time in her life.

She took my hot hands in her bony, cold ones, and wrung them enthusiastically, her whole body shaking.

"I don't know what to say," she cried. "It's just too much."

I couldn't help being embarrassed at the feelings I'd aroused in this normally cold woman and I just wanted to stop her. It was too raw for me to feel comfortable. I changed the subject.

"Look, I'll take some of the floral arrangements and put them in the churchyard in their vases. Shame to waste them when they're still fresh." So saying, I picked up an armful of flowers and headed out to the graves. I held on to the biggest one and placed the others in strategic places, bringing the grey stones to vibrant colour.

As I was busying myself, I heard my phone beep.

A lazy voice murmured, "I want you to come back here, sit with me, and have a long, lovely lunch – or dinner, depending how posh you are – and discuss our future plans. I must warn you, however, that those plans will have to centre around our being together."

"I'll be five minutes. I hope you can wait that long?"

He laughed quietly on the other end of the phone.

It was then that I understood why Ammy had said she was 'so happy she could burst'.

I quickly arranged the rest of the flowers and took the larger bouquet to the grave of Edmund Winter, late of this parish. I whispered, "Rest in peace, Edmund," and, kissing my hand, I bent over and pressed it to the gravestone beside the flowers, hoping I'd played a part in helping him to finally find the peace he deserved.

I did a bit of desultory weeding and tidying up of the long-neglected plot, and told him, this long-dead man, about the amends I'd tried to make to one of his scattered offspring. It was now time to cut the ties I'd imagined for so long and get on with living.

And that was when I felt the hot, almost familiar, sensation of someone slowly running a finger down my spine. I shivered slightly, then smiled and walked slowly back to my future and Greg.